Jamis Bachman, Ghost Hunter

Jamis Bachman, Ghost Hunter

by

Jen Jensen

2020

ISBN 13: 978-1-63555-605-6

THIS TRADE PAPERBACK ORIGINAL IS PUBLISHED BY
BOLD STROKES BOOKS, INC.
P.O. BOX 249
VALLEY FALLS, NY 12185

FIRST EDITION: JANUARY 2020

CREDITS
EDITOR: CINDY CRESAP
PRODUCTION DESIGN: SUSAN RAMUNDO
COVER DESIGN BY TAMMY SEIDICK

Acknowledgments

I am so grateful to my family. Your unconditional support means everything. Special thanks to Leigh for teaching me to read and write when I was just tiny.

Thanks to Sarah, who listened to me talk about this book for hours.

Prologue

She stood in an open field made of light, devoid of mass but clear in form, freed from the noisy confusion of her circular thoughts. There was a woman across from her. She wanted to walk toward her but could not move. Though unable to reach her, the woman's presence gifted her with hope and love, the best medicine for suffering anywhere in the universe. It was enough to let them begin.

She concentrated and willed a projection of her human form into being with the speed of intention. Her last significant memory of herself provided the prototype, and she wore her favorite yellow summer dress. She felt the soft breeze on her bare shoulders and breathed out a wish for grass to appear under her feet. It did and she wiggled her toes between the soft green wedges.

She strained to hear the woman's voice, carried across space and time to her, and smiled as the words touched her ears, "Where am I? Who are you? Am I dreaming?" She'd missed the sound of human voices.

Somehow, in moments of clarity, she created this space. It began with simple questions, "Where am I? What happened?" It felt oddly familiar to dig through emotional pain and confusion, as though she'd pried back layers of dense darkness to find her truth before. It was then she realized she was dead but not finished. It was like everyone she loved waited for her. She could see them but as if they were on opposite sides of aquarium glass.

Then her memory returned, and she relived the moment of her death in vicious repetition, until surrender was her only recourse to make it stop. So, she let go and sunk into her own pain. It was then she knew she was not alone. Someone stood behind her, quiet but seething. She reached out, but her attempt at comfort was batted away. She watched her and knew something connected them.

Then, suddenly, she knew what to do. That always surprised her in life too—how answers assembled themselves, readying for emergence in their own time, without her conscious participation. Everything had always been so much better when she just let herself be.

She called out for help and now saw her. They both had more work to do to arrive to each other, but she knew they would.

Chapter One

Drapes obscured Jamis's view from the hotel room. A heavy fog settled across the mountains in the distance and suited her mood. Jamis had arrived in Sage Creek, Utah, the night before to follow a promising lead about a poltergeist, but instead of excitement, she felt forlorn. She'd been chasing ghosts for so long, without finding proof, her life's vocation was either a grandiose psychiatric delusion or a complicated form of self-destruction. After a few drinks, she often insisted it was both to anyone who would listen.

Her dreams also left her uneasy and tired, like she'd spent the night running through waist high mud. The images were recurrent the past few months, and the same two scenarios played out again and again. In one, Jamis struggled toward a woman, standing directly across from her, and in the other, a hooded figure chased her. The night before gave her both, together for the first time. The hooded figured pursued her and the woman in front moved farther away the harder she ran.

Jamis pushed through the anxiety to focus on something tangible, and opened Facebook to scroll through the comments on the photo of the Salt Lake City skyline she posted the night before.

Bill W.

You're a fraud.

Jamis replied.

But I've been told I have dreamy brown eyes and women love me. Don't be jealous bc you can't say the same. Xoxo, Jamis

The computer chirped with notifications as followers liked her reply. Jamis routinely trolled her trolls and people loved it. She wasn't as confrontational in person, but like the trolls who bashed her, the internet gave her courage. She closed the browser and poked through files to find the video clip that brought her to Utah.

She watched the video at least one hundred times. She often obsessed like that, unable to move forward without resolution. The video began in the doorway of a kitchen. Cupboard doors opened and closed in heavy, jerky movements, out of sync. The fridge door opened so quickly the camera angle dropped to film the floor as the person holding the camera jumped backward to avoid being hit. What she saw on the floor was what drew her to Sage Creek. Between the cupboards and the shadow of whoever held the camera was another silhouette, disembodied from a source. It looked like the book cover of an old crime noir thriller, where an elongated shadow stretched across the cobblestone, framed by the streetlight. The light around it took on a yellowish glow, like it was lit from an old glass bulb.

Jamis zoomed into the image and hit play frame by frame. The figure shimmered into existence in one frame and was gone the next. She replayed the video three more times before forcefully extracting herself from the compulsion to watch it again. The video was obviously from a cell phone camera, and her higher tech cameras would produce better video resolution. She'd visit the house and leave those behind.

Something about the image in the video tugged her instincts. The figure in the middle of the swirling chaos of the kitchen provoked a sense of dread when she watched it in slow motion. It emerged from nothing only to disappear back into empty space. A skeptic might say it was the shadow of the person opening and closing the cupboards and fridge, edited sloppily from the footage. But there didn't seem to be evidence of tampering, and as always, she wanted to assume benevolence and believe.

She needed to see it in person. Jamis slid the laptop into her messenger bag and grabbed the cameras, secured in a heavy steel case, and left the hotel room. Outside, the cold air plunged into her lungs and she coughed. It was wrong to assume Utah would be warmer in early March. Late winter snow sat piled in the corners of the parking lot, soiled with soot, the asphalt wet with melting snow. Pounding startled her. A woman stood at the hotel office window, waving for her to come inside. Jamis held up her finger and put the bags in the car first.

"Morning," Jamis said as the door closed behind her. The woman now sat behind the counter. There was a picture of a Chihuahua in a Santa hat on her sweatshirt. "I like that." Jamis pointed and smiled.

"My son got me this."

"Nice son," Jamis said.

"Well, I kept him."

Jamis jammed her hands in her coat pockets. Her arms felt too long. "What's up?"

"My son checked you in last night and told me it was you. I just wanted to say hi."

"You watched my show?" Jamis smiled, feeling more natural about the conversation. She never tired of talking about *Ghastly Incidents*. It ran for ten years and amassed a huge following.

"Sure did," she said. "It used to come on after the news. Sometimes I'd watch it in bed at night. I'm Tess, by the way."

"Good to meet you," Jamis said.

Tess gazed at her. No matter how often it happened, people's reaction to meeting her in person, after seeing her on television, made her uncomfortable. She always heard, "I had no idea you were so tall."

Jamis braced for something like this from Tess, but instead she asked, "How long are you here for?"

"I'm not sure. I checked in for a week." If the poltergeist was real, she'd stay for however long it took.

"Ghost hunting?"

"Yeah," Jamis said. Jamis liked Tess's energy, a down-to-earth feminine pragmatism. She felt safe and wanted to linger. "It might be something or not. I'll let you know."

"Can't wait. Well, you let me know if you need anything," Tess said.

"I will. Where can I get some groceries? Just a few things for the room. I hate eating out all the time when I travel." A peanut butter sandwich in the afternoon soothed her stomach and psyche.

"There's a place right up the road. Town Market." Jamis queried her phone and held it up for Tess to approve. "That's the one," Tess said. "You'll like the owner, Carmen. Let her know I sent you."

"Will do." Jamis turned to leave and then paused. "Why's it so cold today? It didn't feel like this last night when I drove in from Salt Lake."

"You drove that canyon pass at night?"

"Yeah, it was dicey," Jamis said, understating her terror as the road narrowed, climbed, and then dropped. She pulled off the side of the road at a gas station to recover when it was over.

"You know, there's supposed to be ghosts at the highest point. Soldier Summit they call it. A bunch of Confederate soldiers died there trying to get through in August when a freak snowstorm killed them. You should check that out."

"I will, with a full search and rescue party." Jamis pushed the door open with her shoulder.

"And yeah," Tess said. Jamis paused, half out of the office. "It's cold because we have a few more weeks of winter. It always gives us a wallop on the way out. There's a storm coming soon so be careful." The phone rang behind Tess and she turned to answer it.

In the car, Jamis turned up the heat and watched Tess through the window. She moved her hands animatedly as she spoke into the phone. She was a good local guide for her. She'd get groceries where she recommended later. First, she had a house to visit. If the video was staged, this would be her last ghost hunt. She'd promised her psychiatrist that before leaving San Diego the morning before.

In the rearview mirror, she looked at the faint lines around her eyes and mouth, touched the few gray hairs mixed in the dark strands. They'd arrived with the major depression the year before, after her television show's cancellation. The silent space without her show was more overwhelming than any ghost or paranormal phenomena she ever chased. The emptiness propelled her to a psychiatrist who did talk therapy. The question Dr. Frank asked during that first session still hovered over her head like a dark shroud about to fall. "Are you trying to find your mother, Jamis?"

"I came home from school to my mom dead when I was eleven. I'd say I already found her. Who wouldn't be fucked up by that trauma?" The question struck so close to her pain, lashing out was her only comfortable response.

But she didn't think it was fair to reduce everything to it. Not everything was about her mom. Jamis accused Dr. Frank of being Freudian. She preferred Jung. Not deterred, Dr. Frank insisted Jamis remain in therapy and consider it as a primary motivation. Jamis didn't think the root cause mattered but kept talking anyway, took Wellbutrin each morning, and Klonopin when anxiety ran over her ability to deflect it.

Eventually, her mood lifted enough to shower and brush her teeth daily. Jamis began to engage with her fans on social media again. The cry for help with the video arrived via Messenger late one afternoon. She almost deleted it, somehow sensing the stakes.

Which led her to the front of the hotel, readying to chase one final poltergeist.

What Jamis didn't tell Dr. Frank was that she repeatedly found her mom. The night of her death, Jamis woke to her standing by the window, arms outstretched, mouth moving. The State of California became her guardian then, and her mom followed to all thirteen group homes, and eventually, to her college dorm and first apartment. Until Jamis turned twenty-seven and her mom disappeared. Saturn returns, one psychic told her. It was also the year her show began. Finally, life gave her what she needed to let go of her mom—a chase that allowed her to keep moving, when everything else inside wanted to give up.

So maybe she was looking for her mom. Maybe she was looking for the part of herself lost that day. But Jamis was also looking for answers to reframe suffering. Because if humans were not just finite beings born only to slip into oblivion, then her loss had greater meaning. And it was possible to heal from every horrible thing that happened from that day forward. Jamis didn't think Dr. Frank would understand that. It was always her secret anyway.

She put the car in reverse. There was a poltergeist waiting.

Chapter Two

Jamis dialed Vince's phone number. He and his wife, Darcy, sent the video. After just one ring, he answered. "Jamis?"

"Yes. Hey." Jamis set the phone on her leg, speaker on. "I'm in the car on my way over. Is it a good time?"

"Yeah." He breathed heavily into the phone. Muffled movement obscured his words.

"I can't understand you," Jamis said.

"Sorry. Is that better?"

"Yeah, you're good. Go again."

"Last night was so fucked up. We're leaving to stay with some friends."

"Okay. Just wait there so we can meet in person? I'll be right there." Jamis rolled to a stop at an intersection and glanced at Google maps.

"It's fine now. I can wait," Vince said. "Darcy is ready to move. I think she'll insist we do after this." He paused. A car door shut. Then hinges squeaked as another door opened. "No one can live here."

"I'll be there shortly." Jamis hung up the phone. The hairs on her arm stood on end. If it was scary enough for him to not want to live there maybe it was real.

Jamis parked in front of the house, next to the curb. Brown grass peeked from beneath melting snow. The door opened, and a young man stepped into the yard. Despite the cold, he wore only a T-shirt.

"I'm so glad you're here. I don't know if you can do anything to fix this, but maybe you can understand it." He waved her into the house. "Darcy left and went to the school library to study. Said she couldn't stay here."

Jamis's first impression of a house was always the most important, so she slowed her thoughts and imagined that time held still with them. Vince continued to talk, but Jamis chose not to hear him. Light flooded the living room. Stairs split the room and led to a second level. The kitchen was in the back. The dining room was to the right.

Jamis looked at the space without asking permission. Vince waited for her by the stairs. She walked around the house, one hand stretched outward to touch the walls. It was just a normal house in late morning. She pointed to the stairs, asked permission, and Vince waved her up. She began to climb.

The central air hummed to life. Warm air wafted up from floor vents in the hallway. There were two bedrooms on the right and one on the left, at the top of the hall, and a window at the end. The open doors on the right let in light. The door on the left was closed. Jamis opened it. The room was empty except for a twin bed, positioned in the middle of the wall under a window. Something didn't feel right. The space felt wrong, but she didn't know why.

Jamis stood in the middle of the hallway, hands on the walls. "What happened today?"

"It started about three thirty this morning. Darcy woke me up. There was wailing and screaming. It sounded like someone getting tortured. I got up and came into the hallway and Darcy waited in bed." He rubbed his arms and then his eyes. "I came to where you're standing now." She watched him, looking for signs he was lying. There were none. It was genuine distress.

"I stood right there, looked down the stairs and it was so dark. I mean it was so dark. Like darker than when there is no moon. No, it was like, the dark of hell or something. I swear I'm not making this up," Vince said.

"I don't think you are," Jamis said. She touched his arm to redirect him. "Tell me what happened next."

"I came down the stairs real slow because it was so dark. I got to the bottom of the stairs, and in the middle of the front room was a woman and she was dead. She was on the ground and it looked like one of those scenes in a TV show, you know? When they find a body? And I was like, there's a dead body in my house. How did it get here? But then I realized all around her body was so dark, but there was light from somewhere because I could see this dead body. So, I realized this had to be a dream or something. I looked away, and when I looked back, the body was gone. Then, from the corner of the room, down there," he pointed into the living room, his finger directed at the far corner, "came this horrible thing. I can't even describe it."

"Can you show me exactly how you came down the stairs?" He moved slowly and stopped on the last one. "Is this where you were?"

"Yeah," Vince said. He stepped into the living room so Jamis could stand where he had been.

"Can you pull the drapes?" He hesitated. "It's okay. I want to see the room from this perspective with less light. It helps me understand the causes of things."

"I'm not crazy," he said. "I'm working on a master's in counseling."

Jamis held up her hands in surrender. "I'm not suggesting you are. I just want to start with facts and details. That's all I'm doing. I want to be sure I understand."

"I'm sorry," he said. "I'm really on edge. We both are. I think whatever is here is affecting us. We just didn't realize it." He pulled the drapes.

"It's okay. Can you stand where you saw the body?" He complied, moving to the middle of the room. With the drapes closed, light still spilled into the room from the window in the front door, the kitchen, and the entryway into the dining room. "Was it cold?"

"It was so cold. When I ran back upstairs, Darcy said my lips were blue."

"What did you do when you saw the body and then the figure?" There was nothing he might confuse with a ghost. Jamis didn't see anything that might cast a shadow, either.

"I screamed. Loud. It was running at me. I ran to the front door and hit that light switch." He pointed. "As soon as the light was on, it disappeared." He snapped his finger. "Just like that. Gone. I don't know what I saw. But I swear to God, for a few seconds I saw a dead body in my front room. Then, for a few seconds, something came at me." Vince crossed his arms and clutched his elbows in his hands.

"What did the figure look like?" Jamis opened the drapes again. He waved for her to sit on the couch against the back wall. From there, Jamis could see the stairs, window, center of the room, and the back corner. The room was clean and painted a light gray. She'd attributed many poltergeists to poor lighting, dull paint, and general untidiness. That wasn't the case here.

"This sounds even crazier," Vince said. "It had long skinny arms and legs and a massive belly. Like the belly was bloated or something."

"A hungry ghost."

"What's a hungry ghost?"

"It's Buddhist. At death our souls retreat to the bardo where we remain until we're ready to reincarnate. It's a kind of purgatory, I guess. An in-between place. But some of us get stuck. For many reasons. Desire, fear, pain. We grasp, and in our grasping, we attach, which locks us in place, and we're not able to move on. Hungry ghosts are like addicts—they can't get enough, and they can't let go, so they just stay where they are and suffer. They're depicted with long arms and bulging, swollen stomachs."

Jamis searched for an image and held up her phone for him.

"That's what I saw," Vince said.

It was possible he'd seen pictures like that before and it subconsciously informed his experience. It was also possible he saw a hungry ghost. Jamis saw crazy stuff all the time so there wasn't a reason to doubt him.

"Can you ask Darcy to come home and talk to me too?" Vince pulled out his phone and sent a text. "Thanks."

Jamis wondered if she should push for more information or wait for Darcy. Based on feedback from staff and friends over the years, she knew her habit of asking rapid-fire questions felt like an inquisition. Dr. Frank also urged her to engage with people about normal topics, like the weather and news. Her comfort zone was, "So what do you think happens when we die?"

Jamis just wasn't good with day-to-day feelings. It wasn't that she didn't care. It was just that we lived in an unfathomable universe. The day-to-day was a quagmire that kept her from focusing only on discovering it.

Vince seemed so upset. Nothing sensitive came to mind, so Jamis decided to plow forward. Ultimately, it was always facts and analytical detachment that moved her along. It would work for Vince too. "Can you tell me what else happened?"

Vince reclined in the armchair across the room and started talking. "It started when we moved in about six weeks ago. We transferred to college here for graduate programs in counseling and needed to find something close to the school. We didn't want to drive a lot. This was the only house available in the area. We didn't want student housing or an apartment anymore. We wanted to get a dog.

"Anyway, we saw this place online and just rented it on the spot. We were in Salt Lake and had only been here once or twice. We got here, got our stuff in the house, and the first night we were here, Darcy screamed. She was in the kitchen and I was upstairs putting the books away. I came running down the stairs and found her standing in the kitchen holding a towel over her face, crying. She swore up and down that the cabinet doors opened and closed all around her. When I got there, they were closed.

"Little things like this started happening. We'd leave our keys on tables and they'd fly off, like they were thrown. Or we'd be sitting here watching TV and the lights would flicker and the windows would rattle. Or we'd be in bed and hear steps on the stairs and get up and look and not see anything. But the last few weeks it's been really bad." He fixed his gaze on the corner of the room. "I think we need to move.

"I sent you the video of the cupboard doors opening and closing. That was when the screaming and wailing started. Then the windows began to rattle. The books on the shelves upstairs flew off. I recorded that video, and then we left and went to a friend's house. They probably think we're nuts."

"Everyone thinks I'm nuts. It's okay. What did your friends say about it?"

"Nothing, really. They listened to the story and told us we could stay while we worked it out."

"But you came back, even after?" He shrugged. "Have you heard anyone around you say anything? Like what does your landlord say about the house?" Jamis wanted to see the hinges on the cupboard and impulsively moved to make it happen. As much difficulty as she had with day-to-day feelings, holding still was even harder. In the kitchen, she opened each door to inspect the hinges. They were new. The cupboards, counter, and floor were level. She hoisted herself up to sit on the counter.

"It's a property management company in Salt Lake," Vince said. He followed and stood by the table.

"Everything is new?"

"Everything is or at least we were told. We rented it furnished." The front door opened, and a female voice called out.

Darcy was home. Jamis leaped from the counter to meet her in the middle of the kitchen. "I'm so glad you're here. I used to watch your show with my mom, and I told Vince you were the person to ask for help. I'm not sure anyone else would believe this." Her smile was genuine. She was short but not petite. Pretty in a normal, Midwestern way. She sounded like she was from Illinois.

"Thanks. I swear eighty percent of the people I meet tell me they watched my show with their mom." Jamis smiled and then continued. "Vince told me what happened to him last night, about the other random events, and about your experience with the cabinets the first night here. Is there anything else I should know?"

"Can you make some coffee for us?" Darcy turned to Vince, and he moved quickly to do so. "He makes the best coffee," Darcy said. "I feel weird here. Anxious. Angry. Scared. My stomach hurts all the time. My head aches." She put her hand on her head. "It hurts right here at the top of my head, and sometimes it wakes me up at night. It's not just the cabinets or the screaming. It's something heavy and dark. Sometimes I wake and feel like there is someone on top of me. One night I punched Vince in the nose because he was trying to shake me and wake me up."

The coffee pot gurgled to life. Water spit out through the filter and splashed into the bottom of the pot. The house was cold and silent. All background noise faded away as Darcy spoke and Jamis shivered.

"And that," Darcy said. "It's cold all the time. The thermostat is set at seventy-eight. And sometimes I swear I hear someone crying." Darcy went to the doorway and pointed up the stairwell. "Like it's in the walls." A gust of wind rattled the back window.

"I think that's just a storm heading our way," Jamis said. "The lady at the motel said one was coming."

"I'm not sure about that. At all," Darcy said. The coffee continued to gurgle. "I used to watch your show and think it was just good fun. Oh, God. I'm sorry. I don't mean to be rude. It's just I never really believed any of it. I mean, I thought it was possible, but there is never proof, right?"

"Tell me about it," Jamis said. "And then tell my shrink." Darcy looked puzzled. Jamis motioned for her to continue.

"My mom believed in ghosts. Said her mom came to visit her the day before her heart attack and told her everything would be okay. I'm not Mormon, in case you're wondering, like most in this area. Vince is, but he's not practicing. I don't believe in the afterlife. But in the past six weeks, well, if there isn't proof here, I don't know where there is proof." Vince set a mug of coffee on the counter next to Jamis. She picked it up, used it to warm her hands, took a small sip.

Then Jamis set it down and put a finger to her lips. A sound like a cry filtered in from the front room, indistinct but growing in volume. Jamis opened the Voice Memo app on her phone and signaled for Vince and Darcy to remain where they were. She followed the sounds into the front room, but then they changed their directionality and now came from behind her. She came back into the kitchen, but the sounds changed again. She moved into the formal dining room. In each room, the crying sounds fled to the next ahead of her arrival. It was extraordinary. Finally, they stopped. She hit play, but it had recorded nothing.

"Nothing. Damnit. Did you hear that?" Vince and Darcy were pale, shaken, and terrified and Jamis was thrilled. It said a lot about her, but she was too excited for psychoanalysis. "I think it's best if you stay somewhere else. But I need access to the house, and I want to set up cameras. Is that okay? Can I have a key?" They both agreed and Darcy dug in her purse on the table.

Darcy held out the keys for Jamis. As Jamis reached for them, the front door of the house flew open. Something knocked Jamis forward, and once she regained balance, the front door slammed shut. Then the fridge door opened and Jamis fell back into the table to avoid it. The chair next to her fell. Its legs lifted off the ground and then something unseen slammed it on the linoleum. Darcy jumped away from the table and into Vince's arms. Jamis waited in the middle of the kitchen as the air calmed.

Vince and Darcy retreated to the back door. It opened under their weight. They tumbled outside and landed together in the snow. Jamis ran toward them. Something shoved her, the pressure firm against her back and neck. It felt like a playground bully pushing her off the jungle gym. She tumbled to the ground to land across Darcy and Vince.

"Well, hell," Jamis said. The fall knocked the wind out of her, and she rolled off of them to lay on her side and hold her stomach while she caught her breath.

"Do you see? Oh my God," Vince yelled. "Do you see?" He cried actual tears. Darcy rubbed his face with the arm of her shirt.

Chapter Three

Jamis recorded the day's events and posted a picture of Vince and Darcy in the snow across social media with a brief summary. Then the house began to feel oppressive. Jamis felt like weights were strapped to her legs before a power walk. Her skin itched like she'd been bitten by a swarm of mosquitos.

So, she left to wait in the front yard for Vince and Darcy to pack. Wind raged and the snow on the ground blew around her feet. The curtain in the front room shifted and billowed, but by the time Jamis got to the window, it was at rest, like it never moved.

"What happened now?" Darcy stopped on the porch, carrying a large bag and a purse, her face frightened and anxious.

"Nothing. Just a trick of light," Jamis said. She didn't know if that was the case, but Darcy's expression said she'd had enough for today. Vince joined her and Jamis walked them to their car.

"I'll let you know what happens, okay? We'll stay in touch."

Vince waved as he backed the car out of the driveway.

Jamis studied the house. The numbers on front were new: 32. They didn't appear out of the ordinary in any way, but a consultation with a numerologist might be helpful. She texted a friend who dabbled with numbers to ask. Jamis often told her viewers, "Ask all the questions. Prepare to change your mind."

There was a stillness around the house, as if it existed just outside the space-time continuum she was in. Even the sky looked different in the shadow of the house. Jamis waited outside, watching, but nothing substantial happened so she took the cameras inside. Her energy shifted when she walked from the sidewalk across the street into the house. It was subtle, but she felt it.

Her phone chirped with a texted reply. *Thirty-two is the number that says I must compost and re-form all that I carry. Karmic liberation. Escaping the cycle of samsara. For Pythagoricians it's all about justice.*

The cold from earlier was gone. Warm air gushed from air vents and she shrugged out of her coat, reading the text a handful of times before sending thanks and tucking her phone away. The text wasn't helpful, she decided. Any life well lived required constant reframing. Jamis was becoming an expert with Dr. Frank. She didn't lose her show. She moved on to a new chapter. Talk about composting.

Jamis set a camera at the bottom of the stairs, positioned to record all of the front room. She placed a camera in the kitchen, angled in the back corner of the counter, another in the formal dining space, and one at the top of the stairs. It caught a wide view of the staircase and the upstairs hallway. Jamis tapped the tablet and connected them via satellite. All were set to record with motion.

The cameras were the only tools left in her ghost hunting toolbox. She had night vision goggles to help her see in the dark, but they did little else. On television, Jamis used everything from meters that read electrical impulses to Ouija boards. But they were just props, intended to entertain, so she let them go with the show. Now, stripped bare of everything, she relied on her second sight, and the rare moments when the cameras caught something.

The potential to dip into melancholy rose inside her. Her life was reduced to waiting for the video clip that couldn't be refuted. Despair creeped around the corner, stood on the threshold. Depression was tempting, but warmth enveloped and stopped her. With it came her most vivid childhood memory, and Jamis felt it as though she were there, reliving it. Her mom carried her from the couch to bed, half asleep, safe in her arms, and tucked her into bed.

The blankets were heavy on her limbs. The window was open, the air cool on her nose. The radio, on soft jazz, filtered in from the front room, and while she drifted back to sleep, her mom rubbed her back.

Then something pulled the warmth from her, like the blanket her mom lovingly tucked around her was yanked off with force. Her arms burned like she'd held a bag of ice for too long. The safety of the bedroom faded away. Now she was somewhere else, and her mom's body was on a stretcher, the zipper of the body bag opened just enough to see her face, eyes closed, lips blue.

It was the worst moment of her life. Every night for the next ten years, it was the scene that played on the backside of her eyelids when she tried to sleep. She left a whole chunk of herself in the room that day. The coroner packed it up in the body bag. The grief made her feel like she was clawing at a brick wall, fingertips bloodied. She carried the loss inside, woven into the scar tissue of her heart, and imagined death would come and she'd carry nothing else. Anguish reorganized her into someone different from that point forward.

Jamis leaned over the stretcher to kiss her mom's forehead, heart wrenched. Her mom's eyes opened. Adrenaline flooded her system. Her heart thundered and stomach muscles spasmed. It took a few minutes for Jamis to regain control of her limbs. The image of her mom's death-clouded eyes was prominent as she struggled to breathe. Upset clogged her windpipe. She couldn't escape the vision.

"That was not nice," Jamis said, struggling to leave. "I'd like to help you, but if you keep that up, I'll tell you to fuck off."

The pressure lessened. Jamis was confused about her whereabouts. Her place in time came back to her with the sound of a car horn. The curtain billowed. "Do you want me to hurt as much as you? Is that what you're doing? I don't know who you are, I want to help you, but you need to be nicer." The air remained still and the house silent. Her emotions settled and she struggled to regain composure and change her tone.

"I have this feeling like I've been here before. In this town. Do you think that's possible?" The words surprised her. She'd not expected to say them.

Branches of a tree scraped a window somewhere upstairs. Jamis watched cars drive by and was overcome by a sensation of slipping through the earth. She grabbed the trim around the window, closed her eyes, took a deep breath, and settled her vertigo. When she opened her eyes, the sun shone brightly in the front yard. The cloudy day was gone. Perhaps she was in a different place or time.

There was a hunched figure at the bottom of the porch, its back to Jamis, wearing a dark, bluish gray robe. A car with a large metal bumper and heavy square frame drove by. There was no sound. Other cars drove by as well, but she couldn't hear them. The steps she took were silent. She couldn't even hear her own breathing, which was labored from repeated emotional jolts. Jamis crept toward the figure, covering her eyes to block the glare of the sun, and descended the stairs. Each step reminded her of the dream. Her legs felt heavy, like she waded through waist high mud. The pressure was so intense Jamis dropped to her hands and knees to crawl, struggling to close the space between them. "Did you bring me here?"

The figure turned and there was emptiness where its face should have been. It threw back the cloak and screamed. The mouth opened like a small patch of light inside an otherwise dark room. The sound choked Jamis; she perceived the sensation of hearing physically. A stench rolled off the figure, and then danced in front of her eyes like bright, spinning, chaotic lights. Wherever she was, her senses were scrambled and confused. Smell was sight, and sound pressed against her windpipe, trying to snuff out her life. She lay down on her side, clawing at her throat, thinking there was something there she could pry off. But there wasn't.

She thrashed, pushing back to her hands and knees, finally to her feet. Terror wasn't a good enough word to describe the state where she found herself. There was nothing between her and the oblivion the figure represented. The creature's shadow was so long,

Jamis feared it would consume her. It moved independently, long fingers stretching toward her. Humans were not meant to confront such darkness. Even Jamis was unprepared.

Jamis felt ripped open, like an ax had split her in two, head to toe, right down the middle. She had to get free of its orbit, find solid ground. She closed her eyes, an act of exceptional bravery, and ran into the middle of the yard, putting distance between them again.

It was enough and Jamis jerked back into the present. She was outside in the freezing cold, alone. She rushed into the house, slamming the door. Her watch showed ten minutes had elapsed. Her breath marked the frigid air.

"I asked for that. Was that you?" Heaviness filled the air and fell like a memory foam mattress topper on her shoulders. "It would be nice if you weren't quite so hostile." The pressure mounted again.

"Let's talk more later." The terror of confrontation had left her shaken, unsure of her own sanity. It was enough for the day. Jamis wanted to flee, but the door wouldn't open. Snow blew at the window. Desperate, Jamis connected with the door with her shoulder, throwing all her strength and weight behind it. The door opened, and she sailed through the air.

"Well, hell," Jamis said, as she hit the ground on her back. "You are so rude," she yelled back at the house. The door closed. Jamis held up her birdie fingers. Then she crawled through the front yard on her hands and knees looking for her glasses.

This was a new experience. Heavy, dense, cold air. Unseen force that interacted with objects. Psychic visions and transference between points in time. Jamis experienced them in isolated events in the past, but never all at once. This could be real. She found her glasses, slipped them on, and sat in the snow, looking up at the house.

Despite her excitement, Jamis was energetically drained and her stomach growled. The only thing she needed to think about next was food. Everything else could wait.

❖

It was a little after six p.m. Night descended with taillights glowing in the mist of melted snow, splashed up from tires on the road. The day felt like a dream. The intensity of seeing her mom in the body bag provoked disassociation as Jamis drove away from the house. The poltergeist played dirty resurfacing that memory. Or was it her? Did something in Jamis connect the experience in the house to that formative moment? Maybe she was in a therapy session with the universe and could expect her core issues to get resolved with whatever was happening in Sage Creek. It was a comforting thought, even if absurd.

The grocery store Tess recommended was made of industrial cinderblock, painted dark gray with "Town Market" stenciled on the front. Bright green-and-white shamrocks for St. Patrick's Day were painted on the windows. The bell on the door chimed loudly as Jamis opened it. She lifted a small handheld basket from a stack. There were only six aisles in the store, and Jamis gathered groceries quickly. At the deli in the back, Jamis peered over the counter at a woman placing items in the display case.

"Hello," Jamis said, meeting her dark eyes. Jamis grinned, taking in her short dark hair, streaked with gray. "Tess told me to tell you she sent me here." The woman wiped her hands on her pants.

"Tess did, huh?" She strode from behind the deli counter. "I'm Carmen." Jamis introduced herself. "Why are you here?"

"I'm hunting ghosts."

"Well, that's not something I hear every day." She waved at the small basket Jamis held. "You ready?"

At the register, one with old-fashioned push button numbers, Jamis took the groceries from the basket and set them on the counter. Carmen tallied the cost.

"That's it?" Jamis dug in her pocket for cash. "I only have a card."

“It’s fine,” Carmen said, swiping it. “I was getting ready to close up and go get a beer. Wanna come?”

“Sign me up,” Jamis said. The idea of not returning to the hotel room alone was appealing. Jamis hated being alone, though she often was. “But I’d prefer gin and tonic.”

“Well, it might be called gin and tonic, but I can’t promise what’s actually in it. You’ll understand once we get there,” Carmen said.

CHAPTER FOUR

A single neon light cut through the darkness and Jamis pointed, standing beneath it. "The Silver Nickel?"

Carmen held the door open. The bar was full of smoke. When Jamis walked inside, her shoes stuck to the floor and made squeaking noises. "I thought you couldn't smoke in public places." Carmen shrugged. The walls were covered floor to ceiling with license plates.

"It's a dive, I know, but the beer is good. The gin and tonic?" Carmen raised her hands to indicate non-commitment.

"Whatever you're having is fine." She'd eaten a peanut butter and jelly sandwich in the truck on the way over. Carmen let her use the break room while she closed up. She'd left the groceries in the back of the rental car in the parking lot since it was colder than a fridge outside.

Carmen waved at the bartender, who filled a pitcher and brought two glasses to the booth where they sat. He looked disinterested and turned away without a word. She looked at Carmen who stared into the glass of beer she just poured. "Why did you ask me for a drink?"

"I don't meet many new folks like you. I was headed here anyway. Shot in the dark."

"Folks like me?"

"Queer," Carmen said without apology. "Gay. Lesbian. Whatever."

"To queer, gay, lesbian, whatever solidarity." Jamis held up her beer to toast Carmen. She sipped her beer and grimaced. "But honestly, am I that obvious?"

"Are you serious?" Carmen raised an eyebrow. "It's better here than it used to be, but there's not a lot of us." She drank the rest of her beer. "Or maybe some of it is generational. I'm sixty-three this year."

"No, you're not. Really?" Carmen was striking, and despite her hatred of the word when used to describe butch women, handsome. "Are you single?"

"Yeah," Carmen said. Jamis poured them both more beer. It was already moving to her head, and a fleeting thought told her to stop. But she didn't. Instead, Jamis pointed. "What's with the license plates?"

"I think the decor makes the place. Sets the tone," Carmen said.

"If that wall were in a modern art museum people would be walking around it, saying shit like, 'This represents the vast mobility of American life and its loss of center and roots.'"

Carmen laughed and held her glass up in the air. "So, you're ghost hunting?"

"A poltergeist. Do you believe in ghosts?" Jamis took a long drink and refilled her glass.

"I wish I did. I wish I knew for sure we kept on after this." Sadness settled into Carmen's eyes and crept across the table to Jamis. The pressure of emotion wrapped around her heart and spread into her lungs. Instinctively, Jamis reached across the table and put her hand on top of Carmen's.

"You okay?"

"Yeah, I'm fine. Sorry. Just tired." Jamis withdrew her hand, letting Carmen recover on her own terms. "I've never seen a ghost. But there's lots of stuff I've not seen. Doesn't mean it doesn't happen," Carmen said a few moments later.

"A skeptical open mind?" Jamis was content to allow whatever emotion they triggered to pass. The intensity of it shocked her. What or who inspired such grief?

"Yeah. I suppose." Carmen poured another beer. "Tell me about your poltergeist." Jamis shared the video and day's event. "You really think poltergeists are real?"

"Generally, I'm prone to the unconventional."

"You don't say," Carmen said.

"I think it's possible our consciousness evolves and transitions at death, but some of us get stuck in between forms because of our attachments." Jamis paused to think and drink. "Like the Zen proverb which says we should die before we die. Well, what if we don't do that? What if we can't? What if we carry so much pain and grief, or hold so much love, we can't let go? What happens then?"

"You assume consciousness exists separate from the body," Carmen said.

"Oh yeah. I do. But what if consciousness somehow informs the physical form? What if, as we punched forward into modernity and scientific rationalism, we got some of it right but the most important thing wrong? Who is to say that existence precedes essence? Why can't essence or consciousness be what initiates existence? And what if we're all that spark? What if God is the spark that lives inside all life, urging it to grow and manifest in the physical?

"We can't explain that underlying desire of life to live. What if that creates all of this, and we play our role as the story unfolds? Maybe we're a piece of the whole, and as we grow and learn, the whole changes and evolves with us, but we keep what's unique. I mean, the mystics of all the world's religions are so similar—they can't all possibly be wrong, right?"

Jamis took another drink and switched gears. "What if the aliens we talk about understand more of this and can move in and out of dimensions? What if some ghosts are alien anthropologists? Or what if some ghosts are images of different times that momentarily bleed through? Or beings in other dimensions who somehow slip through into our awareness?"

"Jesus Christ," Carmen said. "I just wanted to have a beer and chat."

"I get a little carried away." Jamis set her glasses on the table. She unwrapped her ponytail, tying it into a bun on top of her head. She put her glasses back on.

"You should hear me talk about organic cheese." Carmen waved to the bartender.

"You're welcome to talk about organic cheese, if you want," Jamis said.

"I think I'm good. But you keep talking."

They wound through the hours in comfortable conversation. Jamis showed Carmen videos of her television show on YouTube. Other customers joined them, recognizing Jamis.

"It's midnight," Jamis said. They were the only two people left in the bar. Carmen scooted lower in the seat. "I've talked nonstop."

"I mumbled and encouraged you." Carmen fell over in the booth and lay on her side. Jamis kicked out under the table at her, and Carmen caught her foot and pulled. Jamis slipped down and they laughed harder, looking at each other under the table.

"How the hell are we going to get home?" Carmen's expression was concerned.

"I might be able to drive." Jamis scooted from the booth and tried to stand. She teetered, laughing. "Maybe not. Can we call a cab?" Carmen's reaction was incredulous. "No cabs, huh?" Carmen shook her head. "Uber? Lyft?" Jamis put her head on the table. The world spun.

"There isn't much public transportation to choose from in Sage Creek. I'll call us a ride," Carmen said.

"I'm drunk at the Silver Nickel and need a ride home." Carmen said apologetically into the phone. She hung up. "She'll be here in about twenty." Jamis lifted her head. "Do you really think there's a poltergeist?"

"God, I hope so. Isn't that crazy? At a certain point, I can't just keep doing this because I don't know what else to do. Something has to pan out. I actually wanted to be an archaeologist, you know? I have a BA and half a graduate degree in it. But I wasn't disciplined enough. I found the process exasperating. I don't like other people's rules."

She sat up. "Give me your phone," Jamis said. Carmen did. Jamis tapped the screen and handed it back to Carmen. "Put in your code." Carmen reached across the table and tapped in her code. "I'm adding me." Jamis texted herself and picked up her phone, showing Carmen. "Now, I've got your number. We are officially friends." She gave Carmen her phone back. They drifted into tired silence, heads foggy.

The door of the bar opened, and a rush of cold filtered in. A woman wearing faded jeans and work boots stepped inside. She took off her knit hat and dark blond red hair fell around her shoulders.

"That's our ride. Johnna, over here," Carmen said, waving.

Time stilled for Jamis as Johnna moved toward them, like a scene in an old movie when the heroine crosses the screen toward the hero for the first time. Jamis heard the crescendo of an orchestra as she approached the table. Behind her, giant strobe lights lit up the license plates on the ceiling. Maybe the MGM lion even roared. It was probably the alcohol and excitement of her day, but her impulse was to ask Johnna to leave with her.

Maybe nothing else was open on a Saturday night in Sage Creek, Utah. Didn't matter. Jamis wasn't beyond sitting in the food court of McDonald's at the twenty-four hour Walmart they passed on the way to the bar. Johnna was so beautiful her presence would make it a five star restaurant. Then Johnna smiled at Carmen and Jamis was close enough to see her green eyes twinkle and the small dimple in her right cheek. After that, she was prepared to charter a plane to take them anywhere together. She'd empty her savings account. Sell off her investments.

Carmen covered her eyes with her hands. Johnna turned to Jamis. "I'm Johnna."

Jamis stuck out her hand to Johnna, who took it. "Jamis." Johnna's hand fit nicely in her palm, just the right length and width, like they were carved to fit together. Jamis stared at their enclosed hands.

"Can I have my hand back?"

"Sorry," Jamis said. "I've had a lot to drink and you're really beautiful." She forced herself to let go of Johnna's hand.

"Watch it, Ghostbuster," Carmen said.

Johnna smiled and sat next to Jamis. The bartender came to the table and mumbled at Johnna. She turned and made eye contact. "I'm fine, Bill, thank you though." Johnna wiped crumbs from the table with her hand and grimaced.

"We got a little carried away," Carmen said.

Jamis thought the color of Johnna's hair was a miracle. Maybe even proof of God. Then Johnna arched and stretched her arms above her head. Her shirt lifted. There was a sliver of skin just above the waistband of her jeans. Jamis felt a flush of desire. It was shocking because it had been so long since she felt anything like it. The previous year was stale and empty. She'd worried the depression had snuffed out any chance of future companionship. No matter the depth of darkness into which she sank, Jamis had found an unending capacity for life to surprise her. What she needed always arrived on time, even if it wasn't always what she wanted.

Carmen pulled cash from her wallet and left it on the table. Jamis moved to take money out of her pocket.

"Nah, I got it," Carmen said. Jamis held her hands together in thanks, bowed her head.

"I can get you home tonight. I'll come pick you up in the morning and take you to the store," Johnna said. She turned to Jamis. "Where are you staying?"

"I'm staying at the motel Tess owns. I'm sorry, but I don't remember the name."

"I know it." Johnna slid from the booth. Jamis followed unsteadily and leaned casually against the side of the bench.

"Jamis is so drunk," Carmen said.

"Am not," Jamis said. "I'm beer drunk, which is only half of gin drunk. I look cool standing here like this."

Johnna laughed and followed Carmen out the door. Jamis stepped consciously behind them, watching Johnna. Her hair fell down to the middle of her back and tiny wisps danced with each step. Johnna had the most perfect walk and hair Jamis had ever seen. Johnna was also kind because she turned to wave to Bill as they left. Jamis needed to get a journal to write down all these things about Johnna to remember when she was sober.

In the truck, Jamis stretched her legs across the back seat. Carmen wanted to get back there, but Jamis refused. Johnna looked at her in the rearview mirror. "Tight fit?"

"I think you should get one of those size limits things like they have at amusement parks and set it in the back of the truck. Cap it at five-nine. I'm about two inches over the limit."

Johnna held eye contact with her via the mirror. Jamis grew quiet as the noise of the day faded away when she looked into Johnna's eyes. They'd arrived at the point in the old movie where the screen faded to black just as the hero and heroine realized they were star-crossed lovers. Either that, or Jamis was approaching a blackout.

Johnna broke eye contact first, and Jamis watched her hands on the steering wheel, long fingers wrapped around it. Jamis rested her head against the window, soothed by the cold. "We're coming up on the motel." Jamis pointed to her room from the back seat, and Johnna pulled into the parking lot. Jamis climbed out of the truck.

She stuck her head in Carmen's rolled down window and kissed her cheek. Carmen pushed her away and she stumbled toward her room. Their laughter filled the dark, icy silence of the night. There were heavy storm clouds in the sky. She opened the door after two tries and turned before she stepped inside and waved. She wanted to yell, "Johnna, don't leave." Instead, the truck faded from view.

Once inside, she slid out of her clothes, fell on the bed, and planted a foot on the ground to stop the spinning until her toes grew too cold. She pulled her leg in, burrowed under the covers, and scooted to the middle of the bed. With closed eyes, she saw the hint of Johnna's stomach peeking from beneath her shirt. She grabbed a pillow from above her, put her foot on it, and shifted back to put her foot on the ground. How would Johnna's skin feel under her fingertips?

Then sleep came and with it, dreams. She walked in the big field. The air was warm, the earth covered in green grasses and tall weeds. A woman waited on the other side. She wore yellow and her dark blond red hair reminded Jamis of Johnna. But when Jamis moved closer, it wasn't Johnna and then she was gone. Jamis stopped and sat on the ground.

She crossed her legs, took a deep breath, and decided to engage with the urgency of the experience. It hadn't been so vivid before. Jamis placed both hands on the grass. She drew power from it and heat flooded her body. Then the woman was back, watching from a distance. Jamis moved to close the distance between them, but with each step, the woman remained the same distance from her, like she was on a treadmill.

Jamis panicked as the woman faded. She dropped to her knees to crawl, just as she did earlier in the day. Something pushed her back. Bitter cold replaced the warmth. She was swept back into a brick building with many hallways and levels. Jamis crawled through them, fighting toward a door. She drew closer to it, until a rush of dark anger rose and blocked her way. She covered her face and fell on her side. The figure she'd seen earlier at the house moved closer, half of its head gone, side to back. It had no eyes, substance, or mass, and yet it was there. Jamis saw more of it somehow, her senses not confused as they were earlier.

Pressure mounted and then the building was Vince and Darcy's front room. She lay in the middle of the floor. There was a grunt, cry, and a thud, followed by a sharp pain in her head. Jamis struggled to sit up. A warm presence lifted her from the ground.

Then there was knocking. Persistent, consistent, knocking.

Jamis opened her eyes, huddled under the covers, heart pounding. She touched the bed to be certain she was awake and forced herself to sit up. The knocking continued, and as her awareness returned, she realized someone was at the door.

CHAPTER FIVE

Jamis opened the door and held her hand across her eyes to block out the sunlight. It was Johnna, wearing jeans and work boots again, hair tied back in a braid.

"Morning," Johnna said, smiling at Jamis. "I brought Carmen down and thought you might like a ride to your car."

"That would be great. I never walk if I can help it."

"I can come back, if you want to get dressed," Johnna said. Jamis stopped her and opened the door wider.

"No, I'm so rude. I'm not awake yet. Come in."

Johnna turned and whistled, fingers in her mouth. A dog ran across the parking lot to her and skidded to a halt in front of Jamis.

"This is Virginia," Johnna said. Jamis knelt and Virginia licked her face from chin to hairline.

"I hope you don't mind if she comes in the room. We're a package deal." Jamis rubbed Virginia's turtle jowls and laughed at the slobber on her hands. "Obviously, you don't."

"I love dogs so much. Is she a pit bull?"

"Brindle pit bull," Johnna said. Jamis motioned for Virginia to come into the room. "I'm sorry I woke you. I get up so early, sometimes I forget other people don't."

"No, it's okay. I'm glad you came. I keep having this recurring dream. You woke me from it."

"Do you want to talk about it?" Johnna's tone was kind, and Jamis turned to face her. In the light of day, she was even more beautiful than Jamis remembered. Johnna studied her with kindness and curiosity, her eyes light and spirit present.

"I don't even know what to say about it, honestly."

"Maybe later," Johnna said. "Don't push yourself. Go get dressed, take a shower. You smell like the Silver Nickel."

"My mouth tastes like an ashtray. I may brush my teeth, too." Johnna feigned to move away. "That's harsh."

"Truth is," Johnna said. Virginia jumped on the bed. She pointed. "That okay?"

"Yes," Jamis said, watching her with a grin. Johnna's eyes were on her and she lapsed into silence, struggling to find something to say.

"Why don't you come meet us at the diner?" Johnna filled the silence. "It's just across the parking lot. Tess's breakfast is awesome."

"Give me five," Jamis said, an unknown sensation coming to life inside. It was expansive. She imagined the blackened tissue around her heart turning pink and vibrant. The beats of her renewed heart echoed through the rest of her body.

"Okay," Johnna said, eyes quickly downcast. Jamis noticed it, hopeful she felt the same way. Johnna called to Virginia and they left.

The thought of Johnna waiting for her at the diner made her regret not waxing her whole body before leaving home. Steam from the shower fogged the mirror. Jamis wiped it with a washcloth and leaned close to pluck stray eyebrow hairs. She looked at her wet hair, holding it in her hand. Did she have too many split ends? Why didn't she take more time to groom? She slammed the brush down. There wasn't time for any of this. She dressed quickly, not wanting to keep Johnna waiting.

She found them in a booth near the door at the diner.

"Yell-o. I'm clean and ready," Jamis said, sliding in. "Thanks for asking me to come."

"Sure," Johnna said. Virginia sat next to Johnna, upright, waiting for her order.

"Does Sage Creek have relaxed public health standards?" Jamis asked, pointing to Virginia.

"Are you suggesting Virginia is dirty?"

"I'm just suggesting that it's the first time in my varied and traveled life that I've seen a dog in a booth waiting to place her order."

"Obviously, you're not that well traveled."

Tess arrived to take their order. "How did you end up with this breakfast date?" She pointed at Johnna. "Might be out of your league."

"Good karma. And Carmen. I like her. Thank you," Jamis said.

"I thought you'd like each other," Tess said, turning to Johnna. "While you're here can you look at Xavier? He's not eating again."

"Of course," Johnna said.

Jamis ordered pancakes and eggs. Johnna ordered eggs for Virginia and oatmeal and fruit for herself. Tess left with their orders.

"Is Xavier a dog?" Johnna nodded. "You're a veterinarian," Jamis said. "That's a real job. I've never had a real job."

"It's all I ever wanted to do," Johnna said.

"Are you off today?"

"Yeah," Johnna said. She didn't offer anything else. She held Jamis's eye contact long enough for her to know she felt the same way. It was like tiny fairies danced and unicorns pranced around their heads. Connections like this didn't happen in real life, only movies and in books that ended with some conflict solved, heroines happily ever after. Jamis rarely noticed anyone in such a way. The draw was deep enough to penetrate the layers of her practiced detachment, even sober. Jamis couldn't stand the idea that she'd leave her after dropping her off to get her car. The surge of emotion in her chest cast her off balance.

"Use your words," Jamis said.

"I'm sorry?" Johnna looked at her with genuine interest.

"I don't know why I said that. Martha, a counselor in a group home I lived in, used to tell me that all the time. I didn't talk much. But I threw a lot of stuff."

"You were in a group home?"

"Yeah," Jamis said, staring at her. Was it too soon to tell her everything? It was, so instead she said, "My brain feels slow this morning."

"Carmen felt the same way. She wasn't very talkative." Johnna let her change the subject but Jamis saw enough compassion in her eyes to know she could talk to her.

"Do you mind if I check in on my feeds real quick? I promise it will just take a minute," Jamis said. She needed to break the spell. Johnna sat forward to peer over the table at Jamis's phone. Jamis opened Facebook, Instagram, and Twitter to thousands of notifications, replied quickly to a few, and then put her phone away.

"I don't have any of those," Johnna said.

"What? Social media?"

"Yeah. I don't like computers. I still read the newspaper and paper books, too. Sometimes I get crazy and watch a DVD. My brother Sam lives with me, and he hooked up an Amazon thingy that plays music, but it mostly creeps me out. There is a TV thing too that connects to the Wi-Fi. It all feels so unnecessary."

"That is so sad," Jamis said.

"Tell me you don't get tired of it."

"I'm so connected, it's hard to understand."

"Well, when I told Sam about you, he went crazy. He follows you on one of the sites. Found a picture of Salt Lake you put up there and showed me this morning before I left."

"My loyal legions of fans," Jamis said. "Did he watch my show?"

"Yeah, he did. He said to tell you he has all the seasons on Amazon."

"It was fun," Jamis said. "Traveling all over the world. Seeing so many different places. Chasing ghosts, aliens, urban legends. You name it."

"Do you miss it?"

"I do," Jamis said. She felt like telling Johnna about her depression. About how her days opened up into nothingness without her show and made her face every uncomfortable emotion she ever avoided. How she spent most of her time alone, without friends, the crew of the show moved on to other things. No one in Hollywood took her seriously as anything other than a celebrity ghost hunter. There was nothing else for her to do. But she didn't say that. Instead, she said, "Carmen is lonely." It was easier to say she was than to admit the depth of her own loneliness.

"I know." The light in Johnna's eyes dimmed, and Jamis immediately regretted being the cause of it. She started to say something to make the light return, but Johnna stopped her. "You need new shoes. You can't walk around Utah in winter wearing Converse."

Jamis appreciated the deflection. But she couldn't stop. "You two seem close. How do you know her?"

"I've lived here my whole life. I know a lot of people." Tess brought their food. She set a plate of scrambled eggs in front of Virginia, who ate them, sitting in the booth. Jamis took a few bites in silence, as did Johnna.

"You just know her from around? Like just from living daily life?"

Johnna set down her spoon and studied Jamis.

"What?" Jamis's fork was midair. Was she sorting through what was appropriate to share?

"Nothing," Johnna said.

"Now I'm going to be paranoid. Were you going to say something about me? Do I have something stuck in my teeth? Hanging from my nose?"

"You're charming."

"Thanks," Jamis said. "That's probably why I was on television. But I don't think that's what you were going to say."

"You're humble, too," Johnna said.

"I know. I'm the whole package." Jamis took a bite. "I'm sorry. I'm working on this compulsive need to ask a million questions. I need to do a better job attending to the present and people's feelings."

"That sounds like something you'd learn in therapy," Johnna said.

"Oh my God, you too?"

"So much therapy. Let's save Carmen and therapy for another time." Jamis agreed with a grin and a thumbs-up. "Tell me why you're here?"

Jamis told her, in between bites and sips of coffee.

"Do you know anything about the house?" Jamis was still hungry. She looked at her plate and then turned to look for Tess.

"I'll get it," Johnna said and waved. "Tess saw me. She'll bring more." She smiled at Jamis. "I don't know anything about the house. But I know who would. When we finish here, let me look at Xavier, and then take you to meet someone. If you have time."

"Nothing but time," Jamis said.

Jamis peered into the office behind the lobby desk. Johnna held a tiny Chihuahua on her lap and talked with Tess. Her hands were gentle and she held perfectly still, listening to Tess. Jamis watched her, feeling like a different light embodied her. Like she existed just outside the frame of energy that contained everything else around her. Everything around her faded from view.

Jamis retreated to the lobby, overwhelmed by her desire to just look at Johnna, and scrolled through the comments on her most recent post. They ranged from, *"Be careful Jamis. Poltergeists OMG!"* to *"WTF you crazy bitch. Google Scientific Method."*

"Jesus sends poltergeists after u cuz your gay. Repent."

It deserved a reply. "*You're. ~Jamis.*"

When Johnna called out, she tucked her phone away.

"I think we're ready," Johnna said. She stepped into the lobby, followed by Tess.

"I hope he feels better," Jamis said to Tess.

"Just stop by the clinic and pick up the meds. I'll text Gloria. She and my part-time vet are there today," Johnna told her.

Jamis pulled her phone from her pocket and responded again. "*YOU'RE. Omg at least get that right. XOXO ~Jamis.*" She looked up in time to follow Johnna outside, and waved back at Tess.

Johnna whistled at Virginia, who jumped into the back seat of the truck. "I texted Sapphire from the restaurant and she's expecting us," Johnna said.

"Sapphire?"

"Yeah. The two of you are a match made in heaven." Johnna stopped right in front of her. She was a few inches shorter and Jamis stepped forward. Johnna lifted her hand and brushed something from the front of Jamis's coat and fixed the collar, before turning away. "Let's go," she said. Jamis touched the coat where Johnna's fingers had been.

Chapter Six

They retrieved the rental car from the market, and Jamis followed Johnna to the municipal building about a mile from the hotel. They parked and entered through a side door, held ajar with a rock. They started down a flight of stairs, until Johnna stopped. "I didn't even ask if stairs were okay."

"Totally fine. I'll take them back up too. I need to burn off Tess's pancakes," Jamis said.

They trotted down two flights of stairs into the building's subbasement. Johnna pushed open a double set of industrial doors. The walls were plain cinderblock and had been painted a light blue sometime during the twentieth century. The floors were light beige linoleum with gray rubber baseboards.

Johnna opened another set of double doors into a massive space. Jamis paused to take it all in. It was the town archives, and it stretched the length and width of the building. A large metal cage blocked the entry room from the archives. Behind the cage, metal shelving overflowed with filing boxes.

"This is amazing," Jamis said, impressed and overwhelmed. "Kismet, Johnna. I needed county records, and instead, I meet Tess, Carmen, and then you."

"Wait until you meet Sapphire." Johnna moved closer to the cage. "Sapphire? Are you here?"

"I am. Hold on." The voice came from far away, obscured by the metal cabinets. Jamis strained to look behind the cage. There were rows upon rows of boxes. They appeared to be sorted by date and type. In the first row she read, “Marriage certificates 1997,” but couldn’t see beyond that. The cabinets were positioned at an angle.

“Sapphire did all of this,” Johnna said. “My brother-in-law, Paul, my sister Sara’s husband, is the district attorney. He helped her secure the space and materials some years back. Before this, the county had stuff stored everywhere. She’s systematically brought everything here. Engineered fireproof systems and security. All of this with fifteen thousand dollars.”

Sapphire came around the corner and unlocked the cage with a key on a lanyard around her neck, immediately greeting Virginia. She had black hair and wore dark blue jeans and a plain red long sleeve T-shirt. She wore no makeup and had a small tasteful ring in her nose and multiple rings in her ears. She wasn’t overweight, but she had enough to keep warm, and her eyes were bright blue. A sleeve tattoo peeked from beneath Sapphire’s T-shirt. Jamis couldn’t wait to compare their tattoos.

“I’m trying so hard to be cool.” Sapphire dropped the file she was holding on the desk, leaped forward, and wrapped her arms around Jamis’s neck. Jamis held her arms at her sides. Sapphire whipped her around in excitement. She let go, stepped back, covered her mouth with both hands, and blushed. “Oh my God. I’m so sorry. It’s just you’re a geek legend.”

“That’s the best compliment I’ve ever gotten,” Jamis said, grinning. She didn’t even mind the hug.

“You never greet me like that,” Johnna said. Sapphire pulled her into a generous hug. “That’s better. Jamis needs help with a house. What was it again?”

“Thirty-two Third Street.”

“I gotcha. I’m your gal,” Sapphire said.

“Well, okay then,” Johnna said, as she turned to leave. “When you both finish here, why don’t you come over for dinner tonight? Sam wants to meet Jamis, and I know he’d love to see you.”

“I’ll be there,” Sapphire said.

“I’ll see you later, then,” Johnna said. She walked down the hallway with Virginia, and Jamis didn’t want her to leave.

"Johnna," Jamis said. She liked saying her name.

"Yeah?" Johnna stopped in the hallway, Virginia at her side.

"I'll see you later then," Jamis said. Johnna waved, and a faint blush stole across her cheeks, but she turned away before Jamis could see more of it.

❖

"Let's start on the computer back here," Sapphire said.

Jamis followed Sapphire past aisles of metal shelves to the middle of the archives. There were four flat screen monitors on a large wooden desk. They were stacked at alternating heights. There was a large desktop computer off to the side of the desk and wires ran from it to two other computers on the side. A laptop and a tablet were connected to all of it via cables and open circuit boards in the middle of the desk. Sapphire tapped on the laptop, and the whole system lit up with screensavers full of floating fish.

"Did you build this? It's amazing."

"I like computers," Sapphire said.

"Obviously," Jamis said. "With this kind of talent, why are you here?"

"I don't like the world. But I like it okay here." Sapphire typed while she spoke, querying a database. She sorted through lines of returned data, pressing a series of buttons on her laptop and then turned a computer monitor to face Jamis.

"There you go. House was built in 1922. Owned by James Davis. Looks like the house belonged to Rick Davis until 1993. Probably passed down in estate. Probably his son. Let's look." She typed and names popped up on another monitor. "Yup. That's his son." Jamis watched, enraptured.

Sapphire scrolled through lines of fast moving data flying at her, pushing information to another screen. "Sold to Michael Alger in 1993. Foreclosed in 1995." She pointed with one finger while she typed. "Then it was sold to an out of town investment group. There's the sale paperwork. Look." The date was July 16, 1996.

Sapphire continued to scroll. "Ooh, foreclosed in February 2002. They didn't pay taxes on it. Look." She put up the tax repossession notice on the middle monitor. "Looks like the county took possession of the house until 2015. Here's the sale paperwork to a Salt Lake City investment group in 2016. Brings us up to date."

"Why did the county have it for so long?"

"Back in 2015, the county sold off a ton of land, property, and such to raise some revenue. It probably got bogged down in bureaucracy." She continued to scroll. "I can't find anything else."

"Would police reports be in here?"

"That's the only thing I don't have in here. They have their own archive." Sapphire said "archive" while making quotes with her fingers. Obviously, it wasn't well managed. "I'm working on getting access though. What are you thinking? Why?"

"Well, if there were disturbances about the house, that's where it would be." Jamis stared at the screen, thinking. "Wait, was it a rental?"

Sapphire turned to type and fell into silence, sorting through data. "Yeah, good call. It was. For a long time, actually." She pushed a picture to a monitor with a swipe of her fingers on the tablet. "Look there. That's an eviction notice for the property in 1973, and ooh, wait," she said. "Check this out. Another one from 1991." She pushed it to the monitor. "Eviction notice served to Stephanie Gardner. January 4, 1991." Sapphire continued to type. "Ooh, another one. Same woman. September 23, 1991."

Jamis looked at the eviction notice. A renter who couldn't pay the rent on time but who was granted a reprieve only to regress again. "Are there any others?"

"Nothing after September 1991. Just the sale records and tax repossession. Nothing about renters." The data moved so fast at Sapphire, Jamis was overwhelmed watching it.

Jamis put her elbows on Sapphire's desk, held her chin in her hands, looked away from the code. "How were you able to get this information? I mean, how is this possible?"

"Well, I rendered every paper record in the county to digital. When I did that, I created a metadata infrastructure and then associated searchable phrases and taxonomy. Even though the record is flat and scanned, in the background I've associated data I can query. It wasn't that hard, really."

"If you say so. Your education?"

"PhD in computer science from ASU."

"That's where I went. I didn't get that far, though," Jamis said.

"When were you there?"

"Late nineties. You?"

"Little after that. We missed each other. Though it's a big school."

"You're extraordinary," Jamis said. Sapphire blushed, rich red flooding her cheeks. Sapphire scooted back to look at her. "So, the house has transferred ownership multiple times since 1992. Before then, it was with one family." Sapphire agreed. "Then it passed hands a number of times and was empty, owned by the county because of unpaid taxes, until 2016 when it was purchased and renovated by an investment company, bringing us up to date."

"Why do you want to know about this house anyway?"

"I wondered how long it would take you to ask," Jamis said with a grin. "It's haunted."

"No way."

"Yup." Jamis shared what happened at the house the day before. "I think things get wonky in the early nineties. Would you agree?"

"I do, actually. Let's see if we can find anything about Stephanie Gardner." Sapphire began to type again. "I'm curious now." Sapphire tossed a death certificate onto a monitor, then pulled up a browser and typed "Stephanie Gardner" into the search engine which returned thousands of hits. "Holy shit," she said.

"Holy shit is right," Jamis said. "Can you go to that one?" Jamis pointed to a search result that linked to a Wikipedia article.

Sapphire clicked on the link and Jamis read out loud. "It is widely believed that Richard Crespin murdered Stephanie Gardner in Sage Creek, Utah, in March 1992. She was found on March 16,1992, though her date of death was undetermined. However, he never took responsibility for this murder before he was executed by lethal injection in Idaho in 2007."

"If that doesn't make a poltergeist, I don't know what does," Jamis said.

"If she was murdered, it would have been really big news. I started archiving the local paper, but I'm only up to 1982. We'll have to go to the library and review the microfilm to see what they were saying about it then. I don't remember anything."

"You can just point me there. You don't have to go."

"Are you kidding me? Like I'm not seeing this through. Let me call and tell them we're heading over. They can get the microfilm ready for us." She spoke into the telephone while Jamis ruminated. Was this an actual poltergeist of a murdered woman? What were the implications of it? Should she document it differently? Call someone? The authorities? Her thoughts whirled. It wasn't like there was a ghost hunting council, though there should be. Or maybe there was, and she wasn't a member. No clubs wanted her as a member.

Sapphire finished talking, hung up the phone and interrupted her reverie. "Oh my God, Jamis, do you think she's the poltergeist?"

"It's possible. It would make sense. I mean, if she was murdered at the house? Or somehow felt tied to the house?" Jamis wasn't certain of anything but felt the excitement of a chase emerging. Maybe Stephanie was the figure from her dreams and her encounter at the house the night before. "I guess we'll just see where this leads us."

A librarian greeted Jamis and Sapphire at the public library. She pulled microfilm from March 1992 through the end of the year. Jamis thanked her profusely, while Sapphire wound the March reel, pausing on the front page to twist the view right side up. "We're looking somewhere in the middle of the month forward. She was found on March 16."

Sapphire scrolled and stopped abruptly, adjusting the image on the screen. It was a black-and-white grainy photo of a semi stretched across US Highway 6 and a car to the side, the front end mangled. She looked at Jamis and wiped a tear.

"It's March 14," Jamis said, reading the date. "Why did you stop here?"

"That's the wreck that killed Johnna's mom and little brother. Crushed Sam's legs."

"I had no idea." Jamis nudged Sapphire who scooted to the right of the machine. "Do you mind if I read?" Sapphire motioned for her to continue. "An afternoon accident took the lives of a local woman and her seven-year-old son yesterday. Two other children were in the car. One is in critical condition at Sage Creek General Hospital. The other has minor cuts, bruises, and a broken arm. The semi-truck driver is also dead. He lost control of his truck and it jackknifed, impacting the car at speeds over sixty-five miles per hour. The highway was closed for fourteen hours as police investigated the scene."

Johnna's mom died too. Jamis put her hand on her chest and sat back in the chair. Did their stitched together hearts recognize each other?

"What are the chances that I'd meet Johnna, investigating a poltergeist who might be the woman murdered around the same time her mom and brother died, exactly twenty-five years ago?" The level of interconnectivity was astonishing. Jamis was nauseous, though, like she pried into someone's diary. "Oh my God, Sapphire, I wish I could unread that."

"Do you understand the statistical improbability that you would meet Johnna, come to me, flip through this newspaper looking for your poltergeist?"

Sadness welled in Jamis's throat. It was consuming. "Are you familiar with Jung's theory of synchronicity?"

"Vaguely. Basically, it says that events that appear unrelated actually are, right?" Sapphire turned back and began to scroll.

"More or less. I think it's when events are somehow related without evident external causation. Events manifest via internal processes, or in quantum dimensions, fields, or spaces we are unable to see. Somehow, unrelated objective occurrences share a common, underlying pattern." Her heart hammered. Johnna's mom died too. "Anyway, I don't need to get stuck there, so yeah, what you said, mostly."

"What does it mean? What does this mean?" Sapphire pointed at the microfilm.

"Honestly, I don't know. I have no idea. It might not be related at all." Jamis twisted the ring on her right index finger, and then worried at the thumb ring. She stared at the desk and focused her eyes on the corner of the microfiche machine. "I think I want to talk to Johnna about this."

"If you're going to talk to any of them, Johnna is the best one," Sapphire said.

"Why do you say that?"

"She's hyperrational and super calm. Sam and Sara, their older sister, are softer. You'll see when you meet them."

"You've known them all a long time?"

"We grew up together," Sapphire said. "Johnna, Sam, and me are the same grade." She stopped the microfilm again. "Here she is. March 16, 1992. Stephanie Gardner is found at the dump. Police are investigating. Her mother is dead. No family." Sapphire skimmed the article. "Not a lot here."

They put the next reel on the machine, skimming through the newspaper for the next few months. When they finished, sometime in October, Sapphire said, "Nothing. I can't believe a murder like this would only be mentioned once."

"No family, no money. No one cared," Jamis said. "Can we get police records?"

"Well, we can, but can you be comfortable not knowing how?"

"I won't ask any questions," Jamis said.

"Give me a day or two."

"Thanks," Jamis said. "No one cared then, but I care now. I want to know Stephanie's story."

"Someone should always care," Sapphire said, winding up the microfilm roll.

CHAPTER SEVEN

In her car, Jamis responded to comments on Facebook while waiting for Sapphire to power down and lock up the archives. Someone wrote, "*You suck so bad. Stupid lesbo.*"

Jamis wrote back, "*That's not what your mom said. XOXO ~ Jamis.*"

Sapphire knocked on the passenger window, startling Jamis. "What are you doing? I texted Johnna. Dinner will be ready about six."

"Want to go to the house?" Sapphire scrunched up her face. "Ah, come on. You said you're a fan."

"I'm going to regret this," Sapphire said, expression pinched. She got in the car and tucked her bag behind the seat.

"You know, you and me could be partners. Like Starsky and Hutch. Cagney and Lacey."

"Buffy and Willow? Mulder and Scully?"

"Oh my God, are you gay? Because if you are, I might ask you to marry me."

"I mean, I might go for you. You're adorable. But sadly, I like men."

"It's better to be platonic, crime solving partners. Romance jacks it up."

"What about Bones and Booth?"

"Well, except for them." Jamis pulled onto the road. "Mulder and Scully had issues." Sapphire agreed.

At the house, Sapphire paused in the front seat. "I don't want to get out of the car."

"Come on," Jamis said. "Please?" Jamis left the car and stood in front of it, hands pressed together. "Sapphire, please?"

"I'm going to regret this," Sapphire said, climbing from the car.

"I can't tell you how excited I am to see what happens tonight." Jamis rushed up the porch stairs. "I've had the video equipment set up since last night. It's set to record with motion, like a security system. I checked earlier and there were no clips, so my thought is the activity happens when someone is present."

Sapphire followed her up the stairs, closed her eyes, took a deep breath, and stepped into the house. "Like the old adage, if a tree falls and no one is there to hear it, does it make a sound?"

"Exactly. It's hard to know how this works," Jamis said. "It's the creating force of observation. We know that particles behave differently when they're observed. Perhaps the force of our observation, and the projection of our consciousness, is what allows ghosts to manifest."

"I have to ask. Do you really believe in ghosts?"

"I do," Jamis said, moving into the kitchen. "I don't have conclusive proof they exist, though. Only evidence. I don't know what they are, either. I mean, is it our consciousness hanging out in another dimension? Our soul? Who knows. I wish there was more formal, scientific, and academic support for paranormal investigation. Because there isn't, it's relegated to outer space, which attracts nut bags."

Maybe that was her. This was the last ghost hunt, she reminded herself. Either this produced enough tangible evidence for her to justify continuing, or it was time to let go. "So, I do." Sapphire still stood by the front door. "You going to come in?"

"Maybe. I don't know," Sapphire said. "Do you have some gadgets? Gadgets might make me feel better."

"No proton packs," Jamis said. "Gadgets don't really do anything, so I gave them up." Sapphire took a tentative step into the house. "Don't think of a marshmallow man, whatever you do," Jamis said. Sapphire held up her birdie finger. The house was cold, but the thermostat was set to seventy-two degrees. "Feel that cold?" Jamis opened the camera case and handed Sapphire the night vision goggles. "You can use those."

Sapphire put them on. "Are you my mummy?"

"You don't love *Doctor Who* as much as I do," Jamis said.

"I've watched every episode since 1963. I've read every book, comic book, listened to every full cast production." Sapphire took the goggles off.

"We're soul mates." A gust of wind smacked into the windows. They rattled, and the curtains shook. The back door opened and hit the kitchen counter. Sapphire moved to close it. As she passed the refrigerator, the door flew open and hit her. She crashed into the kitchen chairs. Jamis grabbed her around the waist before she fell.

Jamis stood in front of her and closed both the fridge and back door. Any heat accumulated in the house was gone. Their breath marked the air. It was twenty-two degrees outside. The house felt below zero.

"I knew I'd regret this," Sapphire said, hand on her heart.

"Come on," Jamis said. "This is fun."

Then the front door flew open with another gust of air. There was nothing on the stoop. Only their footsteps were visible in the fine dusting of blown snow on the sidewalk leading to the front door. Jamis moved to close the door. Sapphire watched from the kitchen. As Jamis lifted her hand to latch the chain, something emerged from the far left corner of the room, right where Vince saw something. It moved from her peripheral vision to direct line of sight. It emerged as a tickle, erupting in her consciousness and sounding her survival alarms. Time stilled, and silence enveloped her again. It was so quiet she heard the blood rushing through her veins.

The room was dark, though it should not have been. Jamis lunged for the light switch near the door, which lit enough of the space that the shadow dispersed. Jamis put her hand on the back of the door to find balance.

"What? What did you see?" Sapphire rushed toward her and followed her gaze.

"Something. Coming from that corner," Jamis said, pointing. "Shit. The cameras."

She grabbed the tablet from her bag and tapped it to life, the sensation of earwigs crawling down her spine. She navigated to get to the footage of the last few minutes, rewinding it to see herself walking to the front door. The back of her head was visible but there was no movement recorded in the corner of the room.

"Are you sure you saw something? It wasn't a shadow?" Sapphire waited in the doorway between the kitchen and front room

"I'm sure. I mean, I'm really sure. I don't know what else it could be. Something came at me. I shouldn't have panicked. Should have kept watching it."

"Maybe it's in pain," Sapphire said. "I mean, that's what you used to say on your show. It means they're scared, really hurting. Like a hurt animal or something."

"Well, if Stephanie was murdered here, it could explain the anger and darkness." Grief and love were the two emotions powering the human experience. Jamis knew that when turned inward, grief turned to anger and despair. In the years following her mom's death, she cycled between despondency and volatility. The instability of foster care and the abuse there added layers of trauma, which then bled into adulthood. It manifested in broken relationships, obsessive work, and depression. Such heavy emotion demanded a recompense. It was true for the living and the dead.

A clock ticked in the background; otherwise, the house was silent. Jamis opened her mouth to speak again, but Sapphire stopped her.

"Jamis, don't look behind you, but there is someone in the corner of the room."

Chapter Eight

The lights flickered and blinked off. Jamis lunged for the flashlight she noticed on the table next to the stairs, pressing the on button repeatedly. It would not turn on, so she threw it at the corner of the room. It moved through whatever was there and hit the wall.

She then struggled to take her phone out of her pocket. Sapphire followed her lead, and they both turned their cell phones to the corner. The illumination was not heavy, but it was enough to light the way.

"What happened to the light?" Jamis moved to stand closer to Sapphire. "Where the hell is the sun? It didn't set yet." They had been surrounded by light, from the windows, from the kitchen, lamps in the front room, and the light above the entryway into the house. Now, there was only darkness. "Did the lights go out? What happened?"

"I don't know," Sapphire whispered. The figure in the corner of the room rose and filled the space between the floor and ceiling. Long arms reached down the walls and fingers stretched through a landscape print hung above the couch. Jamis and Sapphire both screamed. Sapphire grabbed Jamis's arm, squeezing so hard it hurt.

"Oh my God, help us. Jamis, do something," Sapphire said.

Jamis pulled Sapphire's fingers from her arm and pushed her to the front door, taking two steps before she fell to her knees. Sapphire collapsed in front of her.

It felt like her dream. It felt like the day before. The pattern was repeating. Patterns could be changed. She knew from her own life. How different could it be for a dead person? Jamis took a deep breath, closed her eyes, no longer afraid. When she opened them, the woman from the field stood by the front door. Sapphire screamed again, pointing behind Jamis.

"Let go. It's feeding on our terror. Close your eyes. Imagine something that makes you happy." Jamis shifted so they faced each other.

"I can't close my eyes," Sapphire said. "It's right behind us."

"It's not really here. Close your eyes. See something that makes you happy."

Sapphire closed her eyes and was silent. "Jamis?"

The distorted shadow of the being she'd met the day before dissipated. The woman from the field disappeared and the light returned.

"It's gone. You can open your eyes," Jamis said.

"What just happened?"

"I don't know." Jamis retrieved her tablet. "How much you want to bet I got nothing on the cameras?"

"Let me see." Sapphire came toward her.

They watched the clips together. The cameras recorded nothing but the two of them. Jamis stopped the playback.

"Oh, hey, wait. Wait," Sapphire said. She touched the screen and reversed it a few seconds. "There," she said, pointing at the screen. Her finger rested on the front door. A shadow hovered in front of it. "Did you see it in real time? What was it?"

"Yeah. It's this woman from a dream." Jamis tried to zoom on the tablet, but nothing returned. The flicker of movement was almost indistinguishable.

"What?" Sapphire tapped the screen again. "You see stuff from your dreams in real life?"

"Maybe?" Jamis wasn't really sure. Maybe it was wishful projection. But then why would Sapphire notice it on the recording?

"Weird," Sapphire said.

"Tell me about it."

"Can you give me access to your cameras? I have some imaging enhancing software I use for old photos. I might be able to clear it up."

"Take a look. I'll give you the passwords." Jamis handed her the tablet.

"I'll look tonight," Sapphire said.

"I think we need to go. I feel like I've had enough. I can take you to your car," Jamis said.

They left together, side by side, but as Jamis shut off the lights, she paused to look in the far corner of the room. Blue lines, shaped vaguely like eyes blinked at her. Did Stephanie have blue eyes? She felt deep tenderness replace her alarm. What if someone really killed Stephanie in the house? Did she show Vince her body? The lines shifted to red, something screamed. Jamis pulled the door shut.

Her emotions were amped and charged. It wasn't like her to turn away from something like that, but the emotional density of the experience overwhelmed her. Her nervous system felt inflamed, like one more thing would be the last she could take. It was probably because of her ongoing recovery from depression.

In the car, she released the tension. "Fucked up," Jamis said, hitting the steering wheel. "Holy hell."

"I've never seen anything like it," Sapphire said, "but this isn't something I do on a regular basis." Sapphire looked out the window at passing houses and mailboxes.

"I thought I was desensitized." She shivered, thought about her strained nerves, imagined them swollen like a twisted ankle. "I didn't feel desensitized tonight. That was unreal." At a stop sign, she turned to Sapphire. "It was almost like we were somewhere else."

"Yes. It wasn't like it came to us. It was like we went to it." Sapphire drifted away in thought for a few moments. "But how did we get back? By thinking happy thoughts?"

Jamis considered the question as they traveled on together. "You know, hell is a state of consciousness. What if, for whatever reason, this particular being can share its consciousness? What if we are somehow pulled into their illusion?" She stopped again at the end of the street by her motel. "This is as far as I know to go. It looks different at dusk." Sapphire directed her. "Anger, fear, grief create darkness. These energies settle in our bodies and they create attachments to people, things, events. With enough trauma, it's conceivable this being created their own hell and continued to live in it. Now, for whatever reason, it wants to share it or wants to be seen."

"That's really creepy." Sapphire pointed, and Jamis followed the path of her finger.

"But think about it. Serial killers have the worst imaginable experiences as they grow up. It warps their psyche. The most difficult people are the most wounded. Pain needs an outlet so it creates chaos. It cries for help. What if that's what's happening here? What if that being is Stephanie Gardner, somehow reaching out, now, after all these years?"

"Are you a psychologist or ghost hunter?"

"I've just had a lot of therapy. But everything is conjecture and projection with communal consensus. That's what we do with everything. We form laws, customs, and normative standards. Then we tell stories about it. Then those stories form our body of knowledge. The lanes get defined. And within them we project our consciousness." Jamis tapped the steering wheel, when the right question emerged. "Maybe we should ask what you and I needed to see there tonight." Her blood raced to her head with visceral understanding. "What made you feel better?"

"I thought about seeing Johnna earlier, Sam, and my mom when I gave her a new iPad a few days ago."

"I thought about this dream I've been having for months. The one I told you about. There is a woman there. I can't reach her, though." Jamis pulled the car where Sapphire pointed in the municipal building parking lot. "Don't lose me. I'll just follow you."

They drove through Sage Creek as night settled. Porch lights flickered on. Deep purple settled into the fading orange of the sun. Red dirt mountains jutted upward like gothic towers, reaching to the sky. In the distance, a sage bush, grown almost eight feet tall, stood alone in the high desert against the long emptiness of western sky.

Jamis longed to roll down her window, but the peace she viewed was tinged with frigid cold. Sapphire took them from the lights of the city down a long, dark road, and Jamis slowed automatically, unaccustomed to driving without streetlights. A mile or two passed, she was not sure, and they turned down a plowed dirt road that wound for just a tenth of a mile, over a small creek, before opening to a well-lit house surrounded by open space. A light hung in a window of a barn. A chimney puffed smoke. Sapphire waved at her from the front door on the wrap-around porch. Jamis climbed from the car. Was this for real? Did Johnna really live in a place that looked like it belonged in a Norman Rockwell painting?

Light classical music filtered out. In the doorway, a man in a wheelchair said, "Well, come in. It's cold." Sapphire followed him. Jamis hurried behind, relieved to be inside. Warm lighting filled the space. The room was sparsely decorated, minimalistic. The only visual noise was the overflowing bookshelves along the staircase.

"Hi, Jamis. I'm Sam. It's so amazing to meet you. Come in. Relax." Jamis sat in the chair next to the fire and wished the blinds were open on the wall of windows to her right.

"Johnna, Sapphire is here with Jamis," Sam yelled up the stairs.

"Just getting out of the shower and I'll be down." Johnna's voice thrilled and simultaneously soothed Jamis. She didn't think anything that was happening was possible. From poltergeists to a gorgeous woman who made her pulse race. She'd given up on almost everything the previous few years, and certainly didn't have the energy to date. Her focus had been inside, shifting through the emotional debris of everything that came before. Jamis told

Dr. Frank there might not be space to try again with someone. It felt too dangerous, as love becomes after too many failed attempts. If that was true, what was she doing here? With this woman who seemed entirely too good to be true? Was it a delusion? She needed to slow down, be sure.

Virginia bounded down the stairs, nails clacking against the wood. She saw Jamis and leaped, landing on her lap.

"I've missed you too." Virginia licked her face before collapsing to pant happily on her back, stretched across Jamis's legs.

"Are you kidding, Virginia?" Virginia looked at Sam and wagged her tail. "I mean, I can't blame her. This is the biggest thing to happen to us in years." He moved toward the kitchen. "I shouldn't admit that. Don't tell Johnna I did." He waved at Sapphire. "Come see my new bird. Do you want to come?"

"I'm going to sit if you don't mind. It's been quite the day." They left and Jamis kissed Virginia on the mouth. "Mauled by a pit bull."

Jamis stretched her legs in front of her, shifting Virginia. The walls were painted light yellow and made of plaster. They looked like the dress in the dream. A washing machine ran in the background. The sound of water rushing into the machine filled the silent spaces in the music. She closed her eyes. The low murmur of Sam's voice behind the closed door wove itself with the sounds of the house, and her consciousness retreated into sleep.

Jamis was in the field again. The sun was lower in the sky. The woman was closer now. Jamis called out to her, tried to walk toward her. The woman took a step toward her and Jamis smiled, excited. "Yes, walk to me," she said, pushing forward like a runner on the starting blocks of a race. But then there was pressure on her shoulder, like a hand.

"Jamis." She heard her name. "You fell asleep. Jamis?" She was dreaming and needed to wake up. For an unfocused moment, as her eyes opened, Jamis thought the woman in the dress was closer. The yellow paint of the wall shone around her head, reflected by the light behind her. She shifted her focus and reached to touch her face.

"Who are you?"

"It's Johnna. You fell asleep. Remember, you came with Sapphire?" Johnna touched Jamis's hand on her face and nudged Virginia who slept soundly. "Go on, you. Get down. You probably put her to sleep."

Jamis dropped her hand, pulling back into herself. "I'm sorry," she said, "Was I drooling or snoring? Anything embarrassing?" Johnna's green eyes were soft and kind.

"No. But you were in a really deep sleep." Johnna knelt on one knee next to her. "I was no more than ten minutes upstairs. It's strange you fell to sleep so hard. Have you struggled sleeping lately?"

"I don't sleep well at all, normally, so I nap a lot. But I keep having this dream."

"You said that this morning." Johnna's shampoo smelled like eucalyptus and mint. "Do you want to talk about it?"

"I'm not sure I can." Her words caught in her throat. "There's a field. It's beautiful and peaceful, but I'm not able to move. There's a woman there. She's closer now. It feels important, but I don't know why." Johnna's presence magnified Jamis's senses. They were so close, touching her was possible, but Jamis hesitated. They'd just met the night before. Was she healthy enough to get involved? Did she have enough to offer? A retired ghost hunter, who was popular, but also a pop culture joke. What if she asked and Johnna said no? Would she dip back down into the grand abyss from which she just emerged?

"Come on. Let's eat. We can talk about it later, if you want."

Johnna turned on the kitchen lights. The cabinets were white, simple, and clean.

"You're okay? No health issues?" Johnna lifted a pan out of the oven and set it on the counter. It was baked ziti and it smelled divine. She could cook too.

"Nope. Not that I know of, anyway." Jamis made her way to Johnna's side. "You're a doctor. What's wrong with me?"

Johnna reached to adjust the pan on a wooden block. Her arm brushed Jamis's hip, and both of them stopped to register the contact. Johnna leaned against Jamis's shoulder before returning to her own space.

"I'm a vet." Johnna laughed. "Take that to the table?"

Jamis picked up the pan with the hot pad. She lifted at the wrong angle and the pan burned her skin. "Ouch," she said, setting the pan down.

"Did you burn yourself?" Johnna grabbed her arm, fingers soft on her skin. "Oh, you did," she said, pulling Jamis's arm forward. She turned on the cold water and eased Jamis's arm under it. Jamis was silent, the touch of Johnna's fingers on her skin drowning out the pain. "Keep your arm under the water. Let me get some aloe." Johnna opened a cupboard door, pulled down gel, turned off the water, dried Jamis's arm with a towel, and gently put aloe on the burn with a fingertip.

"I think you'll live." Johnna smiled and turned away, but Jamis caught her face gently with her free hand, turning her back. It happened before she knew what she was doing. Johnna paused, and Jamis tugged her forward, her desire drowning out any wise thought about timing, location, or appropriateness.

"Jamis," Johnna said, breaking the spell. "I, it's just…" Jamis let her go, stepped back.

"Johnna, I am so sorry. I don't know why I did that. You were just so kind. And you're beautiful." Jamis smiled at her, strangely vulnerable, and picked up the hot pad. "Let's see if I can do this without injuring myself."

Sam opened the door and came toward them with Sapphire. "There's lots of birds in there."

"How many is a lot? I can hear them," Jamis said. She needed to recover the situation from her emboldened trespass on Johnna's obvious boundaries.

"About twenty, but don't judge. They're rescued," Sam said.

"Sam, I hunt ghosts and believe aliens influenced ancient earth culture. It's all relative." Johnna laughed and Jamis turned to face her.

"Ask me about aliens," Jamis said to Johnna.

"Some other time," Johnna said, handing her a salad bowl, meeting Jamis's eyes, as if to tell her it was okay. Jamis nodded and turned to set it on the table.

"You won't believe what happened," Sapphire said, interrupting to share the story of their day. Sapphire and Jamis agreed to leave out details that would lead to the date of the worst day of their lives until they knew more.

Sam opened the fridge. "My sister is a vegan. She sucks the joy from all my favorite home cooked meals, but I insist on my dairy ranch dressing. Even if she makes me eat fake cheese."

"There are non-dairy alternatives," Johnna said. "Everything tonight is cruelty free."

"Prepare to feel guilty, all the time, Jamis," Sam said.

"I've always thought I should be a vegan," Jamis said.

Johnna pointed at Jamis. "See?"

"Oh God, not you too," Sam said.

They fell silent as they dished up food. Jamis didn't speak until she was on helping number two. "I was so hungry."

"Maybe because of what's happening," Sam said.

"That's a good point. Out-of-body experiences burn a lot of calories. I met a shaman once, in Mexico, who told me that after a trance, he ate over three thousand calories to feel satiated."

"I'm starved tonight too," Sapphire said.

"There's some cake in the fridge," Johnna said. Sam pushed back from the table to get it. "Do you really believe you saw something in that house? Something otherworldly?"

"I do." Sam cut the cake and handed Jamis a piece. "I'm starting to think I'm being pulled psychically into something bigger than me. Sapphire was tonight too. Because the moment I realized it was happening, I was able to make it stop."

"That's why there is nothing on the video," Sam said. "Because it's all happening in your head."

"This could be why there is no proof of ghosts. Evidence. But no proof. Because it's all a complicated web of consciousness and manifestation in quantum states of physicality we don't understand." Jamis took a bite of cake.

"That's totally something I could hear you say on your show," Sam said, raising his hand to give her a high five. Jamis met it with a smile.

"That was good. Gotta write that down," Jamis said.

"Well, just keep your hell dimension consciousness away from me and Virginia. We're happy here on planet Earth, third dimension," Johnna said, touching Jamis's hand.

"I'm not," Sapphire said. "Take me to a dimension without Donald Trump."

"Sapphire hasn't been the same since the election," Sam said.

"Who has?" Johnna left the table. "I'm in denial."

"We're working out our shadow," Jamis said. "It's ugly when that happens." Johnna made coffee. Jamis relaxed watching her. Sam nudged Sapphire with his elbow. She cleared her throat, catching Jamis's attention. Jamis flushed and pushed crumbs of cake around her plate. They both laughed at her. In the kitchen, Johnna rinsed pots, waiting for the coffee to brew.

"I'm going to Salt Lake tomorrow to pick up some new equipment," Sapphire said. "Do you want to come with me, Sam?"

"I was going to go help Sara with this church thing."

"Do you really want to do that?" Sapphire pushed her fork in front of her and spun it on the table.

"No. He doesn't," Johnna said from the kitchen. "He does it out of guilt and obligation. It's my dad's influence."

"That's actually true, so I won't argue." He paused, thinking. "Yeah, I'll go. It'll be fun to get away. It won't be a problem with my wheelchair?"

"Why would it?" Sapphire smiled. She turned to Jamis. "Do you want to go?"

"I'm good. I've got so much to do." Jamis stood to help Johnna with the coffee. In the kitchen, Jamis remembered touching her face, the impulse to kiss her, and kept her distance. Together, they brought four cups to the table.

"What? Am I not invited?" Johnna sipped her coffee.

"Johnna, do you want to go?"

"No. Not at all," Johnna said, smiling. The lights flickered. "That keeps happening. I need to call an electrician."

Jamis spun around in her seat. There was a flash of yellow in her peripheral vision, in the corner by the windows. No one else noticed.

CHAPTER NINE

Jamis pulled back the blinds a few hours before. She'd spent the morning capturing her thoughts about Stephanie and hadn't left the hotel room. A snowstorm arrived and fell heavy from four a.m. until noon, and then abruptly stopped. The world outside was silent.

The clock on the nightstand read two twenty-five p.m. She scooted down against the pillows and set the alarm to wake her at three thirty. Dust hovered in the sunlight from the window and cut a path to the end of the bed where a triangle of the quilt was bright with light. Jamis stuck her toe in the sun's path, and then her whole foot, and drifted to sleep.

She slept effortlessly. She was in the field again. Given her previous experiences, she didn't try to move. Instead, she rested, present, aware of a sensation of infiniteness. Where was she? The woman was back. This time, she moved toward Jamis, her skirt billowing behind her. Her face shifted just beyond Jamis's sight, as though she was standing behind frosted panes of glass.

Jamis spoke. "Please come closer. I can't move toward you. Who are you? Can I see you?" She moved closer, but was still obscured. Her fingers closed around Jamis's wrist. The fog lifted. "You're so beautiful." The woman smiled, kissed her forehead, and then moved to leave. "No. Please don't go. Who are you?" Jamis tried to run, but her legs buckled, as though gravity quadrupled. "Please. Tell me who you are." She faded from view.

Jamis willed herself to wake. The clock read three twenty p.m. Uncertain what else to do, she left the hotel room without a formal decision and found herself in the parking lot of Johnna's clinic. Sapphire had pointed it out to her the afternoon before when they drove by. She'd obviously made a strong mental note of it.

She also remembered Johnna declining Sapphire's offer to go to Salt Lake because of her office hours. It was three fifty, which seemed close enough to closing time to drop in. Jamis pushed through the large door of the clinic, stopping just inside. Johnna was in the lobby with a middle-aged man in worn jeans and boots and an adolescent girl, who held a gray parrot in her coat. Jamis smiled. "I'm party crashing."

"Hi." Johnna met her eyes and smiled. The response was simple and direct, but warmth rushed through Jamis, erupting in her chest.

"I just wanted to chat," Jamis said. Why had she come?

"Sure. I'll be done here in just a minute. You can sit." Jamis took the chair across from her, crossing her legs. "Come on in," Johnna said, and the girl and man followed Johnna into an exam room. Jamis heard the bird squawking in the room and enjoyed the low murmur of Johnna's voice through the door. Jamis scrolled through social media as she waited, responding to a few positive comments, avoiding her trolls. She wasn't in the mood. Johnna and the pair came out of the room.

"Um, Johnna, what do I owe you?" The man stood awkwardly in front of Johnna.

"It was nothing, Jim. Really. Don't worry about it."

"I didn't bring her to get somethin' free." Jim looked at his boots.

"I don't even know how to charge for that, and Gloria has gone home so I guess you just have to accept it, huh?" Johnna put her hand on his arm.

"Did you ever get your fence run all the way?" Jim asked.

"No. I didn't. I ran out of steam on the east side of my property." They stopped by the door. Stacey stood next to him. He put his arm around her shoulders.

"I'll come this spring and help you finish it up," Jim said.

"It's a deal." Johnna flipped the bolt behind them as they left and turned to face Jamis.

"You are so cool," Jamis said. "But where is Virginia?"

Johnna opened the exam room door. Virginia catapulted toward Jamis, who caught her midair.

"Glad to see where I stand," Johnna said. Jamis set her on the ground, laughing as Virginia zipped around the waiting room, smelling for the bird. "Are you free for dinner?"

"I am," Jamis said.

"Let me lock up and we can go."

"Where are we going?"

Johnna stopped at the receptionist desk and turned back to Jamis. "Just come home with me. I'll make something."

"I've never had vegan mac 'n' cheese," Jamis said. She watched Johnna cook from a stool at the kitchen counter. "I didn't even really know such a thing existed."

Johnna dumped three bags of vegan cheese into a saucepan. "It's good. Different. But it works," she said. "I think dairy is worse than just eating the animal."

"This whole ghost business and quantum states of consciousness stuff might get snagged up on the fact that we slaughter animals for food," Jamis said. "I mean, do they ever turn into ghosts?" A piece of the non-dairy cheese fell from the pan and Jamis picked it up. Johnna stopped her with a gentle tug on the wrist, and then rubbed her thumb absent mindedly on the back of her hand, before letting go. Jamis viewed it in slow motion and thought about pulling Johnna toward her, to meet her over the counter for a kiss. It was the same impulse from the day before.

"You won't like it like that and then it'll ruin your willingness to try my dinner," Johnna said. Jamis dropped the cheese, embarrassed that Johnna wasn't thinking about kissing her too.

Johnna wiped the counter with a dishrag. “If they became ghosts, we’d be overrun.” Maybe she was because her gaze was downcast, movements jerky.

“Maybe only complex consciousness carries over.”

“What’s complex, Jamis? The mammals we eat share similarities with us. They have the same nervous systems. Have you ever seen a cow waiting in line for slaughter?”

“No,” Jamis said. “I don’t want to. Should I?”

“There’s a slaughterhouse on the other side of town. I’ll take you if you’d like. They feel fear just as we do. You can see it in their eyes. They stand in line and cry.”

“I just became a vegan,” Jamis said. “I don’t eat meat, by the way. But eggs and cheese, really?”

“I’ll take you to the dairy farm and show you the rows of veal crates.”

“Okay. Stop. I give.” Jamis held up her hands.

“You started it.” Johnna opened the oven and slid the pan in.

“It wouldn’t take much. Honestly.” Jamis followed Johnna to the front room. Virginia shifted on the couch to roll into her lap.

“What else did you learn about your poltergeist with Sapphire yesterday?” Johnna faced her on the couch. She’d showered and changed into a white V-neck sweater and jeans. The skin where the V tapered was really pale, like it never saw sun. Jamis kept thinking about the moment in the kitchen the night before and wondered if she should bring it up. She didn’t. Johnna didn’t seem to want to talk about it.

“The house was once occupied by a woman likely murdered by a serial killer,” Jamis said.

“No way.”

“I’m not making this up. We went to the library and looked at microfilm of old town newspapers.”

“So that’s your ghost then? Case solved?”

Jamis stilled, her heart raced. She didn’t want to hurt Johnna, but she felt compelled to tell her. “Her body was found on March

16, 1992." Johnna shifted in her seat. "The actual date of death is undetermined."

"That's just days after my mom and brother Jacob died. In a car accident. When Sam was hurt," Johnna said. Her tone was dispassionate, detached. Practiced. Jamis recognized the mechanisms that allowed it. But despite her efforts, Johnna's eyes darkened, and she pulled her legs up to her chest, wrapped her arms around them, and scooted back into the corner of the couch. She kept her eyes on Jamis, wary.

Jamis touched Virginia's toenails and rubbed her foot. She didn't want to be responsible for Johnna's sadness. But she was. Might as well continue. "I know. I saw the newspaper article." Jamis expected Johnna to react, but she was silent. "I didn't mean to. It just came through." Johnna still said nothing. "I'm really so sorry. I wish I could unread it. I feel like I pried into your diary or something."

"You don't need to apologize," Johnna said, stretching her legs and arms back out, as if just now aware of retreating. "The timing is so strange, isn't it? I don't remember a murder around that time, but I suppose with so much happening…" Her voice trailed off. She turned away from Jamis and stared out the window. "Is this why you came by today?"

"No. God no. I just wanted to see you." This time, she touched Johnna, hand on her arm. "You're not an investigation, Johnna." Johnna accepted her reassurance with a slight nod. "Sapphire told me if I wanted to talk to anyone about it though, it should be you."

"Sam and Sara don't talk about it," Johnna said. "I really don't either. I'm sure you can imagine."

"My mom died when I was eleven."

"She did?" Jamis felt Johnna's compassion spread through her like a drink of warm coffee before six a.m.

"It was just the two of us." Jamis shifted and pulled Virginia tighter. "Overdose. She was addicted to painkillers. I don't know why, really. I was too young. I didn't know my dad. We didn't have a lot." Virginia kissed her chin.

"She knows when you feel sad," Johnna said. "She always knows when I am."

"Sometimes, though, I forget how she looks. Do you forget how your mom looks?"

"Fortunately, we have pictures. She was really photogenic."

"I don't have any pictures," Jamis said. Through the windows, the blue of the sky turned bright orange and red as night crept toward them. Did she like Johnna because on a subconscious level they recognized each other's wounds? Or was there more there?

The oven timer buzzed, and Johnna jumped up. Jamis watched her walk to the kitchen. "Are you a vegan because you love animals or because you saw your mom and Jacob die?"

"I think exposure to death at such a young age would make anyone oversensitive. Adverse childhood events, multiplied."

"I think the trauma of my mom's death created space in my psyche. It's how I do what I do. See what I see. Think how I think. High sensitivity, introversion, queerness, and trauma fused to give me a different view of the world."

"That actually makes sense." Johnna brought two plates to the couch, handing one to Jamis. "Queerness," Johnna said with a smile. "You're not just gay. You're queer in a lot of ways, I think."

"Is that good or bad?"

"Certainly not bad," Johnna said. "I like it." She held eye contact with Jamis, smiling, and then turned away. "But not that you had trauma, to clarify."

"I sometimes doubt what I see, think, and feel."

"Mental illness and trauma do that," Johnna said quietly. "It's hard to learn to trust anything. I spent a lot of years waiting for the next bad thing to happen. Then I think I just kind of gave up trying for anything more than I needed…" She trailed off in thought, her gaze distant. Jamis wanted her to come back.

"I used to see my mom every night." Johnna balanced the plate on her knees and turned to face her. "I didn't know if I was just seeing things or if my mom was really there, you know? I thought I was crazy. Then I saw something else, on a trip to

Jerome, Arizona, when I was in college. At a haunted hotel. It was so profound, I got obsessed after."

Johnna took a few bites of food, silent, staring out the window. Her energy shifted after talking about her mom, and Jamis felt it. She wished it were possible to unwind time, go back, make it better. "I probably shouldn't have brought up your mom," Jamis said, addressing it directly.

"No," Johnna said, returning to her. "You had to, didn't you? It wouldn't be right not to."

Jamis thought that was true, but there was a fine line between a right to know and protecting people when you have the chance. Johnna's reaction was generous. Abruptly, Jamis shifted gears. "Are you single?"

Johnna finished chewing and turned to look at her. "Get right to it, don't you?" Jamis shrugged, waiting for her answer. "Yeah. I am. For a long time. So long I barely remember it being any other way." Johnna shifted away. "You?"

"Of course, yeah." Jamis committed to the course she set and asked, "You're gay too, right?"

"Yes, I am. Are you done now?"

"Just being sure," Jamis said. "Should we change the subject?"

"Why? I was hoping you'd pass me a note."

"Pretend I have paper," Jamis said. "I hand you the note and it reads, 'Do you like me? Yes, No, or Maybe.'"

"Okay. I have the note." Johnna pretended to look at invisible paper in her hands.

"Well? What's your answer?"

"I can't find my pencil," Johnna said, smiling. "You'll need to wait."

"That's fine," Jamis said, leaning forward to set her plate on the coffee table. "I'm patient."

"No, you're not," Johnna said.

"You're right. I'm not. But I'm working on that too." Jamis crossed her legs. "I have a feeling you're worth it."

"Why are you interested in me?" Johnna's question was direct, but her tone was soft, tentative.

"What do you mean?" Jamis set the plate on the table.

"I mean, why are you pursuing me? Sam showed me your social media. There are a lot of women there."

"I like you," Jamis said without thought but with genuine emotion that wrapped itself around her heart and made her feel poetic and wish for words to better explain it to both of them.

"Right," Johnna said. "For the moment? The trip? The week?"

"No," Jamis said. "I mean, I hadn't thought about things that far."

"I read some of your comments on Facebook," Johnna said. "You're flirtatious."

"It's all good fun. I've not dated anyone for a long time." Johnna said nothing. "I've really been focused on myself. We can compare adverse childhood event scores, if you want."

"I'm sure yours is higher," Johnna said. Jamis shrugged. "I don't mean to put you on the spot. It's probably more my insecurity than your issues."

"I just like you," Jamis said. It was true. She noticed her and thought every small detail was worth noting, analyzing, and holding close.

"Maybe," Johnna said, watching Jamis skeptically. "It's just, I'm nothing special." Jamis moved toward her, but she retreated.

"Johnna," Jamis said. "You can't possibly think that." Johnna watched her, gaze intent. "What?"

"I don't do things quickly," Johnna said. "It's been a long time and I don't have a ton of experience dating. The gay scene in Sage Creek isn't exactly hopping. I mean, there's only seventy-thousand people here in total."

"There's no rush," Jamis said. "I shouldn't have tried to kiss you. In fairness, I've not tried since. Also, you put aloe on my arm."

"Is that an aphrodisiac?"

"Obviously," Jamis said, grinning. Jamis waited, unsure where the conversation was going.

"Can we just get to know each other? It would be nice to just get to know each other," Johnna said. "I mean, I want to, I just—"

"Yeah," Jamis interrupted, hoping she sounded nonchalant. "Johnna, it's fine. We'll get to know each other."

"Okay," Johnna said, tension releasing. "I'll try not to use any aloe." Johnna stood to take their plates into the kitchen, returning with second helpings. Jamis watched her with new understanding. She didn't say no, just hold on, slow down, make sure. "If you know how to work the Netflix thingy on the TV, we can watch something," Johnna said.

Jamis turned on the television and the sun settled behind the mountains. "Ever seen *Babylon 5*?"

CHAPTER TEN

Jamis turned in her sleep and fell from the couch. She landed on her side and scrambled up, falling back over as her feet tangled. She rested for a moment on her stomach, less frantic, before rising. The sun shone brightly through the front windows. She was in Johnna's home. She must have fallen asleep, though she had no memory of it. The clock on the wall near the dining table told her it was after nine a.m. There was a cup on the counter and a note.

Jamis,

You fell asleep during episode three of that ridiculous show you made me watch. :) I decided to tuck you in. I hope you slept okay. Coffee in the maker. It might be cold so feel free to make a new pot. Just lock the handle when you leave. Thanks for a lovely evening. I hope you keep showing up.

Johnna

Jamis held the note in her hands and ran a finger over Johnna's signature. Her handwriting was neat and simple, like her. She folded the note carefully and tucked it into her pocket. She never wanted to leave. She'd not dreamed.

Jamis parked the car in the grocery parking lot. She hopped over a pile of snow to land firmly on the sidewalk. The sun was out and the cold not as bitter. The weather app on her phone said it was thirty-six degrees. It was nearly balmy.

She'd texted Carmen the night before but had not heard back. Johnna told her Carmen often neglected her phone. Inside the store, Jamis picked up a container of chocolate coconut brownie bites and held them close. She was hungry and wasn't leaving the store without them.

She wound through browsing patrons and made her way to Carmen, who stood on a stepladder, lifting cereal boxes to a shelf above her head. Jamis stopped at the side of her, far enough away not to startle her. Jamis waved at Carmen. "Do you know what text messages are?"

Carmen looked down at her. "I don't live and die with my phone."

"What's wrong with you?"

Carmen made a noise and continued to put boxes on the shelf. "You found me anyway, didn't you?"

"Have you always been this ornery?"

Carmen laughed and tossed a bag of rice puff cereal at Jamis, who caught it, but dropped her brownie bites doing so. "You made me drop my bites," Jamis said, dramatic and loud. A few shoppers turned to look and Jamis held up her hands. "All is well. Don't be alarmed. The bites are fine."

Carmen climbed down from the ladder and took the rice puffs from Jamis, who bent for her bites. From behind her, a customer said, "Oh my God, that's Jamis Bachman." Jamis turned, saluted, offered a half curtsy, and the woman giggled and waved.

"Bring your bites," Carmen said. Jamis tucked them under her arm, grinning at the customers. They stepped into a small office in the back of the store. Carmen took a seat behind a desk.

"Can I eat a bite before I pay for them?" Jamis opened the container.

"Yeah, go ahead. Just have them." Carmen pushed against the face of her phone with a single finger, touch heavy.

"You are the best. Jesus, you're going to break your phone." Carmen ignored her. "Can I have some coffee?" Jamis ate a brownie.

"Go get some." Carmen pointed. Jamis poured coffee from a small pot in the corner of the office, and then looked over Carmen's shoulder at her phone.

"Seriously?" Jamis asked. "How many are there?" She took the phone from Carmen. "There are twenty-two unread text messages here." She handed it back. "Lesson learned."

"What did you want?" Carmen set down the phone. Jamis took a sip of coffee and put another bite in her mouth.

"Nothing." Jamis shrugged. "Just saying hi. Seeing what's up. What you doing? You know. Normal stuff."

Carmen watched her seriously. "You're lying."

"Ha." Carmen was right to the point. She could work with that. She could work with anything today. The night with Johnna was perfect. She took a picture of the mountains from Johnna's porch. When she posted it on social media earlier that morning, she set her location as "bliss." "Really, it started as that, but then I wanted to talk to you about something more serious. I talked to Johnna."

Carmen's body became rigid. Jamis noted it but pushed on. "I was researching the poltergeist house. Stephanie Gardner was the tenant and she was murdered. Her body was found on March 16, 1992." Jamis waited quietly and took another drink of coffee. "I was just wondering if you knew her."

Carmen poured coffee for herself. "I did, actually. She went to school with my youngest sister, Maria. She knew her." She perched on the side of the desk, facing Jamis. "I remember when she was found."

"Do you remember anything about her that might help me?" Jamis put another bite in her mouth, the taste exploding. The chocolate was divine, and she worried a little piece of coconut between her teeth. Carmen stared at an unfixed location near the door, eyes distant and dark with the heavy sadness she'd seen at the bar. Jamis's desire was to fix it, so she tried to distract her. "Oh my God, these are so good, Carmen."

"I can give you my sister's phone number. She's in Denver. I'll tell her you're calling." She pulled a piece of paper from a pad and wrote down a number. Then she picked up her phone and sent a text.

"So, you do know how to text. You just don't." Carmen ignored her, but she seemed less unhappy. "You have the number memorized?"

"It's my sister," Carmen said.

"I don't memorize anyone's numbers. I'd be fucked without my phone. Completely lost if I couldn't get to my Gmail backup contacts."

"I don't understand anything you just said." Jamis took the paper from her outstretched hand, using it as an opportunity to check her energy. It was lighter, but still not as buoyant as when she came in.

"These are perfect. How have I not had them before?" Jamis ate the last brownie bite. "Do you know Sapphire?"

"Yeah. Of course," Carmen said.

"Those county records down at the municipal building and courthouse are, wow," Jamis said. "Have you seen what she's done down there?"

"Are you going to move here? It seems like you're ready to become a permanent resident," Carmen said.

"Do you have a spare bedroom?"

"Jesus," Carmen said.

"Is that a no?" Carmen left the office, not answering, but Jamis saw her smile and felt relief. "I'd pick up my room on a regular basis. I could help clean and do other chores," Jamis called after Carmen. She finished her coffee before leaving with Maria's number in her hand. She waved to Carmen on the way out. In the car, Jamis dialed Maria's number.

It rang twice before a woman answered. "Hello?"

"Maria?"

"Yes. Who's calling?" Jamis heard Carmen in her voice.

"Jamis Bachman. Carmen texted you, right?"

"Yes, she did. Just a few minutes ago. She didn't give me much to go on, though. Just that the famous ghost hunter needed to talk to me. You'll need to tell me. You made an impression because she told me about you yesterday when we talked," Maria said, laughing.

Acceptance felt like the brownie bites tasted. Carmen liked her. "I'm investigating the murder of Stephanie Gardner in March 1992. I'm just looking to talk to people who knew her. Carmen said you did."

"She was troubled. Her mother was a prostitute, though we didn't talk about it in those days." Maria's voice had a flutter of hesitation. "We didn't even call her a prostitute. But we all knew. I'm pretty certain that the men her mom brought home took liberties with her too, if you know what I mean." Jamis did and felt sickened. She turned down the heat in the car. She unzipped her coat and tugged at the neck of her T-shirt. It felt constrictive.

"I guess nowadays we'd say Stephanie had borderline personality disorder and be able to help her some. Maybe with some therapy and medication or something. But then, during those times, we just stayed away from her. That's about all I know. The boys took advantage of her. There were rumors she slept with the whole football team. Who knows what's true. We all grew up and left school. Stephanie stayed in town and got a job at the bowling lanes on Washington Street. I saw her there once after graduation. I lost touch with her after that."

"Do you know anyone else I should talk to about this? About her? Anyone closer to her?"

"I think most people will tell you the same thing. A lot of guys got close to Stephanie, but I don't think she was close to anyone. It's just so sad."

"It is, Maria. Thank you for talking to me," Jamis said.

"One more thing. When I heard what happened I felt so bad. I felt like I should have done something. Like we were all to blame. Children can be cruel." Jamis let Maria gather her thoughts. "Anyway, I don't know what I was going to say. Just that I wish we did more to help people like her."

Jamis thought about this and silently agreed. Stephanie was trapped in a cycle of abuse and exploitation. She learned a certain way to be in the world and the energy of those early lessons informed the rest of her life. Without interruption, she simply dwelled in the same energy, creating and re-creating the pain in endless repetition. Jamis understood it all too well.

"Me too, Maria. One question, before I let you go. What is your last name? And would it be okay if I quoted you in my final thoughts about this on my website?"

"Could you not use my last name?"

"Of course. Can I still get your name?"

"Well, I kept my name. Ojeda. Our dad came to Utah from Mexico. Our mom is Native American. Navajo." It was the remnants of the Spanish and Navajo Jamis heard in their words, and she loved it. She kept thinking about sending in her own DNA, to learn more about her heritage, but never got around to it. Dr. Frank urged her to do it, so that was why she didn't. Some sort of adolescent defiance. She returned to Maria.

"Thanks, Maria. Would it be okay if I called you again if anything comes up?"

"Yes. That's fine, and, Jamis…" Her voice drifted away. "Never mind. Yes, of course. Call anytime." She hung up, and Jamis put her phone in the cup holder. It chirped and she picked it back up. It was Sapphire. *I have your files.*

Jamis texted her. *OMW.*

She dropped the phone back in the cup holder and backed up. While waiting to turn, she picked the phone up and texted Johnna. *Hi. Thx for tucking me in. I ate a box of brownie bites with Carmen. Don't need to eat for six days. I hope you're having a good day.* She put the phone back and pulled into the street.

❖

Sapphire waited on a small bench upstairs at the municipal building. The light filtered through the stained glass windows in the brick building and danced across the shiny tile. The play of stained glass and shadows made it look like a dance club. Jamis followed dancing flecks of blue, red, and gold as they moved across the floor to Sapphire, who wore a pair of tan corduroys and a dark blue sweater. Her hair was pulled up on top of her head, now dyed a deep purple. Jamis stopped in front of her. "I love your hair."

"Me too. But it was a bit of an accident," Sapphire said, pulling a face. "I did it last night when I got home. I should have waited."

"Did you drive in the storm?" Jamis followed her down the stairs into the basement while she unlocked the cage.

"Oh, yeah. Not a big deal at all. Winter and I are foes. We do battle and I win when I want to go somewhere."

"Winter cosplayer." Jamis laughed, following her inside the metal gates. Sapphire held her arms in the air and pumped them.

There were stacks of paper everywhere, and they stepped around them to get to the computers. Jamis cringed at the photo of Stephanie Gardner wrapped in a tarp on the center monitor. Sapphire noticed. "I know. It gets worse."

Sapphire picked up a folder, slid papers in it, closed the clasp, and handed it to Jamis. "I made a copy for you. I scanned all of it here." She turned to her keyboard and then swiped her tablet. A police report appeared next to the gruesome photo. Jamis pulled a stool next to her and read the report.

"She was found by a truck driver. He got out of his truck to move something so he could pull by and noticed her foot. Otherwise, she would have likely never been found," Jamis said.

A deep sadness enveloped them both. Jamis put her hand on Sapphire's arm and took a deep breath. "She suffered blunt force trauma to her head, and there were signs she'd had sex, though no body fluids were recovered." Fury moved through her body like an army platoon marching into battle. "Signs she'd had sex. They didn't even suppose she'd been sexually assaulted."

"It was 1992. Practically a different world," Sapphire said. "We didn't even have social media."

"I wonder if they even considered it."

"I've read this whole file and saw nothing about sexual assault." Sapphire took a deep breath. "I feel pretty sick. I mean, really sick."

Jamis felt nauseous too. "The official cause of death is the blunt force trauma. If I was raped and bludgeoned in the head, I'd be a fucking poltergeist too."

Sapphire pulled up the second page of the police report. Jamis read it.

"Looks like they spoke to her neighbors, Sue and John Giffords and Ethel Waters," Jamis said.

"Before you ask, Sue and John live right next door in present day Sage Creek, Utah." Sapphire pulled up an online directory of residents and addresses. "Ethel died in 2011."

"Okay, can you believe it never occurred to me to talk to the neighbors?" Jamis asked Sapphire, laughing. "Here I am desperate for info and I run all around instead of walking next door."

"Sometimes, it's the simple things that elude us smart folks," Sapphire said.

Such was the story of Jamis's life. "There isn't much more here. The unofficial notes in the file said they assumed a drifter killed her. Put the case on the shelf. An addendum was added in 1995 when Richard Crespin was captured, and they worked with Idaho police to try to link her murder to him. They never could. Technically, Jamis, it's still unsolved."

"Want to go talk to her neighbors?"

"I'm your partner these days, aren't I?" Sapphire clicked the computer screens off.

CHAPTER ELEVEN

Sapphire and Jamis walked gingerly up the sidewalk to Sue and John Giffords's house. The snow was shoveled, but not well, and the result was small pockets of iced, packed down snow. Jamis held lightly to Sapphire's shoulder. Sapphire warned her not to take her down. They giggled en route, fast friends. Jamis had never had a best friend growing up, but had she known Sapphire then, it would have been her. Jamis knocked on the front door and kicked the snow off her Converse.

The door opened with a gush of warmed air and an elderly man squinted at them. "What do you want?"

Sapphire spoke before Jamis could. "Mr. Giffords, I'm Sapphire Neugent. I work in county records at the municipal building. We wanted to ask you some questions about the house next door and a woman who used to live there. Stephanie Gardner."

"I don't want to dig any of that stuff up. Now you two go on." He began to shut the door, but a female voice behind him called out.

"You ornery old bastard. Let her in." He grumbled and opened the door again, stepping out of the way, retreating back into the house, leaving the door open.

Jamis stepped tentatively inside. An elderly woman sat on the couch with a blanket over her legs and a cat on her lap. She muted the television and called them in. "Sit, both of you." They took two chairs by the window.

Sapphire introduced them. "Are you Sue Giffords?"

"I am. I thought you looked familiar when I saw you outside the window. I used to watch your show." Jamis thanked her. "And I knew Sapphire's dad. We used to work together at the grocery store. How is your mom, honey?"

"I thought you did, Mrs. Giffords. She's good."

"Well, tell her I said hello."

"Mrs. Giffords," Jamis began.

"Call me Sue."

"Sue, what can you tell us about the house next door?"

"You know that girl killed by a serial killer, Stephanie, lived there. We always wondered if it happened there. But the police never found nothing. I remember. Is that why you're here in town?"

"I'm not really sure, yet," Jamis said.

"Is it haunted by her ghost do you think?" Sue continued without pausing to let Jamis answer. She was excited to share. "It's been vacant a long time, I can tell you that. Then some investment company came and bought it last year, woke me up every day at five, pounding on nails, ripping out flooring. Before then, it's bounced around."

"I saw that in the county records. At the time, it was a rental. Were there a lot of tenants in and out of it before Stephanie? Or after her?"

"You know, after Stephanie no one really lived in it long. Some young fellow bought it from Rick, but he wasn't there long. It sat empty for years." Sue looked from Jamis to Sapphire, serious about the information she shared.

"Did you know Stephanie well at all?" Sapphire shifted in her chair, opening her body language to Sue, a silent encouragement to talk.

"Well, I knew she was loose. A chippie my mom used to say. Legs open to anyone." Jamis gasped. Sapphire leaned even closer in a conspiratorial gesture. Sue lowered her voice. "I don't want John to hear. But I used to see men in and out of there all the time, all hours of the day and night. Up through that back door. I could see it from my bedroom." She stopped talking, held her body stiff, satisfied with her disclosure.

"Can I see before we leave?" Jamis wanted to see the house from this angle. While uncertain what it would accomplish, she felt desperate for any insight.

"Sure you can," Sue said.

Jamis smiled at her. "Thanks. The men you saw. Did you ever see anyone you shouldn't see?"

Sue looked from side to side again to be sure John wasn't coming in the room. "I used to see the police chief's son, Mitch, in and out all the time." She grinned and looked at Sapphire. "You remember Mitch Jr., honey?" Sapphire said she didn't. "Well, you may be too young. Your mom probably does."

"Do you think the chief's son was having an affair with Stephanie?" Again, Jamis pressed her for information.

"I wouldn't call it an affair, but I think he was dipping his quill in her ink." The imagery was startling. "And he was making ink blots. Not writing the alphabet." Jamis stared at Sue, momentarily stunned. Down home descriptors of sex and infidelity left her speechless. It took a lot.

"Is there anything else we should know about the house?" Sapphire jumped in, helping her.

"Is it haunted? I've never heard or seen anything, and I'll be damned if I've been missing it all these years."

Sapphire spoke again. "Jamis thinks something is going on and related to Stephanie. Will you let us know if you think of anything else?"

"I sure will." Jamis stood and Sue pushed the cat from her lap, grabbed a cane next to the couch, rose on wobbly legs, and pointed to the stairs. "You just head right up those there, turn right, and go straight to my window."

Jamis took the stairs two at a time, moved briskly through their bedroom, and pulled back the sheer curtain. The entire house was visible. The backyard splayed at a slight angle. The kitchen door, which opened up to the outside, faced her. The imprints of their bodies in the snow and the vague outline of her footprints around the perimeter were still visible. She turned to leave and caught a movement in the upstairs window out of the corner of her eye.

She turned abruptly, but nothing was there. A sharp pain struck her stomach, and she bent over. All warmth was sucked from the air. It was difficult to breathe. The edges of her vision darkened, and she tried to move but fell to a knee, holding her stomach. She put her hand on the dresser, trying to steady herself.

Darkness swirled and became a road that pulled her in. She was leaving the second-story bedroom on Third Street through a dimensional portal. There was a sound like roaring engines and the smell of burning coal. A massive bird dropped down toward her, talons exposed, and tried to grab her face. She fell to the ground and covered her head.

"Jamis." Warm hands held her shoulders. "Oh my God, Jamis. Are you okay? What's wrong? Do you need an ambulance?"

"No. I'm okay. I don't know what happened." She struggled to stand. Sapphire held on to her. "I just looked out the window and I saw something move, and next thing I know, I had this pain, and then I was in a tunnel. With engines." Sapphire raised an eyebrow. "I know. It sounds nuts."

"Maybe it's bad gas," Sapphire said, trying to be funny.

"Let's get out of here," Jamis said.

Sapphire wrapped an arm around Jamis's waist and together they left the room.

"You okay up there?" Sue waited for them at the bottom of the stairs.

"Jamis just had a light head from low blood sugar. Do you have a banana?"

Sue moved quickly to the kitchen, on a purposeful mission.

"Thank you," Jamis said, barely a whisper, to Sapphire. Sapphire took the banana from Sue. The television was back on and Jamis recognized it as *NCIS*.

❖

"Have you ever had stuff like this happen before?" Sapphire replied to text messages while she spoke and adjusted the air vent in the car.

"Yeah, sometimes. Not this intense, though. I feel skinless."

They'd moved to the driveway of Stephanie's house, but Jamis didn't know how wise it was to get closer. "Do you think it's medical? Should we get you checked out?"

"Can Johnna look at me?"

"She's a vet, Jamis. Are you a golden retriever?"

"I'm dark and almost six feet tall. I think I'd be more of an Irish wolfhound."

Sapphire waved her hand. "Oh my God, are we playing what kind of dog would we be? I'm a corgi, short legs, round bum, big belly." Jamis laughed. "How about an urgent care? You looked whacked when I found you. Like fucking whacked. Not quite in sync with the earthly plane. It's hard to explain."

"Tell me about it. Maybe the more it happens, the more I'll understand. The pain in my stomach is gone." Jamis looked down at her legs and feet. "I'm not quite sure, honestly. What's next? I feel like I'm making progress, but I don't know what I'm solving."

There was a shadow standing in the upstairs window of the house. Jamis put the car in reverse. She wasn't in a space to deal with it. She stopped them by the college campus, a few streets over. Trees without leaves were silhouettes against the early afternoon sun. The shadows of students walking from building to building left temporary marks of black against the white of the snow.

"I think I'm going to send a copy of the police files to a friend of mine. She owns a forensics lab down in Phoenix," Jamis said, searching for positive solutions.

"That's a good idea," Sapphire said.

"Then, I'm really just not sure. I wish we could somehow re-create Stephanie's last few days. If she was found on March 16, she likely died that week before."

"How do we do that, though? It was so long ago," Sapphire said.

"I've never done this much work. I mean, solve a murder or something. The writers always gave me the overviews, mostly exaggerated truth, honestly. But I've watched enough episodes of *Criminal Minds* to feel like I should know how." This was a problem to be solved, nothing more. The solution to all of this was within her reach. She could figure out anything for herself. Always had. She was a foster kid with nothing and no one who ended up a television star. This was nothing in comparison to the effort it took to climb out of her childhood.

But if that was entirely true, why was Jamis so scared that the specter haunting her dreams was there to demand a recompense for everything that came before? The pressure on her neck mounted. Something demanded her attention. She just didn't know what.

"Emotional detachment," Jamis said.

"What?"

"Me, I need to chill out. I feel emotional," Jamis said, talking for herself more than Sapphire. "Okay, let's think. We will send the files to the lab. Can we get phone records?"

"Mountain Bell was the provider here then. Back when phones were utilities and managed as a monopoly. I remember the phone bill coming in the mail. We called them Ma Bell. But they've since been broken up and splintered off. I'm sure I know someone who worked for them. I don't know what they would have archived and for how long. Let me work on it. I can't promise anything."

"How did you get the police reports?" Jamis was suddenly curious.

"It's really better if you don't know," Sapphire said, typing on the phone.

"Are you sure? You should implicate me if there are issues. I don't want you to get into trouble."

"There is absolutely no one around with my skill. To catch me and prosecute me they'd need someone smarter than me to get evidence." Sapphire tucked her phone away. "Not sure there is someone like that. So, good luck proving it."

"Overconfidence is a deadly sin."

"It is not," Sapphire said.

"It is. I'm sure of it," Jamis said. She poked Sapphire's shoulder.

"Do you mean pride?"

"Well, I feel like overconfidence is its modern equivalent," Jamis said, moving the car into drive, mood lifting.

"I don't think the deadly sins are open to your interpretation."

"Whatever."

"I feel gluttonous," Sapphire said, and Jamis giggled.

Jamis took Sapphire back to work. In the hotel room, she scrolled through contacts on her phone and dialed Maggie Kirkpatrick. "Hello?" Jamis's heart lurched when she heard her voice. Should it do that? It was the emotional charge she attached to the end of their relationship, nothing more. She'd not been in love with Maggie for a long time. A decade or better. The voice just triggered unprocessed emotion. Jamis sometimes imagined her insides were like a battleground with landmines. One wrong step and everything would blow.

"Maggie," Jamis said.

"Hi, Jamis." She said nothing else.

"I hope you're well," Jamis said. At this time of day, Maggie would be in her lab, wearing a lab coat, khakis, and a button-down blouse. Did she still wear glasses, or had she switched to contacts? Last time Jamis saw Maggie, her black hair was cut in a short angle and rested just below her ears. That was over five years ago.

"You don't just call to see if I'm well. Usually, it's because you want something." Jamis wanted to deny it, but then stopped short. It was true, though she wished it were different.

"I know I hurt you. I could deny it, but what good would it do? I'm sorry, Maggie." She wasn't able to hold still then. So many things could hurt people who cared. Her inability to commit was as harmful as betrayal.

"My God, have you grown up, Jamis?"

"Don't get carried away," Jamis said. "I do want something. I do hope you're well. Those two things don't need to be mutually exclusive."

"I got married late last year," Maggie said, with some force.

"Well, she's lucky. Really lucky." She meant it, even as she searched inside for hidden or residual emotion. A few years ago, saying that would have been like chewing glass. Now, it was all gone. She'd let go. "I'm happy for you."

"Right. Thanks. Now, how can I help you?" Her tone was cold, but she wasn't hanging up. Maggie might have ample reasons to avoid contact, but her curiosity always triumphed. She knew if Jamis called, it was something interesting.

"I'm in Utah. I've stumbled into a really strange situation. I've got a potential poltergeist at a house and a twenty-five-year-old murder. We managed to get a copy of the police records from back in 1992. They linked the death to Richard Crespin, but he never confessed. I was wondering if you could look at the autopsy files and tell me what you think."

"Send me everything you have."

"I'll have a friend email them to you. Look for something from Sapphire Neugent shortly." Jamis paused.

"I'll call you after I've had a chance to look at them."

"I appreciate it, Maggie." Maggie hung up without any other words, and Jamis cringed. It'd gone better than she thought it would. She was pleasantly surprised at how quickly she agreed to help her. Jamis texted Sapphire with Maggie's email address, asking her to send the scanned files. Sapphire responded via email within minutes. She cc'd Jamis.

She turned on her Kindle Fire and connected to the internet in the hotel, scrolling through Netflix and Prime. She chose *30 Rock* and hit play. She rested the tablet in her lap and willed herself to relax. She brought her awareness into the present moment, drawing attention to her feet, then her legs, moving up her body with deliberate concentration. Jamis drew a deep breath but didn't focus on it. If she paid too much attention to her breathing, she hyperventilated.

Something was happening in her life. It started with Dr. Frank, the dreams, and brought her to where she was. Perhaps the weight of the past finally exceeded her capacity to carry it. Maggie married. Why wouldn't she? Normal people did that. They met someone, married, bought a house, mowed the lawn on Saturdays and filled out living wills. Jamis knew it would never work, even when she wanted it to be possible. It was difficult for her to imagine a normal life because it wasn't something she'd ever known. The life she created drew from the well she knew. It's what everyone did, until they got conscious enough to choose differently.

Was Johnna normal? It seemed like it. She owned a house and probably mowed the lawn. But something in her eyes suggested that what she expected from life was different from someone like Maggie. Was there something about Johnna that spoke to her past traumas? Was her attraction as simple as that? She'd known her for three days. Before meeting Johnna, she lived forty years. If she did the math, the percentage of time barely registered. So why did she feel like nothing happened before arriving here?

Then the pressure around her body intensified. It was hard to know how long it had been there. She'd been lost in thought. Where was she? Was it still the old hotel room? The wood paneling was still dull with time. There was a television on the laminate drawers in front of her. But the light filtering into the room looked different. A sharp, white light cast a path across the room, ending abruptly by the bathroom door.

Jamis looked out the window. There was nothing outside. Her chest tightened, heart rate accelerated, and she rushed to the door, fumbled with the chain, and yanked it open. It slammed against the wall. Jamis stepped from the motel room and felt like a current pulled her under. But there was no water, though she felt pressure heavy on her body. It wasn't day or night. She was somewhere without matter or form. The door closed behind her. She lurched toward it, panicking, but the nothing under her feet gave her no traction. Jamis plummeted, grabbing the door handle just before it was out of reach.

She lost her grip, slipping downward, grabbing the bottom of the doorjamb, hanging on with both hands. Her feet dangled. She pulled up so half of her body was outside the door and half was inside. The chair next to the window worked as leverage and she tucked her legs up next to her and rolled into the room, scrambling across the floor to rest against the bed.

Then Tess was in the doorway. “What the hell is wrong with you? Are you high?”

“Did you see that? Everything disappeared.”

“What the hell are you talking about? I was sitting in the office over there, looked out the window to see you thrashing around on the ground like a damned fool. I thought you were having a seizure. From drugs or something.”

Jamis looked behind Tess. Cars moved up and down the street. Her rental car was outside right where she parked it. The sun shined and the snow melted. Jamis looked down at her clothes. They were dry. The sidewalk was covered in salt and damp with melting snow. There was no salt or moisture on her. She pointed at the sidewalk and then at herself.

“What the hell?” Tess grabbed her shoulders. “I’m telling you I saw you thrashing all over the ground out there.”

“Something is happening to me. It happened earlier today too, but it was different. Sort of. I don’t know.” She rubbed her eyes. Her stomach growled.

“Just sit still. Let me get you something to eat. I’ll be right back.” Tess’s form became smaller as she crossed the parking lot. The sun glared off the glass windows on the front of the restaurant, and only vague outlines of people were visible inside. Jamis’s vision flickered, like an antenna struggling for reception. The walls of the diner shook and shimmered, before settling into solidity. The parking lot asphalt quivered, as though unfurled like a rug. Then it settled into solidity as well.

A car alarm sounded somewhere in the background. A small drip outside caught her attention and Jamis walked to investigate. An icicle hung on the metal gutter, small droplets of water splashing to the sidewalk. The space around Jamis was solid and good. Whatever happened was over, and she let go of her fear, turning back into the hotel room, defenses lowered. The figure from the house was at the foot of the bed. Her instinct was to flee, shout, cry. Her muscles contracted, ready to move. But it was Stephanie, and she knew it now. The gray robe was tied around her waist with a rope, and her feet were bare and bloodied. Her arms hung at her sides, and her fists clenched and opened, repetitively.

The outline of the hungry ghost was present in her flickering form.

Instead of retreating, Jamis moved closer. "Stephanie?"

She turned to look at Jamis and the hood fell off. It was Stephanie. She moved toward Jamis, lifting her gaze. Her eyes were darkened, cloudy, vacant, but something in them stirred to life. Just a small spark of emotion. Anger allowed her to manifest before, but if Jamis was going to help her, she needed something more. The choice to trust after betrayal was as weighted for the dead as the living.

Jamis held out her hand, committing not to flinch. The contact required absolute acceptance. Stephanie touched Jamis's hand, manifesting into form, fully visible. Her head was gouged open, brain matter peeking through. Jamis pulled back instinctively. Stephanie jerked back and shrieked. Air rushed around Jamis, and the drapes on the windows fluttered. Stephanie screamed louder.

"No. Please don't. I'm sorry. I want to help you." Stephanie threw Jamis back against the doorframe in punishment. She doubled over.

"Who the hell is screaming? What's happening now?" Tess called from the parking lot, holding a tray in her hand. "Are you okay? Christ, I was gone ten minutes."

Stephanie was gone.

"Tess, how crazy would you think I am if I told you the poltergeist of Stephanie Gardner was standing right there? And that you heard her scream?" Jamis pointed to the middle of the motel room. "The cops say that she was murdered by that serial killer, but I don't think so. He died. She should be settled, don't you think?" Jamis put her arms above her head, struggling to catch her breath.

"I'd say you've got low blood sugar." Tess pushed Jamis inside the motel room and shut the door. "I don't need you chasing off my other guests." She pointed to the chair by the window and Jamis obediently sat in it. Tess set the tray down and pulled the metal cover from the plate with a grilled cheese and French fries. Tess sat on the chair across from her. "This is crazy. All of it. But shit if I didn't hear someone scream. And it wasn't a normal scream."

"She was right here." Jamis took a bite of grilled cheese.

Tess looked at her, expression serious. "I don't want poltergeists chasing off my paying guests."

"I'll leave tonight. I'm sorry. I had no idea this would happen."

"Well, now, no. You forget it. Where you going? A Holiday Inn? They'll call the cops on you. You're nuts, flailing around outside like that. Hell." Tess waved her hand. "They'd lock you up in the loony bin."

Jamis laughed, but it wasn't real. It was just all she could think of doing. "Honestly, I think I'm being pulled into another dimension or something. I think she's doing it to me."

"Stephanie Gardner? The lady who got murdered by a serial killer? Whose poltergeist you say you saw right in here, just now?"

"Yes," Jamis said. "You get it."

"You realize how nuts that sounds?"

"It's an occupational hazard." She finished the grilled cheese and sipped her soda, thirsty from interdimensional travel.

"Do you walk around all the time with everyone around you thinking you're nuts?"

"Yeah," Jamis said. There wasn't anything to add to it, so she didn't.

"Okay, well, try not to flail around outside on the sidewalk tonight, okay? And if something nuts happens, you call me. I'm going to write my home number right here by the phone. Just dial it."

"Tess, I'm sorry," Jamis said. "I really didn't mean to do that. I appreciate you coming for me."

Tess pulled the drapes. "For whatever reason, I almost believe you and I don't want to chase you off. But I also don't want to hang out with you right now. Okay?" Jamis gave her a thumbs-up. "So, just stay inside and try to keep it down. Maybe you should text Johnna or something." With that, she was gone, closing the door firmly behind her.

It was almost six p.m. It was closer to four when it started. She fell back on the bed. She'd lost two hours, but Stephanie manifested in the hotel room. They made contact. Suddenly, thrill replaced her fear. She documented the encounter.

She wasn't ready to share, but she would. She texted Johnna. *I got sucked into another dimension and then Stephanie Gardner manifested in my hotel room, and Tess heard her scream while she was bringing me a grilled cheese. I think she wants me to leave because I'm going to scare off her other guests. She might have a valid point. How's your day?*

She hit send. Then she wrote, *I hope you don't think I'm crazy because I think you're really pretty.*

What would happen if Johnna didn't respond? Could she reset the last few days and pretend they never met? It took time to get in so deep the idea of not seeing someone surpassed the risk of letting go. Surely, it was too soon to feel so invested in whether or not she'd get a text reply. Even if she did try to kiss her.

After an agonizing five minutes, her phone chirped with a reply from Johnna. *I don't think you're crazy. I'm off tomorrow. Can I tag along?*

Jamis replied affirmatively and then her phone rang. "Jamis, it's Vince Shire. I just wanted to let you know we've decided to move out of the house. We went back to get some things today and it was whacked. Cold. Creepy. I can't explain it. We got what we could and will get the rest tomorrow during the day. We found an apartment and we're done. We're fighting it out with the property management company, but whatever."

This would limit access, but Jamis understood. They were normal people, who wanted a life that made sense.

"Jamis? Are you there?"

"Yeah, sorry. Of course, you should move out. I'm sorry and I totally understand. Can you text me the property management company's number? I'll see what I can do about the lease. I want to know what's going on."

Vince agreed. She hung up and opened her laptop again, reviewing the police report again. She fell asleep at eight with a photo of Stephanie open on the computer screen.

Chapter Twelve

Jamis was on her way to Johnna's house. She kept looking over her shoulder and in the rearview mirror. Nothing followed her but the wet spray of salt from the car's tires. Her nerves were amped and oversensitive to everything around her, but she felt followed. Probably because a poltergeist kept pulling her into other dimensions. Jamis wondered if she was crazy, if Dr. Frank's hints were on to something. It wasn't the first or last time she questioned it.

She pulled into the driveway. The blinds were open, but the glare of the sun kept her from seeing inside. Jamis was momentarily worried about seeing Johnna. She looked at her reflection in the driver's side window, smoothed the T-shirt under her coat, then zipped it again. Perhaps jeans were a better choice than the dark green cargo pants she picked. They were wrinkled. Johnna probably wouldn't notice, but the pocket that bent up and wouldn't fasten on her leg seemed like an insurmountable obstacle to intimacy.

She took her time walking to the door. Took more time ringing the bell.

"Come in," Johnna said, barely audible.

"Johnna?" Jamis was in the entryway and there was no sign of Johnna.

"I'm on the floor of the kitchen, stretching." Virginia was on the floor behind the table, her chin on her water dish.

"What did you do to Virginia?" Virginia rolled onto her back. Jamis knelt down to rub her belly.

"We just finished our run."

"How much?"

"Eight miles today," Johnna said.

Jamis peered over the counter. Johnna's right leg was in the air. She dropped her leg and looked at Jamis. "I must be running late." Sweat ran down Johnna's chest and arms. Her shirt was soaked. Jamis stared for a moment and then watched Virginia.

"I'm early," Jamis said. "I woke up super charged."

Johnna filled a glass of water, drank it, then bent forward, hands to her feet, stretching.

"I'm so excited to be off today. It's new for me, having time off. I'm always on call, always working." Johnna filled another glass. "I hired a new vet. She's just out of school. I think it might work out well." Johnna's eyes were bright green in the new light of day. Her face was flushed from exertion. "You don't mind if I tag along?"

Jamis looked away from Johnna. She wanted to look down her shirt, but Virginia's gaze was constant. It was hard to look down someone's shirt with their dog staring. "Do you really want to?"

"Of course," Johnna said.

"I was feeling insecure about taking you ghost hunting."

"Why?" Johnna moved to stand in front of Jamis.

"What if you think I'm crazy?"

"Who says I don't already?" Johnna's smile was slow but earnest.

"Do you?"

"No," Johnna said. "But I'd like to get to know you better. Understand."

Jamis pulled a small rock on a chain from her pocket and handed it Johnna, who took it with interest. "It's moonstone," Jamis said. "For new beginnings. New friendship. It's for you. I bought it at the airport in California while I was waiting." Johnna pressed it in her palm.

"Thank you," she said. "I'll go get cleaned up and we can head out."

Jamis watched her climb the stairs, two at a time. Johnna's movements in the world were considered. Jamis hadn't noticed before. Often the noise of her own issues drowned out those around her. Johnna was real and lived a simple life that protected her. She wouldn't let down her guard to have an affair. If she crossed that line, Jamis needed to be sure. Jamis's world was upside down, liable to change in any direction at any time. Would she keep chasing ghosts? Or hang up her shoes, settle down, and mow the lawn? Did she want to do that in Utah?

Until she was sure, risking Johnna's heart wasn't the right thing to do. Johnna was too wise to give her the option anyway. She'd be on her best behavior. Stop flirting. Make a friend. The moonstone necklace was a safe gift. It was a positive step in self-actualization. Recognizing emotions without getting carried away by them. Jamis scrolled social media and replied to trolls, desperate for distraction.

Mitchell K.

God had Noah save two animals, male and female for the ark. That proves homosexuality is wrong.

Jamis replied.

Did you know the story of Noah is pre-dated by an ancient Sumerian tale called the Epic of Gilgamesh, likely derived from a Mesopotamian account of a flood? Probably not because you're a homophobic dumb-ass. ~ Xoxox Jamis

Jamis was pleased with her response and resolved to behave with Johnna, until she came down the stairs, freshly showered, wearing jeans and a knit sweater, padding barefoot across the polished wood floor. Her face was scrubbed clean. The arms of the sweater were pushed halfway up, showing light blond hair and a scattering of freckles. She was beautiful.

What was at the root of attraction? What combination of chemical, hormonal, and emotional processing came together to say, "That one." How much was conscious? And how much of it was her subconscious mind, organizing stimuli and input, making Johnna look like an angel? Desire spilled through her, all her resolutions gone.

"Hi," Jamis said. "I'm glad you came back."

"Well, you're in my living room." Johnna put on socks and shoes. "So, take me ghost hunting."

"Your wish," Jamis said. "Anything you want." She meant it.

❖

"Where are we going?" Johnna pushed her seat back to get more leg room.

"First, Sapphire," Jamis said. "She's got some stuff."

"Sapphire loves my brother, but he's an idiot."

"I thought so," Jamis said. A phone rang. Johnna felt around in her pants and then looked in her bag. She held up her phone. It was dark.

Jamis struggled to pull her phone from her pocket and answered too late. She waited for a voice mail and read the transcription quickly. "It's the leasing company," Jamis said. "I'll call them back later." Jamis started the car and pulled forward.

"The leasing company?"

"Yeah, for the house. The couple who lives there wants to move. I was seeing if I could get it month to month, until I sort out what's happening. Talked to them this morning about it. They were checking."

"You'd move in?" Johnna sounded surprised.

"Yeah, I mean, why not, right? It seems like Stephanie wants me here and wants to talk to me, so I'd like to make it as easy as possible."

"Did they say they had a hard time renting it?"

"Yeah. Apparently, Vince is tenant number three in six months."

"You'll leave eventually, right? When you figure it out?"

Jamis slowed her speed and stopped at the intersection to the main road. She turned to Johnna. "I guess so. I mean, it's inevitable, right?"

"Nothing is but death. Except with you. Then maybe that's not even inevitable."

Jamis considered it. "It's so cold here."

"You need better clothes. You dress like someone from LA visiting the Mountain West."

"I am from LA visiting the Mountain West," Jamis said.

"Exactly," Johnna agreed. "Listen, turn right instead of left. Let me show you a shortcut."

Jamis followed her instructions as they wound through streets lined with houses like Stephanie's. Jamis talked about the terror in Stephanie's eyes before her involuntary reflex rejected her the night before. "It's harder to be loved when you're different," Johnna said.

"Do you feel like that? Different? Because you don't look it or seem it, but that doesn't mean a lot, I've learned." Jamis pulled into the parking lot of the municipal building.

"Inside. Yes." Then she paused. "I hope you find what happened to Stephanie, Jamis. She deserves more." It was warmer in the car and the noise from the street around them faded. Johnna closed her eyes. "Did it just get warmer here?"

"Yes," Jamis said. "I guess we're ghost hunting." It wasn't just warm though. Jamis felt embraced and the certainty of her course was clear. She was where she should be. Together, they stood and looked at Sage Creek's main street. It was like the movie set of an old western. Brick and mortar buildings, but gentrified and busy.

"Pretty, isn't it?" Johnna pointed at a building. "They say there are ghosts in the tunnels under that old Woolworth. From prohibition. They give tours in summer."

"Will you go with me? On a tour?" Jamis turned to look at her and shoved her hands in her coat pockets.

"Maybe," Johnna said. "If you're here."

They walked side by side to the records room, hands touching as their arms swung at their sides. Jamis slyly linked their pinkies together, and Johnna allowed it, leaning into her shoulder. It felt natural, like it was something they always did. They stopped at the iron cage to look inside. Johnna called out.

Sapphire emerged, distracted, unlocking the door without greeting them.

There were towering columns up and down the aisles.

"What is all this? It wasn't here Sunday," Jamis said, pointing.

"I'm working with the state to index all the state records now. They bring them in, I do my stuff, and they take them away and send more. I got a grant for it. More arrived yesterday." Sapphire puffed out her lips, blowing air. "It's such a mess right now. Anyway, I got some info for you."

"You're amazing, Sapphire," Jamis said. Sapphire waved away the compliment and turned to her computer, pushing back the sleeves of her T-shirt, a hint of her sleeve tattoo showing. Sapphire was tense, distracted. It bothered Jamis.

"We need to compare sleeve tattoos," Jamis said. She shook off her coat and pushed up the sleeve of her light sweater. "Here's a teaser. That's the *X-Files* logo."

Sapphire spun around. "You don't have the *X-Files* logo on your arm."

"I do," Jamis said. "Plus some other cool original art. Paranormal phantoms, cool places I've been." Sapphire motioned for her to pull her sweater up and took hold of her arm, looking at it. Johnna joined.

Sapphire showed Jamis her sleeve. "All my favorite stuff. Sci-fi. Computers. Radical anarchist leftism and the destruction of capitalism."

"Is Bernie Sanders on there?" Jamis now held her arm, looking at each piece.

"Don't joke," Sapphire said, taking her arm back. "My heart still hurts from that. I'm grieving." Johnna leaned to kiss her forehead. "Thanks." Sapphire turned back to the computer, mood only a little better, despite Jamis's efforts.

"I managed to get access to some additional records from that time," Sapphire said.

"How is that even possible?"

"Well, I went down to the police station yesterday after we finished up. I told them I didn't feel satisfied with the police report and I really wanted to see everything they had on Stephanie Gardner's murder. It was a different counter clerk. I've never met her before. She and I went down into their basement archives and dug around some. I found another box of autopsy photos, which I scanned and already sent to Maggie. But I also found this report, with information blacked out with a marker. It's an investigator summary from that time."

Sapphire tapped, displaying the report on the largest monitor in the middle of the screen. "I scanned the report and ported it into this image software. I basically told the software to identify the different color gradients in the text that's blacked out." She tapped more keys and then touched the tablet on a display that showed multiple colors in bars, with small buttons in the middle to adjust.

Sapphire's hands moved deftly across the keyboard and the display on the tablet. Jamis mouthed to Johnna, "Genius."

"I can see your reflection in the monitor," Sapphire said. Jamis laughed.

"I don't know how to use Netflix," Johnna said. Sapphire grinned and tapped more. Then the image blurred out of view and blurred back in, without the black marker obscuring the text.

"Neighbor Ethel Waters confirms seeing Mitch Reynolds Jr. at the deceased's house the early morning of March 13, 1992. Mrs. Waters claims Mitch Reynolds Jr. left through the back door loudly, and the deceased chased him, yelling at him. This happened about four a.m., according to Mrs. Waters. Mitch Reynolds Jr. denies being at the deceased's residence, though admitted in questioning he had been having an affair with the deceased." Jamis read the text out loud.

Sapphire held up her finger. "Just wait. I already ran the other blacked out report through the software." She clicked and swiped, and another report appeared. "Gordon Little came to the police station on March 18, 1992, to provide information about Stephanie Gardner. This is his testimony. You can read it, but it says what Ethel Waters said. He told the police that Stephanie told him she was pregnant with Mitch's child and asked him to go away with her. He refused, of course. She was at the bar on March 12. That was the last time he saw her. He said that she told him whether Mitch went with her or not she was going to take her baby and go somewhere else. Start over. She just needed to get money together."

Jamis and Johnna both read the detailed testimony over Sapphire's shoulder. Sapphire flipped the page with a swipe on the tablet. "Gordon is a bartender at the college bar, by the way. He's still there."

"I'll talk to him," Jamis said.

"He goes on to say he thinks she might have been looking to get money from other men she'd been involved with. He said he told her to be careful. He said he had a 'bad feeling' about what she was doing. He said that he knows for certain Mitch Reynolds Jr. was having an affair with her. He told them to do a paternity test. In subsequent notes, it seems as though he returned to the precinct a number of times over the next few months to repeat all this information before he abruptly stopped."

"Is Mitch her killer then? Who is Mitch?" Jamis was certain she was close to something. Her body hummed with possibility.

"The police chief's son. Or was. His dad retired a while back," Johnna said.

Sapphire pulled up a notepad with notes. "He's at Shady Oaks retirement home. And to make our luck worse, Mitch Reynolds Jr. died in a car wreck in 2003 at the age of forty-nine." She scooted back. "Guess what? They never did a paternity test. This testimony was blacked out, instead of destroyed. But the handwriting on the upper corner of this is different from the writing on the report, so

I think someone tucked these into another folder, maybe hiding them for future use. Someone with a conscience."

Sapphire pointed at the screen, agitated and angry. She was upset about Stephanie, nothing else. Jamis liked her even more. "Mitch had plenty of reason to kill her. He was married with six kids. He taught economics at the college. His dad was police chief. If she went to him, told him she's pregnant with his kid, pay up or I'm telling everyone, well, that's motive, right?"

"I want to talk with Gordon and Mitch Reynolds Sr.," Jamis said.

"What about Mitch Jr.'s wife?" Johnna sat on the corner of the desk, legs dangling.

"I checked," Sapphire said. "She's still alive and here in town. She lives just up from the house, actually. They didn't live far from Stephanie. Same house as then." Sapphire tapped on the screen and minimized everything. "I wasn't able to find detailed phone records from that far back, Jamis. But I did find one more thing." Sapphire pulled up a report on the screen. "Rick Davis owned the house while Stephanie lived in it. It looks like both eviction notices were filed by Dan Abbey."

"Really," Johnna said animatedly, with a smile. Jamis liked the expression and moved to stand closer to her.

"That's Paul's uncle. Johnna's brother-in-law. Rick is Matt's dad. Matt is our childhood friend. We are so entangled," Sapphire said.

"These guys are a rich old white man's club," Johnna said. Sapphire agreed.

"Would it be weird for you to ask for access to these old white men?" Jamis turned to face Johnna directly.

"Do you want me to ask Matt?" Johnna asked Sapphire, who nodded. Johnna texted Matt.

"Matt will do it for Johnna because he's in love with her," Sapphire said. Johnna kicked out her foot at Sapphire without looking up from her phone.

"We've been friends since we were three," Johnna said.

"He finally gave in and married his wife when it became clear Johnna wouldn't marry him," Sapphire said to Jamis. "Unrequited love runs deep in these parts."

"Sometimes you just have to be crazy blunt about things," Johnna said, looking at Sapphire.

"Wait, who is Matt? And he's in love with you?" Jamis felt a surge of jealousy, possessiveness.

"No, he had a crush on me when we were little. Sapphire never lets me forget it." Johnna put her phone back in her pocket. "He responded and said he'd call his dad and let him know we were coming by."

"That was fast," Jamis said.

"See? Love." Sapphire grinned, turning off the computer. "Can I come today?"

"I can't imagine a better idea," Johnna said. She held her hand out to Sapphire and pulled her up. Sapphire locked fingers with her, shoulders touching, and they moved together from the room. Jamis watched their connectedness with warmth and some jealously. Johnna's connections seemed so present and genuine, and her warmth was undeniable. But Jamis wondered how much of herself she actually allowed other people access to and how much of it was only externalized feeling.

"You coming?" Johnna startled Jamis from her reverie. "You looked so lost in thought," Johnna said, holding the cage door open.

"Almost out of body," Jamis said, rushing forward.

CHAPTER THIRTEEN

Johnna knocked on the large mahogany door. Jamis turned her back and looked at the front yard. The house, from her estimation, was at least six thousand square feet. The front yard was at least a manicured acre. From the stoop, Jamis could see all of Sage Creek. The Castle Mountains around the valley were imposing and covered in snow. "I can't wait to see this place in summer," Jamis said.

"Your clothes will work then." Johnna turned to her.

Jamis grinned as the door opened. It was Rick Davis, wearing dark gray slacks, a maroon sweater, and leather slippers. His eyeglasses were rimless. He smiled and stepped to allow them in. "Johnna, Sapphire, so good to see you." He shook their hands as they passed. Jamis stopped as he took her hand. "You must be Jamis."

"I appreciate you talking to me."

He motioned for them to come in the front room and sit. "Of course. Matt said you're looking into a murder from many years ago."

Jamis told him what they'd learned about Stephanie. "You rented the house to her in the early nineties. Served her with two eviction notices but didn't evict her, so much as we can see. I'm just curious if you remember anything."

He crossed his legs. "Obviously, I remember her murder. It was a terrible spring." He looked at Johnna. "So much loss. But I didn't manage my rental properties directly. Around that time, Dan worked for me and took care of over twenty properties across the state."

"Dan Abbey," Johnna stated.

"Yes. Paul's uncle," Rick said.

"That's why he signed on both requests for eviction then," Sapphire said.

"Yes. He would have done that. Now, I know he urged me to sell the house not long after she died. I'd held on to it for a number of years because it was my dad's place." His tone softened. "I was being nostalgic. I wish I could tell you more than that. I think you could probably chat with Dan today. Old retired men have a lot of time on their hands."

"I don't want to keep you any longer, but it was good to see you, and I appreciate it," Johnna said, standing up. Jamis and Sapphire followed her lead.

"I will, Johnna, thank you," Rick said.

Johnna waved to Rick, watching as he shut the front door. She turned to look at Sapphire and Jamis. "I think we should talk to Dan."

"Can you get us there?" Jamis said.

Dan Abbey opened his front door. He wore a button-down shirt with the sleeves rolled up. There was an angry white scar on his forearm. Jamis noticed it immediately. He saw her gaze and unrolled his shirt.

"Dan, thanks for talking to us," Johnna said. "Did Rick call?"

"Yes, he did." Dan waved them in. He didn't invite them to sit, though. He put his hands in his trouser pockets. "What can I do for you? I'm getting ready to head out, so I'm afraid I don't have a lot of time."

"Do you remember Stephanie Gardner?" Jamis jumped in.

"I do," he said. "She was found dead. From a serial killer they thought. She rented one of Rick's houses in the nineties. She was living there when they found her."

"You served two eviction notices to her," Jamis said, stating fact, not asking him.

"Did I?"

"Was she able to pay the rent?" Sapphire moved closer to him now. "We saw one in January and September."

"I have no idea. I managed so many properties for Rick then. What I know is just about what I've told you." He tucked his hands deeper in his pockets. "Long time ago. Lifetimes, it feels like."

"You're sure you don't remember anything else?" Jamis stared at him.

"I don't remember anything else." He opened the front door. "I need to get going." They moved to leave, but Johnna paused in the doorway.

"Will I see you at Paul's party tomorrow?"

"Sure will. Wouldn't want to hear from your sister if I didn't show up," Dan said. It was the most comfortable he'd been since they arrived.

"Thanks again, Dan." Johnna smiled and stepped from the house. He waved and shut the door. Johnna froze, staring at the front door.

"You okay?" Jamis moved toward her, hand on her forearm.

"Is it me or did he seem weird?" Johnna still stared at the door.

"I don't know him that well, so it's hard to know," Sapphire said.

"What are you thinking?" Jamis still held Johnna's arm.

"I don't know," Johnna said, moving from the steps. "Something just feels strange. He's a strange dude, though, so it could be that."

"Dude," Jamis said. Johnna smiled. Small lines crinkled around her eyes and mouth. Jamis didn't think she'd seen them before. The lines on her face were stories waiting to be told. She wanted to hear all of them. Jamis wanted to grab her, arms around her waist, pull her forward and kiss her. Could someone really be this calm, thoughtful, and genuine?

"I guess that leaves Mitch Reynold's dad, wife, and Gordon," Sapphire said, oblivious to Jamis's thoughts. "And don't forget to stop at the newspaper. The editor has been there for years."

"Got it," Jamis said, breaking her concentration on Johnna. "Come with me?"

"I should probably get back to work," Sapphire said. "I don't want to, but I probably should. You saw the boxes."

"I'm going to go to the house tonight, if you want to come by," Jamis said.

"I'm going to regret it again, but yes," Sapphire said.

"We have to eat before we talk to anyone else," Johnna said. "I'm starved. I ran eight miles this morning."

"Well, that's your fault," Jamis said as they pulled away.

Jamis dropped Sapphire at work and Johnna at the office. Midway through lunch, Johnna's phone rang. Someone needed help with a horse. Jamis finished her Taco Bell, morosely alone. She didn't really want to talk to Barbara Reynolds. So, it would be Gordon, and then the newspaper editor. She punched the address Sapphire texted her into Google Maps. It was just a few blocks away.

It was a square cinderblock building painted a dark black with blackened windows. Graffiti art covered the side walls in patterns of brilliant colors and shapes. Jamis parked directly in front of the doors. Except for soft rock music, the bar was quiet and empty when she stepped inside. A bar ran the entire length of the room. She could imagine it packed with college kids on a Saturday night.

"Hello," she yelled from the end of the bar closest to the entrance.

A swinging door opened in the back of the bar. A tall man stepped through. His shaggy blond hair was pulled into a ponytail, and he had scruff on his cheeks. He stopped at the sink near the middle of the long bar. "What you having?"

Jamis looked at the cabinet behind him. "Gin and tonic?" He put a glass on the bar. "Extra lime. Are you Gordon?" Surprised, he looked up at her. "I'm in town investigating a murder. Stephanie Gardner?"

"What about her?" He poured her drink, set it in front of her.

She sipped it. "So good. Thank you," Jamis said. "I read some redacted files today. I don't think someone intended for anyone to see them. They had your name all over them. You went to the police a number of times to share what you knew about Stephanie."

He crossed his arms and leaned back against the counter behind him. "Why do you care?" His tone was hostile, agitated.

"You may think I'm crazy if I tell you." He shrugged. She told him the story, as far as she knew. "There's something going on. I'm a ghost hunter. I used to have a television show, actually." She hoped it added credibility, but he didn't blink. "I think Stephanie Gardner is the poltergeist." She paused. He stared at her, unblinking. "Right. I know. It sounds crazy, but it's not. She can't rest. I don't think Richard Crespin killed her."

Gordon stepped toward her and Jamis retreated back instinctively. "She had the worst life. We grew up next door to each other. Her mom let the men she brought home do whatever they wanted to her for extra money." He picked up a glass from the sink and wiped it with a towel. He put it in the strainer. "Then she let any man do the same when she got big enough to do different." Jamis felt sadness constrict her throat. "I knew he didn't kill her. I think Mitch Reynolds Jr. killed her. His dad was the police chief. She was pregnant, you know."

"I know," Jamis said. "But only because you told them."

Gordon's eyes watered. "No one cared she got killed. I just kept going, but no one would listen to me. Then, one day, Mitch Reynolds Sr. showed up here with two cops. They turned over my bar. They arrested a bunch of kids on Saturday night. Then the old man cornered me back in my office and told me to drop it or he'd see me out of town. My old man gave me this place. I had to take care of my mom then." He threw the towel down, wiped tears from his eyes. "It just didn't matter what I did then. Stephanie was dead. Her baby was dead."

Jamis looked into the glass she held between her hands. She swirled the ice cubes, and they clanked against the sides of the glass. She sipped it again and looked up to make eye contact with Gordon. "Did you love her?" The question rose so unbidden, so spontaneously it surprised her.

He put both hands on the bar in front of him. "Yes," he said, voice low.

The front door of the bar flew open with so much force it banged against the wall and rattled. The glasses hanging above the bar clanked against each other. Then, as quickly as it began, it was done. The door closed and the glasses stopped moving. Jamis, who had turned to look at the door, turned slowly back to Gordon. "Well, hell," she said. Gordon clenched the counter. She touched his arm and he loosened his grasp. She felt for him, in the way that only someone broken and rebuilding could. Life was so dangerous, for so many. "I suppose it's safe to say she heard you."

"Find who did this to her. Please. I gave up." He covered his eyes, trying to hide his upset and shame.

"We tell ourselves all kinds of stories so we can survive. You didn't do anything wrong. You tried. Because you did, I'm here now. I think Stephanie heard." He took his hand from his face, met her eyes, vulnerable, grateful. "She has a fierce temper, though, I'll give you that."

"She was a doormat," Gordon said. "She wanted to be loved so bad she'd do anything, for any man. That's why I never asked for anything from her."

"Because you loved her."

"I guess so. I mean, I didn't think I'd marry her, but I guess when we got older, when everyone else saw a whore, I saw the eight-year-old who used to color and draw with me when her mom left her at my house." Jamis took her hand from his arm. "She loved to draw. You want more?" He looked at Jamis's glass. Jamis put her hand over the top of it.

"I'm good. I appreciate you talking with me," she said.

"Yeah." She was halfway out the door when he called to her. She paused, the door in her hand, and looked over her shoulder. "Let me know what you find?"

"I will," Jamis said. She stepped outside, held her hand at her brow to let her eyes adjust. The newspaper was next. Sapphire had texted her the address earlier. Jamis drove without a lot of conscious thought. Her mind wandered to Stephanie.

At a stop sign, she watched a group of teenagers cross the street. They wore backpacks perched on their shoulders. She thought about Gordon and Stephanie, walking home from school together. A surge of warm air circled her, and she closed her eyes, momentarily at peace. When she opened them again, the hunched figure of Stephanie Gardner was in front of her car. She yanked the hood of the robe down, opening her mouth to scream.

The teenagers who just crossed the street screamed and pointed. She put the car in park and looked behind her. There were no cars coming in any direction. When she turned around, Stephanie was gone. Jamis climbed from the car.

One of the male teenagers came toward her in the street. "What was that?"

"You heard it?"

"I heard you scream. Are you okay?" He had braces, a light dusting of facial hair, a generous helping of acne. He squinted at her, leaning close, worried and gallant. "Do you need help?"

"It wasn't me." She looked around him at the other kids. "Did any of you hear it?" There were four of them, all of whom raised their hand. "Did you see anything?" The young man right in front of her shook his head. A girl to the back and the side of the group raised her hand tentatively.

"What did you see?" Jamis moved toward her. The girl shrugged and looked to her friends for reassurance. They didn't speak, but stepped away, forming a circle to watch her. "No one will think you're crazy. Right?" The kids agreed.

"Just for a second, I swore someone in a gray cloak was standing in the middle of the road." Her friends' murmurs rose in the air. A lone crow squawked from a barren branch and took off in flight.

"Yeah, me too." Jamis turned back to the road. "I saw it too." She turned back to the group. "I gotta move my car, but thank you."

She jogged back to her car. The teenagers meandered away in animated discussion.

"Stephanie," Jamis said out loud. "I'm working on it. I really am."

CHAPTER FOURTEEN

The newspaper was called the *Sage Creek Advocate*. The poster on the wall said it had been operating since 1918. The afternoon light filtered through the windows. There were half a dozen desks in the small, open space, but no receptionist. The walls were a dirty cream color, covered in framed newspaper prints, interspersed with small awards. A single person typed, back to the door, the clicking of keyboard keys the only sound. There was a dying rubber tree plant next to the man's desk. It smelled like stale coffee. It was like a scene from a comic book. She half-expected Spider-Man to drop from a vent in the ceiling.

She tapped the lone man on the shoulder. He jumped from his seat and knocked the keyboard from the desk. It swung by the cord and snapped against the metal.

"I'm so sorry," Jamis said.

He took off his headphones and picked up the keyboard. He wore a white short-sleeve shirt with a tie, loosened. His hair was completely gray. She introduced herself.

"Ghost hunter?" Jamis nodded. "Yeah. I thought so. Sampson Birch."

"Pleasure. Do you have some time to talk?"

He looked at the computer, at the clock, and back at her. "A few minutes."

"Do you know anything about Stephanie Gardner?"

Sampson pushed back in his chair. He slid a chair to her. "Have a seat." There was a large, yellowish color stain in the middle of the brown fabric. Jamis looked at it, then looked at Sampson, and decided the desire to talk outweighed her revulsion. "She was murdered. I wrote the article about it. What do you want to know?"

"It's unsolved," Jamis said.

"Is it?"

"Yeah. It is. I've been digging around a bit. Seems like maybe the police didn't really do a thorough job." Jamis avoided touching the armrests of the chair.

"When was that again? I was here, in case you're wondering." She was. "Probably the only one still here."

"Yeah, where is everyone?" Jamis looked around the empty office.

"I do most of the heavy lifting. No need for a big staff. Print newspaper is dying. My online contributors just post from home. Honestly, I think I'll close this office down next year."

"That's really sad," Jamis said. He shrugged. "Stephanie. She was found on March 16, 1992. I have reason to believe the police chief willfully covered up his son's involvement, impregnation, and her murder." She shared details and waited for him to add to it.

When she finished, he turned to his desk and pulled a file from the bottom drawer, almost six inches thick. Paper bulging out the sides, and a large rubber band held it together. "This is my file on Mitch Reynolds Sr., the police chief then. He did whatever he wanted, or didn't do whatever he wanted, for close to thirty years. Nothing stuck. People down in Arizona get worked up about Sheriff Joe, but that's because they don't know Chief Reynolds. These guys are from a different era. They're outlaws, as bad as the guys they chase. The world changed and outpaced them."

"Are you saying Mitch Reynolds was corrupt?"

He pointed to the file. "I'm saying that there is plenty of shit in there to suggest he had his own set of rules and he played by them. He was an old western chief and likely saw Stephanie as a whore, nothing more. If you're asking me if it's possible he covered up her death, for his son or someone else, the answer is yes."

"I was going to go talk to him and his son's wife, Barbara."

"He won't give you anything, even with dementia. But you can try."

"Thanks," Jamis said, readying to leave.

"Hold on," Sampson said. "If you get enough to take this to the police, you come right back here with it too. I'll write about it, print it, and make sure something happens."

"Is that all altruistic? Because you want justice?"

"No, it's not. I want the story. If justice comes with it, amazing for everyone." He turned back to his computer and Jamis let herself out.

Jamis was on the sidewalk in front of Stephanie's house. She felt nervous and uncertain. She knocked to be certain Vince and Darcy weren't home. When no one answered, she tried the handle. The door was unlocked, and it opened. She stepped into the house and closed the door behind her.

"Hello," she yelled, but no one responded. The house was empty except for furniture. The Shires moved quickly. Jamis sat in a chair in the master bedroom and looked out the window. She imagined Stephanie sitting there or lying in the bed near enough to see out of it. Jamis thought about Stephanie's life, considered the depth of sexual abuse, and how much courage it took to decide to leave town. She wondered about Mitch Reynolds Jr. and resolved to talk to Mitch Reynolds Sr. and his wife. At some point, she would need to take her findings to the police, but that wouldn't be today.

"Stephanie. I'm here. I get it now. I understand. I want to find who did this to you. If you can help me, you should."

The house was silent. Somewhere, a board creaked and a faucet dripped. Jamis rested her head against the back of the chair and closed her eyes. She'd not dreamed for a few days and longed for the field and woman. How was that possible or rational? She opened her eyes, expecting to see Stephanie in front of her, but no one materialized. The house rested. Then there was a knock on the front door, and Jamis raced down the stairs.

It was Sapphire. She held a computer tablet in one hand and a box in the other. "I'm probably going to regret this. Didn't I say that already?"

❖

Sapphire scattered the contents of the box she carried around the room. "I assume your cameras have night vision?" She didn't look up from what she assembled.

"Yes." Jamis was in the chair, facing the corner of the room. If anything moved, she wanted to see it.

"Well, I was thinking it might make sense to see if a modified sensor could pick up anything. I downloaded some software earlier that the military uses to read heat and such. Then I found some other cool radar stuff too. I don't know what it will do, but I thought it might be interesting for us to try. So we will try to read heat and bounce some sonar around. Yeah?" Sapphire set a black box on the table, shifting from her tablet to the laptop.

"When you say things like 'software the military uses,' does that mean you stole it?"

"Well, technically, I suppose at some point, someone stole it. But I picked up the code in open-source sharing platforms on the dark web." Sapphire bent to take a smaller box from the larger box, setting it in her lap. "Really, money is stupid. The accumulation of wealth hoarding technology is the crime. Ever heard the term rent-seeking?" Sapphire looked up and met Jamis's eyes.

"No," Jamis said, shifting into a comfortable position in the chair, enthralled.

"Thank Gordon Tullock and Anne Krueger. It's when someone who isn't really adding any great value to humanity hoards wealth only by virtue of their ownership. If I buy land, then I take other people's money and add to my wealth just by owning it, I'm not actually contributing anything new to society. I'm not bettering humanity. I'm creating income inequality. Capitalism isn't really merit based. If it were, you'd know the name of the person who invented the World Wide Web. That's how the one percent in America got rich. Not because they really do anything. Because they know how to earn rent and patent."

Sapphire returned her attention to the device in her lap. "Tim Burners-Lee. He didn't patent the World Wide Web. He wanted it available to everyone. If he had, it would just have come off patent. Can you imagine what we would have lost the past twenty years developing the World Wide Web? Meanwhile, pharmaceutical CEOs make millions every year defending patents to medications created with public funds to protect corporate profits. Rent seekers." She plugged in another cord. "I take liberally from rent seekers." She smiled, a glimmer of mischief in her eyes. "Wanna see?"

Jamis was impressed and jumped up. "I tapped into your cameras here." She pointed at her tablet and held up a device. "The sensor reads heat and the sonar bounces off stuff. I figure we might get lucky and it'll bounce off something paranormal and we will read it here. I don't know." She held up her hands. "I've modified this program to read what it's scanning and return it in images you'll understand."

"Do you think it will work? Nothing I've used before shows anything," Jamis said.

"How should I know? You're the ghost hunter." She walked around the room with the sensor. "Watch on the tablet there. See if anything weird jumps out."

Jamis watched the screen with anticipation, which gave way to disappointment. Sapphire's efforts returned nothing in any room. But then something blinked on the screen and Jamis felt a surge of excitement. "What's that?"

She pointed at the screen, then saw Sapphire point the sensor at her. "Oh, that's me." They laughed together.

"Well, it works, at least," she said, setting it on the coffee table.

"Let's keep it on, just in case something happens." Sapphire nodded. "I was thinking about Stephanie today. I talked to Gordon." Sapphire listened to the details of their conversation. Then Jamis summarized what they knew. "She's pregnant. She asks Mitch to leave town with her. He probably says shit like 'How do you know it's my baby?' She's upset. Angry. Hurt. Decides to break the cycle. Leave town. Give her baby a better life. But she needs money. She decides to blackmail some other men."

"Would she do that?" Sapphire looked genuinely distressed. Jamis knew it was one thing to read about things in the news but to step into the story like they were was emotionally draining. Holding the space for compassion was the ultimate test of empathy, especially when self-preservation urged her to turn away. She understood how Sapphire felt and watched her breathe through the density of emotion.

"Of course, she'd do that. Wouldn't she? These men treated her as little more than an object. Why should she value them any more than they valued her?" Her phone chirped. Jamis picked it up and typed back. "Johnna got dropped off at home. She and Virginia send their regrets."

"Johnna had enough peopling for the day," Sapphire said. "It doesn't take a lot of peopling to be enough." Would Jamis's extroversion drain Johnna over time? She never got tired of talking. It might be problematic. "But she seems happy enough to spend time with you."

Heat flushed her cheeks. Was she that obvious? "Let's talk about ghosts, okay?"

"Sure, yeah, or Johnna, you know, whenever you want," Sapphire said, teasing.

Jamis ignored her. "So, yeah, I think Stephanie would. Why wouldn't she? We create from the place we feel the most comfortable. For Stephanie, in this incarnation, she only knew men as objects or as objectifying. I think she would have gone to them for money." Jamis shifted the subject, uncomfortable.

"If that's the case, Jamis, it's not open-and-shut that Mitch killed her. Any number of men could have killed her." A strong wind howled outside. The trees in the front yard shook with the gust. In the declining light of day, the bare branches cast eerie shadows. "Is there another storm coming?" Jamis looked out the front window. "Big clouds are rolling in. Do you need to get home?"

"I'm fine. I'm in for the long haul," Sapphire said.

"I thought it was kind of nice today," Jamis said. "The sun was out. It wasn't horribly cold."

"Spring is fickle here. We're rolling into it now, but winter doesn't go down without a fight." Sapphire turned on her laptop and began to type. "You should stick around. Even after this is done."

Jamis turned away from the window. "Why?"

"Seems like you could belong here."

Jamis looked down at her phone in her hands. She wanted distraction. She had one thousand notifications on Facebook and too many to filter on Instagram.

"I've considered hacking your social media," Sapphire said.

"Why?"

"Your trolls. I've seen some of those comments. I could chase them down. Ruin their lives. They're mean to you."

"You might be diabolical, and I'm glad you're on my side," Jamis said. Sapphire continued to tap on her laptop. "Did it ever occur to you that all of this is just an unfolding matrix of manifestation and synchronicity? It's almost like this is a computer operating system, constantly upgrading. Right now, we're like WordPerfect 95."

"I liked WordPerfect. I feel like everything else overcomplicated the simple beauty of the word processor," Sapphire said with a grin. "Oh, hey, I forgot to tell you I tried to clear up that image from the other night." Jamis must have looked uncertain because she clarified. "Our incident, when you thought you saw something in front of the door."

"Right. Yeah. Did it show anything?"

"No. Just a blur of yellow. Faint yellow. Then it was gone."

"In my dream, the woman is in a yellow dress."

Jamis had more to say, but a strong gust of wind hit the house, and something crashed above them. Wood squealed as it split apart. The dining room window cracked. Jamis jumped to her feet and Sapphire followed. They ran to the bottom of the stairs, even as thunderous noise echoed above. The wind in the house howled, and they turned to look at each other.

"Well, holy hell," Jamis said, taking the stairs two at a time.

Sapphire followed behind, sleeves pushed up, a fierce look on her face. At the top of the stairs, Jamis said, "You look so cool right now." Sapphire laughed and shoved her forward. Jamis stopped at the end of the landing.

A tree had broken through the side of the house at the end of the hallway. Branches smoked and sparked.

"Lightning," Sapphire said.

"Looks like it," Jamis said. Sapphire crept closer, her back against the wall. "It looks like it came down right into the hallway. Took out the doorway to that bedroom." Sapphire reached across the hall and flipped on the light switch. It flickered and then blinked out. Jamis reached into the bedroom next to her and turned on the light. Some of it drifted into the hallway. Jamis turned on her cell phone flashlight for more illumination. "It got some of that wall too. What is that?"

Sapphire stepped, the floor cracked, a board splintered under her weight, and she plunged. Jamis dropped her cell phone, leaped, and grabbed Sapphire under the shoulders, yanking her upward. Sapphire pushed to get up, and boards splintered under her.

Jamis grabbed her by the hips. "Hold still." Sapphire complied. "Let's scoot back slowly." Jamis moved backward across the floor with Sapphire, pulling them back to the end of the hallway. Sapphire pushed off her and then turned to pull her up. "I dropped my phone."

Sapphire crept forward. “I see it. It’s right up there. I think I can get to it. I see where the boards are splintered now.”

“Let me,” Jamis said, getting to her feet. “Don’t get hurt.” She nudged Sapphire from her path and edged up the hallway, against the left wall. About two feet from her phone, Jamis stopped. “Sapphire, can you see up there?”

Sapphire inched forward and leaned around Jamis without moving her feet from where they were planted on solid flooring. “What is that?” There was a hole in the wall. “Was there a door there?” Sapphire stepped across Jamis, who held on to her waist to help her keep balance. “There are stairs.” Sapphire stepped onto the floor near the window at the end of the hall.

“The tree hit the wall and made a hole, where there are stairs. You’re kidding?” Jamis picked up her phone and shined the light in the hole. “It’s an attic. It looks like it was closed up.” She turned to Sapphire. “This can’t be a coincidence.” That’s why the space hadn’t felt right to her. She sensed it was off balance somehow.

“I don’t think so,” Sapphire said. “I mean, what’s the probability?”

“I’m going to go up there. You don’t come. It might not be safe.”

“What are you? A gallant lesbian knight? Shut the fuck up. I’m going.” Sapphire nudged her forward. “Go. Go up the stairs.”

CHAPTER FIFTEEN

Jamis stepped through the small hole carefully and peered over her shoulder as she did. The tree struck the house at the perfect angle to expose the attic stairs. The emerging night blanketed the backyard in darkness, but a single streetlight cast enough glow to see where the lightning struck the tree. The house groaned under the weight of it and then quieted as the wind calmed. "Watch the glass," Jamis said. "There are some big pieces."

Sapphire stepped into the hole behind Jamis. "Should we go back down for the night vision goggles?"

Jamis held her phone up higher, trying to see more of the space. "Probably, but I don't want to," Jamis said. She stepped on the first stair. "I feel like I should just go up here." She held the light down on the stairs and moved forward. She smacked her head.

"God damn." The ceiling arched at the peak of the stairs and was about three inches shorter than her.

"Should've let me go first," Sapphire said.

Jamis rubbed her head and cast the light around. Boxes lined the walls to her left. There were three trunks in the middle of the room, and a wardrobe next to a metal cabinet in the far right corner. "I think it's safe. Come up here and look at this."

Sapphire walked ahead of Jamis and pulled a cord hanging in the middle of the room and light filled the space. There was a desk by a boarded up window.

Sapphire pulled open the doors on the metal cabinet. There were Christmas decorations, Halloween jack-o'-lantern candy dishes, and a pile of magazines on the bottom shelf. Sapphire lifted one delicately. "Old *Ensign* magazines."

"What?" Jamis opened the wardrobe.

"It's a Mormon magazine. The church publishes it. These are from 1991." Sapphire held it up to Jamis. "These belonged to Stephanie."

"What if all of this belonged to Stephanie?" The light flickered. Jamis twisted the bulb tighter and it steadied. A heavy canvas covered the desk. Jamis pulled it off. She coughed, inhaling the dust.

There was a clown's head on the corner of the desk, next to a carousel. Jamis picked it up and turned it over in her hands. It was made of heavy plaster, with a signature on the bottom. *S. Gardner 1983*. She held it up in front of her. The paint was immaculate and vibrant. The detailed coloring around the mouth and eyes was gorgeous.

"Stephanie made it." Sapphire turned from where she crouched in front of the cabinet. Jamis held the clown for Sapphire to see. "She signed it."

Sapphire took the clown from her and delicately turned it over in her hands, studying it. Jamis picked up the carousel, but the pieces shifted. She caught a horse on a pole right before it fell, setting it gently back on the desk. She removed each carousel animal. The horse, unicorn, and elephant were cracked with missing flecks of paint. She took the top off the carousel, which was painted red and white, like a traditional circus tent, and set it next to the animals. She picked up the base, which was attached to the pole in the middle of the carousel and turned it over. It was made of heavy wood. The pole was iron. It shocked her with its weight. "E. Gardner 1979," she read, and turned it to Sapphire to see. "Why is this stuff up here? Why didn't it get hauled away when she died?"

Sapphire had put the clown head down and was in front of the wardrobe. She pried the doors open and took a step back. "I have no idea. Why would anyone save her stuff up here and then seal it up?" She touched the clothes. "These are women's clothes from the eighties, I think." There was a small shelf with a black case above the rod. She opened it. There was a small black book inside.

"Jamis, look." There were vivid patterns drawn across every inch of the page with a blue ballpoint pen. "She was an artist," Sapphire said and turned the book to Jamis.

Jamis thumbed through the pages delicately, as if she were unearthing an archaeological treasure. She handed it back to Sapphire. "Is there a code in there?"

"That's what I was just thinking, but I think it's just doodles. Do you think it's okay if I take this?"

"Well, technically, the Shires are still tenants, but the house is furnished. I was going to rent it, but I don't think they'll let me rent it now. I suppose all of this would technically belong to the property owners, but since they're rent seekers…" Jamis trailed off and grinned at Sapphire. "Let's sort through the rest of this stuff and see what else is here."

Jamis bent to unlock the trunk. She pulled blankets from it. They were polyester blends, rose and dull beige, popular in the seventies and eighties. She tossed two on the floor. A breeze filtered up the stairs from the hole in the wall. She tossed another blanket over the stairs, blocking the flow of air. She sat on the blankets and opened the first box.

Jamis put her hand on her stomach as it growled. Sapphire looked up from a spiral bound notebook, eyebrow raised. "They're progressing in intensity." Jamis tossed the notebook into a pile with others. "So far we've opened every box here and uncovered nothing of importance. Secretly, I was hoping to find an old phone bill or something, but nada. Nothing." She put her hands on the small of her back and stretched. Something cracked and Jamis grimaced as she tossed her notepad into the pile.

"We've been up here for hours. What time is it anyway?" Jamis shimmied on the floor to pull out her phone. "It's after nine," she said. "Do you want to go get something to eat and close up for the night?"

"God, yes, please." Sapphire said, wiping her hands on her pants. "I feel filthy."

"Twenty-five years of dust will do that," Jamis said.

"Do you think we should put all this back?"

"No. I'll call the property management company tomorrow and tell them about the tree. Then I'll get movers to come move this into a storage shed until everything is sorted out." She moved toward the stairs and pulled the blanket off the opening. A gush of cold air struck her, and she shivered. Sapphire whined. Jamis turned to pull the string on the light in the middle of the attic but then stopped, thinking about the clown head and carousel.

She picked up a small empty box and a few old T-shirts and wrapped the clown head and carousel in them. Sapphire appeared with two pillowcases and helped Jamis without question. Jamis tucked the edges of the box together and picked it up. "She made these. I just feel like they shouldn't be left."

"You are not a rent seeker," she said.

"I am very wealthy, though," Jamis said. "But I don't do much with it. I will though. When I'm done. For Stephanie and women like her." Sapphire put her hand on her shoulder, and they moved slowly down the stairs. The evening air pressed against them, cold and unforgiving.

Once downstairs, Jamis checked the cameras and feed, but she didn't expect to get anything from them. Sapphire checked her sensor and showed Jamis how to connect to the program online. She finished setting the parameters to capture movement and changes in heat and gathered her things to go.

There was crying.

"Do you hear that? That's what I heard the first day." Sapphire held the sensor in her hand and scanned the room.

"Yeah, it's real," Sapphire said.

Jamis accessed the video feed and waited impatiently for it to load. When the room finally emerged, through night vision and sensors, Jamis waved her arms at Sapphire. "Stop. The middle of the room. Go back."

There was an indistinct blob. Sapphire moved closer to it. Jamis turned off the lights.

"Step carefully," she said. Sapphire stopped at the edge of the room.

"You getting this? You can screen shot it. Look for the little button on the tablet there." Jamis snapped a picture before whatever it was shifted away.

"Where did it go?"

Jamis sighed, disappointed. "I will chase ghosts my whole life and never find proof. It is my sad destiny."

"Did you get a picture of that?"

"Yeah, but…"

Sapphire stopped her. "Are you serious? You don't think you have proof? Look upstairs. Look at what you've seen. Look who you've met. There is something at work here that is not coincidental. It's why I'm here."

"I didn't think about it like that. Why not?"

Sapphire opened the door. "Because you're too close to it. Because it's not objective proof in objective reality. It's relational, psychological, and full of synchronicity. Our methods of collecting proof are not sophisticated enough to capture it."

Jamis unpacked the clown and carousel and set it on the small table in the corner. She'd eaten voraciously at Denny's with Sapphire and texted Johnna, wanting to see her but too tired to make it happen. A hot shower, pajamas, and bed were the only things in her immediate future. She slipped into sleep easily, satiated and warm, her eyes on the carousel.

Sleep took her to the field. She touched the grass under her and began to move, shocked when no resistance met her. A bird soared above her, swooping and graceful. It landed on a pine tree, on the east edge of the field. Then the woman in yellow was at the edge of the field. Resistance began to build as Jamis moved toward her. "Please," she begged. "Please talk to me. Tell me who you are. Tell me where this is. Tell me why I keep seeing you."

The woman came toward her. She heard her voice, but her facial features were out of phase. She moved her hands when she spoke, but those were blurred as well. "This is the in-between, the place of remaining attachment."

"The bardo of hungry ghosts," Jamis said, suddenly alarmed.

"Not all hungry ghosts are angry. Some of us just can't let go. Love binds us, just as much as fear and hatred. It just feels different. Looks different. Is nice to dwell in. But you're not meant to stay in it. Even if you want to. All life wants to change and grow. We're meant to let go. We're meant to evolve." She blinked in and out of phase. "This place shifts quickly. I made this for you, but we can only stay a while. I bring you here to me."

"Why? Why are you doing this?" Jamis tried to move closer.

"I saw you. I called you. I knew you'd come." Her image shimmered in front of her. Jamis saw her like a buffering Netflix feed. "I've known you before. In other lives. But it all leaves when we manifest. I don't know why that happens."

"But I don't know who you are," Jamis said. "Can you tell me who you are?"

"I've forgotten. I know sometimes, but then I forget. When I'm not here, I remember, but when I bring you here, I forget. We all do that, no matter where we are. We all know everything we need to know, but then when we manifest, we forget. It's because we search for words to communicate here and on Earth. It takes so much energy we can't remember. But I know that I can't let go. There is so much undone. I feel so much here," she said and put her hand on her chest. "I was just alive, like I was just born, and then I died. I didn't want to go. I wasn't supposed to go."

"Can you touch me?"

"I don't know," she said. Jamis took her hand. She steadied in front of Jamis, and for a split second, Jamis saw her. "I concentrated so hard to see you tonight. I am watching you, but it's like I'm far away and the voices are muted. But I saw something I had to tell you. I don't know what it is."

"I don't know you," Jamis said. "I know Stephanie, but not you. How can I help you if I don't know you?"

"You are helping me. I just can't remember my name here. But you do know me. You do." Her voice became weaker. "It takes a lot to bring you here." Her image blurred again, and Jamis held on to her hand. "Somehow, we're getting closer to each other. I don't know how, but we are."

"How? Why did you do this tonight? Why can we talk?"

"Because I have to tell you something important. I remembered it, but it's gone now. I really concentrated so I could talk to you." Jamis felt growing alarm. She was warning her. "You have to watch who you don't expect. Someone is coming for you."

"Are you okay? Don't be scared. I can help." Jamis held her shoulders, pulling her closer. "Try to concentrate."

"I'm running out of energy. I'm so sorry." She started to fade, and Jamis pulled her close, felt her in her arms, heard her whisper, even as she faded from view. "Someone is coming for you and you must watch. Tell Carmen." Jamis grasped at her, desperate, but she faded from her arms. "Tell Carmen."

The field disappeared and Jamis sank into darkness. She floated in emptiness and fought to climb back to the field, but then she sank, landing with a thud on cold dirt. The smell of mildew choked her. The air was sticky, like Alabama in summer. She scrambled to her knees and wiped dirt from her hands. There was a blinding light to the left. She stumbled back as Stephanie screamed at her from inside it.

"Stop," Jamis yelled back. "Stop screaming. I'm trying to help you." Stephanie came toward Jamis, arms swinging at her sides, skin gray, hair matted with blood. She made eye contact before disappearing into the light. Jamis moved slowly around the darkened space, hands out, feeling for walls and doors, finding nothing.

There was a phone ringing. It was her phone. She was dreaming and needed to wake up.

Chapter Sixteen

Jamis grabbed her phone. "Hello," she mumbled, not quite coherent.

"Jamis? It's Maggie. Is it too early?"

Jamis looked at the clock. It was after ten. "No, Maggie. It's fine."

"You sound like you were sleeping."

"I was. I was up late and slept in."

"I got your stuff and took a look at it last night. Stayed up half the night. Gruesome and horrible." Jamis nodded, though Maggie couldn't see her. "Anyway, I don't think Richard Crespin did this. He used to bash the heads of his victims in with a hammer. It leaves a very distinct pattern behind. These wounds to Stephanie's head looked like they were inflicted with something curved and circular. Then there's another wound that looks like someone inserted a rod into her brain, probably caused her death."

Jamis grimaced. Maggie heard it. "I know. Good morning to you. But the thing is, when I look at all the photos, it looks like she was strangled, too. I can make out faint marks on her neck, even though the images are not the best. We did some enhancement work and I think they're finger marks."

While she spoke, Jamis pulled a bottle of water from the mini fridge. She fumbled to begin a pot of coffee. "You're saying that someone hit her with something curved and circular and then killed her with a rod to the brain? But before that, they strangled her?"

"Yes. Based on the reports, I would think there was sexual assault before her death, too. The hits on her skull look erratic, crazed. There's no methodical pattern to it. I'm guessing whoever did this used something close by, and when he realized it wasn't enough to kill her, he improvised further. It's not Richard Crespin. This is disorganized. Chaotic. Personal."

Jamis imagined Maggie standing at her kitchen counter, sipping coffee. She'd hurt her, but she'd moved on. Jamis could beat the regret into endless submission, only to watch it come back again. Dr. Frank insisted their breakup was a result of not being able to meet each other's mutual needs, but Jamis internalized it as her fault for years. She did that with many things.

"If you can get enough of this evidence together, with some reliable witnesses, and take it to the police to reopen the case, I'll assist with an autopsy. We need to exhume her body and see if we can collect any DNA or additional information."

"Would you fly up here?"

"Yes. The poor woman deserves justice." Maggie paused. "This has nothing to do with you."

"Yeah. I know." Jamis took a sip of coffee and it burned her tongue. "But I appreciate it."

"Yes, well, enough of that. Stephanie Gardner was not murdered by Richard Crespin. Of that I am sure. I'm going to type up my analysis and send it over to you today. In the meantime, what are your next steps?"

Jamis filled her in on the details. "I'm going to talk to Barbara Reynolds and Mitch Sr. today. I'll wait for your report and go to the police tomorrow."

The clown and carousel on the table looked solemn and sad in the dim light of morning. "Maggie, how heavy would something have to be to crack someone's skull like that?"

"Pounds don't really matter. It's all about force, angle. With the right amount of both, I could puncture someone's head with a penny. I've seen it happen. Why?"

"I have a crazy hunch. I'm going to send you a picture of something. Hold on." Jamis snapped a picture of the carousel and texted it to Maggie. "It's coming now."

On the other end of the line, Maggie transferred her to speaker. "Am I looking at a carousel?"

"Could that do it?" Jamis's heart pounded like she'd just read Edgar Allen Poe. Maggie was silent for a few moments.

"Yes. I think so. Where? How?" Maggie stammered. "Where is that from?"

"A hidden attic in the house."

"Send that to me. If there is even one cell left on that, I can get it with our OneTouch equipment."

"I will." Jamis was more tired than when she went to bed. "Maggie, I've had a lot of weird stuff happening to me—"

Maggie interrupted her. "Jamis, you lost the privilege to share your burdens with me when you left me for your television show. Do you remember that? I'll help you put people to rest and solve mysteries, but don't confuse it."

"I didn't leave you for my television show. I left you to be me. I couldn't be who you wanted."

"I don't want to get into this, Jamis," Maggie said.

"I'm sorry. You're right. It was habit. I'll let you go." She hung up the phone and dropped her head, face in her hands. Perhaps Stephanie and the woman in yellow found her because, like them, she was a hungry ghost.

Jamis stopped at the UPS store as her first priority. She helped the clerk wrap the carousel and its pieces. It was hundreds to send it same day air and worth it. If that proved to be the murder weapon, after all this time, then there was another mystery to solve. Who kept it and the rest of Stephanie's stuff and moved it upstairs, only to seal it up? It was a textbook guilty move. Someone regretted her murder and couldn't part with her belongings. If she answered who kept her stuff, she'd know who killed her.

Next, she called a local moving company owned by Tess's nephew. They committed to moving the stuff out of the attic that afternoon and into one of their storage pods. Fortunately, moving companies were desperate for work at the end of winter in the Mountain West. She was uncertain of the legalities about who owned the stuff, but wouldn't lose time figuring it out. She'd act and face consequences later.

Jamis bought a cup of coffee at Starbucks for Johnna and stopped by her clinic. The bell on the door sounded when she stepped into the lobby. An elderly woman greeted her.

"Hi there. Did you have an appointment? Johnna's in surgery."

Jamis's hopes fell. "No, I just got her some coffee and wanted to say hi. You're Gloria?"

"I am. You must be Jamis. Sam told me about you. He's here. Got a full house for grooming today." Gloria scrutinized Jamis, toe to head.

"I didn't realize or I'd get him coffee too," Jamis said.

"Sure," Gloria said.

"Well, I'll leave this here. Tell her I stopped by?"

"I will," Gloria said, taking the coffee from the counter. Jamis turned to leave.

"Your intentions had better be honorable."

Jamis spun around. "It's just coffee."

"It's never just coffee," Gloria said. "But I'll tell her it's here."

In the parking lot, she felt like a teacher had just scolded her for using too much Play-Doh. She dug around her coat pockets for the car keys. She climbed into the front seat when a voice called out. Johnna jogged across the parking lot to her, wearing scrubs, hair pulled back.

"Hey," Jamis said, twisting to get out of the car. Johnna came up to the open door, and Jamis remained perched on the seat.

"I saw you on the security camera," Johnna said, cheeks red from the cold.

"You don't have a coat on." Jamis rubbed Johnna's arms. Johnna watched and then looked up at Jamis. Jamis yearned to pull her close. She dropped her hands.

Johnna eyes were still downcast, but Jamis saw her struggle for composure. "Gloria gave me the business," Jamis said, breaking the tension.

"She's formidable," Johnna said, looking back up at Jamis. "I just wanted…" Johnna pulled her bare arms close. "I just saw you and didn't want you to leave without saying hi."

"I'm glad you did." The door to the clinic opened. It was Gloria.

"Johnna, you have a call."

"Okay," Johnna said over her shoulder, still standing close to Jamis. "I'll see you later."

"Yeah," Jamis said, grinning. Johnna waved to her, stepping into the door. Sprouts of new love opened inside her, in places long barren. Shy glances, anticipatory emotion, longing, and giddy smiles. Who knew it was possible this close to forty?

Jamis still felt uncertain about talking to Barbara Reynolds, so chose Mitch Sr. She called the retirement community ahead to be certain of visiting hours. Upon arrival, a woman in a white uniform, behind glass, greeted her at the reception desk. She pushed a button to talk to Jamis through a speaker. "Can I help you?"

Jamis smiled and introduced herself. "I'd like to talk to Mitch Reynolds, if he's available. Please tell him it's in regard to an investigation. I think he'll be interested in it."

The woman picked up the phone on the desk, dialing. She set the phone down after a few minutes and hit the speaker again. "He says he'll see you. Room 234. Down the hall, to your right, then left." She buzzed open the door for Jamis.

Jamis moved quickly, hopeful neither she nor Mitch changed their minds. Room 234 was ajar. Mitch sat in front of a television. "Mr. Reynolds, thank you for seeing me."

He didn't stand, but he waved her to him. It was one room with a small studio kitchen, two chairs, and a small bed. She took the seat next to him. The television was on Fox News. He picked up the remote, hit mute, and turned to her. "What do you want?"

"I want to talk to you about Stephanie Gardner," Jamis said. It felt like the temperature dropped by twenty degrees in seconds. There were goose bumps on her arms. She thought about Sampson and his corruption file.

Mitch rested his hands on the armrest of the chair. "Damned shame, that girl."

"I don't think Richard Crespin killed her. And I don't think you did a very thorough job investigating her death, and I'd like to know why."

"She was going to do a lot of damage, that's why," he said and turned up the television volume.

"What do you mean?" He stared at the television, a vacant look in his eyes. He sat quiet, unmoving. Jamis took the remote from his hand, muting the television.

"What do you want?" He turned to her.

"We were talking about Stephanie Gardner. You said she was going to do a lot of bad," Jamis said, reminding him.

"Damned shame, that girl." He drifted back to the television. "It's too bad about her, but the damage was done. No use doing more damage."

"Damage to who? Who were you protecting?" He took the remote from her hand, turning up the volume again. Sean Hannity yammered about something and Jamis took the remote back again, muting the television. "Mitch, please tell me who you were protecting." She'd hold the remote hostage for answers.

He looked at her, at once present and gone. "My worthless son." Jamis waited to see if he would offer anything else. They sat together in silence for fifteen minutes before he turned to her again. "What do you want?"

She handed him the remote and rose to leave, shutting his door quietly. He willfully neglected his duties as police chief to protect his son, who killed a woman claiming to carry his baby. Now, he'd lost his mind. In terms of justice, though, it still didn't seem severe enough.

❖

Jamis parked in front of Barbara Reynolds's house. It was just four streets west of Stephanie's house. Jamis rang the doorbell. There was noise behind the door. Voices murmured, rose in intensity, and then dropped off. Jamis felt anxious. Barbara's husband died and now a stranger showed up on the doorstep, asking about his infidelities. Even her practiced analytical detachment couldn't ignore the potential pain associated with her actions. But she wanted answers, and Stephanie deserved them.

Finally, an older woman opened the door. Her hair was brown with gray roots she'd not dyed recently. The bags under her eyes suggested sleep issues, and the wrinkles around her mouth and eyes were exaggerated. Stress aged people and it certainly had aged Barbara Reynolds.

Jamis introduced herself. "I'm in town working on an investigation. I was wondering if I could ask you a few questions. Are you Barbara?"

Her reaction was slow and dull. She nodded and opened her mouth, but a man stepped from behind her.

"What do you want?" He wore a baseball cap and stood at least six inches taller than Jamis. It was rare for her to meet someone that much taller.

"I'm investigating the death of Stephanie Gardner. I've already spoken with Mitch Sr. I realize it might be a hard conversation, but it appears as though I've gathered enough evidence to reopen her case. I plan to take it to the police, but I'd like to talk to Barbara first."

The man stepped forward and shoved Barbara behind him.

"Hey, don't shove her," Jamis said, moving toward Barbara. He blocked her with the door.

"We know what people said about Mitch Jr. when that whore got killed." Jamis jerked back at his words, furious. She needed to start carrying a stun gun. "It was all lies. She was trying to blackmail him to get money. We've got nothing to say to you." He moved to slam the door, but Jamis stopped it with her foot and shoulder. She pushed it back open and he stumbled, shocked. They made eye contact and froze. Jamis imagined them at opposite ends of a dusty main street, hands on their pistols.

She was pissed. "It's going to come out, sooner or later. The past is restless and wants to be heard, Mr…?" she trailed off, asking his name.

"Reynolds," he spit. "Bobby Reynolds. He was my brother. It's enough he's dead. We won't have you soiling his good name and hurting Barb any more than all those lies did all those years ago. Now get your foot out of my house before I call the cops." Jamis moved her foot and he slammed the door.

"Well, hell," Jamis said. She wanted to see Johnna. She texted her and began to drive in her direction.

Jamis talked about her day. Johnna had graciously invited her over to her house again.

"You think Mitch Jr. did it?" Johnna set Virginia's food dish on the floor.

"I do. I'll take everything I've found to the police tomorrow once I get Maggie's report."

"I hope this stops the dimension jumps and vivid dreaming," Johnna said.

"You hope it does? Jesus Christ, me too." Jamis picked up the cup of freshly brewed coffee in both hands. "The dreams are weird though. There are two women. They're so different. Stephanie, I get."

"Is this the field? The woman, right?" Johnna perched on the couch, as if she'd move soon. Jamis settled back, happy to be still for a moment.

"Yes. I'm just remembering that she talked to me last night. But I can't remember what she told me. I remember it and I don't." She put her coffee on the table. "I can see her when I'm there but not really. When I wake up, I can't remember her at all." Johnna placed her hand on her forearm. Jamis looked down at her hand. Johnna moved it, as if she hadn't realized it was there. "I'm terrible at this, so you know. I've only had one serious relationship in my life, and it imploded. I was a rogue for a while after that," Jamis said, wanting to be honest.

Johnna left her hand on her arm. "I can't say I was expecting that." She smiled slowly and held eye contact.

Jamis was embarrassed and pulled her arms to her sides. She scooted back flat against the couch. She peered at Johnna from the corner of her eye. "I have issues."

"I actually picked that up on my own," Johnna said with a smile. Jamis smiled back. "I have issues too. Attachment issues. Abandonment issues. Intimacy issues. Feelings of overwhelming responsibility. Suicidal ideation, in phases." Jamis turned to her, alarmed. "I run six days a week because it helps my depression. I don't eat animals. I struggle for meaning. Because I watched my mom and brother die." Jamis listened, her own incessant inner chatter quieted in compassion. "It's hard to believe in any transcendent purpose after something like that happens." She put her hands in her lap, folded them.

"So, it is possible we are two seriously damaged people. But I hope after you finish up with Stephanie, you consider staying around," Johnna said, pushing off the couch a little too fast. "I have to get ready to go to Sara's for a party. She told me to tell you to come."

"Okay," Jamis said, new certainty about her feelings for Johnna organizing inside. She wondered if she could gather them up, put them in Johnna to best explain how she felt. The depth of feeling was terrifying, and for a second, she wanted to flee.

"Let me get ready and we'll go," Johnna said, heading up the stairs. Jamis watched her until she faded from view.

She could just leave, not come back. Head out of town, go back to California. Something had shifted, and Johnna was opening to her. If it was what she wanted, why did she suddenly want to flee? Find a reason for it not to work so she didn't have to try? It's one thing to think she wanted something and something else entirely when she actually got it. She stayed, breathing through the urge to run.

Jamis patted the couch next to her and Virginia leaped. She rubbed her belly. "Virginia, I get so sick of myself."

CHAPTER SEVENTEEN

Jamis laughed as Johnna drove over an embankment of snow to park in Sara's front yard. "I don't want to park down the street." Jamis followed closely behind Johnna, into the house, then as they navigated the crowded front room.

"I miss Virginia." Jamis felt strange without her.

"She doesn't love children, though. They overwhelm her. She'll be fine dozing on my bed." They stepped through the carpeted front room into the kitchen which had a long bar running down the middle of it. "There's Sara," Johnna said, pointing at a woman.

"What is this for again? Should I have brought a gift?" Jamis worried about social expectations more than was healthy, but it was because she attended so few of them.

"It's Paul's birthday, Sara's husband. It's fine. I gave him his gift a few weeks ago." Sara came to them, and Johnna hugged her.

"You must be Jamis. My brother has been bragging about you all night," Sara said. Jamis saw the resemblance between the sisters. It was the way they held themselves, the tip of their heads when they looked at someone, their smiles. Sara was shorter than Johnna, and pretty in the exact opposite way that Johnna was.

"If you want to grab something to eat, let me run and say hi to my dad and I'll come right back and join you," Johnna said. Sara turned away, called by someone.

"I want to meet your dad," Jamis said.

"Maybe after you've known me for five years. He's not ready for you and I don't want to scare you away." Jamis couldn't imagine anything doing that, but she respected her boundaries. Jamis filled a plate with food and wandered into the front room, taking in all the people in groups and conversations. There were fifty or more people in the house, and she felt momentarily claustrophobic. Someone recognized her and squealed, and Jamis wiggled her fingers while eating cheese cubes.

"Do you always inspire this reaction in people?" Sapphire said, at her side, surprising her. "I mean, it borders on the insane. Do you remember how I reacted to you?" She punched Jamis in the arm. She wore dark jeans and a long sleeved V-neck sweater. Her hair was down.

"You look gorgeous," Jamis said.

"Shut up," Sapphire said, flushing.

"For Sam?"

"I've given up. But thank you. That's kind of you." Sapphire's eyes were sad, and Jamis wanted to fix it.

"Oh, hey. Walk with me to the wall of pictures," Jamis said. "Tell me who they are. I love family photos."

They stopped in front of the wall and Sapphire pointed. "Sara and Paul's family here." Sapphire pointed out Paul, who she'd yet to meet. Young Paul was next to his mother and father in a larger family photo.

"That's Dan," Jamis said, pleased to recognize someone.

"Yup." They moved down the wall as Sapphire constructed a genealogical narrative. "Look at Sara, Johnna, Sam." Jamis got closer to the wall. There were four of them. She presumed the youngest was Jacob. She looked to the right and took an abrupt step back before leaning in closer.

"Who is that?" Jamis pointed to a woman in the photo with her arms around Johnna.

"Emma. That's Johnna's mom. Isn't she the most beautiful human you've ever seen?" Sapphire said, almost reverent. Jamis followed her through the photos to the end of the wall. Her heart pounded. Her vision blurred and darkened, and she dropped her plate. She stumbled, close to falling. Sapphire grabbed her arm and steadied her, looked around to see if anyone had noticed, but they hadn't. Sapphire pushed Jamis backward onto a folding chair tucked in the corner of the room. "Oh my God, don't do this here. Stop it. What's wrong?"

"I don't know. I saw her picture and I couldn't breathe. I…" She looked around. "Sapphire, I think she's the woman in yellow."

"From your dream?" Sapphire was incredulous. "But why would it be her? You must be confused. This is about Stephanie."

"I just saw her last night. I think that's her," Jamis insisted.

"You're probably superimposing Johnna's features on the woman. She looks like her mom," Sapphire said.

"I'm not," Jamis said.

"This is insane, Jamis." Sapphire sounded exasperated.

"Don't tell Johnna, please. I want her to like me."

"Come on. Follow me." Sapphire took Jamis into a room in the back of the house. Jamis said she felt better, but Sapphire brought her a plate of potato salad, chips, and macaroni and cheese, forcing her to eat. She washed it down with an orange soda and almost gagged.

"Sorry," Sapphire said. "I was worried and grabbed whatever I could find. Did your blood sugar drop?"

"I don't have blood sugar issues," Jamis said.

"Are you sure?"

"I was being pulled into another dimension that day," Jamis said, feeling defensive.

"Is that what happened today?"

"No, I just felt like the wind got knocked out of me. I was shocked. I'm seeing Johnna's mom in my dreams," Jamis said.

"I can't believe it. Why? Why would Emma be talking to you?" Jamis shrugged. "Maybe once you go to the police all this weird stuff will stop happening."

"You don't believe me, do you?"

"Thing is, I do. But I don't understand," Sapphire said. They eased into a few minutes of comfortable silence. "You okay?"

"I think so, yeah," Jamis said.

"Let's go back. We can work on it tomorrow." They returned to the party. Sapphire introduced Jamis to Paul and others in a flurry of movement and conversation, including Matt Davis, the man in love with Johnna, and she couldn't dislike him. Jamis urged Sapphire to mingle, begging to sit down.

She approached Dan Abbey on the couch. "May I?"

He motioned to the seat next to him. "We met yesterday, didn't we?"

"We did. Johnna did most of the talking," Jamis said.

"You did okay," he said, taking a drink from a red plastic cup. "These parties. My wife comes and disappears, and I end up sitting on the couch all night by myself."

"Well, I guess you're lucky tonight. I'll keep you company." He held up his cup to Jamis.

"Sorry I had to run off so quickly yesterday. I had a meeting."

"No problem. I don't think anything else you might have shared would have mattered," Jamis said.

"Really? Did you find something?"

"I've found a lot. Nearly enough to open the police file again." Her phone chirped. She held up a finger and pulled it from her pocket. It was Sam, asking where she was so he could make his way to her. She responded. "Sam is trying to find me."

"Hard to believe you've made so much progress in such a short amount of time." Dan shifted to turn toward her.

"Well, I think I've had a lot of help." The conversation trailed off when Matt and Sam approached. She drifted through the rest of the party with partial consciousness, laughing when appropriate and sharing when necessary.

But a question worried her. Why was Emma talking to her in her dreams, and what had she said to her the night before? Sweat ran down her sides, and finally, when she could take no more, Johnna arrived at her side and said, "Let's go."

❖

Jamis was in Johnna's living room again with Virginia stretched across her lap. Johnna was next to her. Jamis wanted to hold her hand but felt unbelievably nervous, her hesitation blocking her desire. Jamis looked at her and considered telling her she spent the night before talking to her mother but hesitated. Johnna might reject her. "I should probably head out. It's getting late and I don't want to keep you."

The front door opened. Virginia jerked awake and gave a half bark from the couch as Sam came in. He smiled, seeing Jamis on the couch. "Hey there."

Jamis pulled her hands into her own lap. "I was just leaving before you came in, so don't get any funny ideas."

"Never, but you can stay, if you want. You're so welcome," Sam said.

"Sapphire loves you, and she's amazing so stop being stupid," Jamis said in a rush of emotion. Johnna covered her mouth with her hand. Sam looked at Jamis, shocked, and put his hands in his lap.

"We're just friends. We…she…"

"I couldn't help myself, dude. Really, get on that before she finally meets someone new. She can't wait forever, even though she has. Didn't you notice? She loves you. Just text her, ask her to go get coffee, and propose marriage. There is no one better for you in the world. She's like one in a bazillion." She turned to Johnna. She felt hyper and chaotic. Her emotions were organizing a revolt and soon she'd have no control. It was best she retreated. "I appreciate the offer to stay, though. I have to get the information organized and typed up to go to the police."

Johnna rose, gaze uncertain. "I'll walk you out." She touched Sam's shoulder. "She's right," she said. He was silent, unmoving, processing the information.

Jamis stopped on the stairs of the porch and tucked her hands in her pockets. A bitter wind blew, and she crouched into herself. Jamis wanted to hug Johnna but didn't.

"You need a better coat," Johnna said with a small smile. "Are you okay? Is all this just wearing on you?" She stood on the top step of the porch, Jamis the bottom.

Jamis heard, "*Tell Carmen*." She said out loud, "Tell Carmen." Johnna tipped her head, uncertain. "Tell Carmen is what I heard last night. What would I tell Carmen?"

"Maybe your mind filled in some blanks," Johnna said, leaning on the porch rail.

It was possible. "I just feel like I'm missing a big piece of this. A connection that's vital." She met Johnna's eyes. Once again, the question rose unbidden. "Who is Carmen to you?"

Johnna stepped down to the bottom step, right in front of her, and tugged on her coat collar, pulling it tighter around her neck. She smoothed it down and stood on her toes to kiss her cheek. She wasn't much shorter than Jamis. She imagined they'd fit together well, their legs intertwined.

"Carmen is the woman my mother loved," Johnna said. Jamis was shocked. She'd forgotten she asked the question. "Let me know when you get back to the hotel."

Johnna slipped back inside and Jamis finally moved when a gust of wind challenged her balance. She drove to the hotel as her mind fired with connections and possibilities. But she was unsettled, out of sorts, like pieces of her rattled out of place and struggled to find their way back where they belonged.

At the hotel, she gathered her printed copies of Stephanie's police report, redacted files, autopsy photos, and Maggie's analysis, articulating her understandings in a document on her desktop. She posted a brief update without specifics across social media.

Something was wrong. Something was missing. Frustrated, she opened the curtain, hoping to be pulled into another dimension. It was just a parking lot full of cars under the orange glow of streetlights. She was putting together a puzzle without all the pieces and without a final picture to guide her. She should feel happy. Johnna kissed her cheek. Maybe she'd found someone, someplace, and her lifelong homelessness would end. She didn't need a lot.

Instead, she felt hopeless and rummaged in her backpack for a Klonopin. She'd not taken the medicine since arriving in Sage Creek, but the panic welling up in her held the promise of pulling her under the tide. Anxiety was her constant foe, emboldened by the fresh emotions of the day. A wicked panic attack was the only way her body knew how to process intense emotions. Shock. Connection. Fear. Love. It didn't matter. When it got like this, the only thing she needed was sleep. Jamis stretched out on the bed, felt the medicine as it flooded her limbs. Stephanie chose that moment to show up by the door.

"Don't you dare scream," Jamis said, eyes heavy. "I mean it. I'm trying to help you." Stephanie was silent, watching Jamis. Her head wasn't gouged open. She stayed while Jamis fell asleep.

Chapter Eighteen

Jamis woke with her eyes crusted shut and dried spit on her lips, feeling like she'd been ripped through the fabric of time. The Klonopin did its job. She'd dreamed of Emma, off and on, throughout the night. The images were a blur, her dreams confused, but Emma was always there, standing to the right at the bowling lane with Maggie in Phoenix. Behind her, while waiting in the security line at the airport.

Jamis went directly to the shower, opened her mouth under the water, and scrubbed her face. "What are you trying to tell me, Emma?"

Jamis was in touch with people who died, legitimately communicating with Stephanie and Emma. Only the noise of her own dysfunctions kept her from this possibility before. Her mom, the person in the Jerome hotel, other beings over the years. It was absurd it took her so long to accept this aspect of herself. What else might have been possible if she'd allowed it?

While her body rested, Emma connected with her consciousness and had been doing so for months. Why she did, Jamis was uncertain. Their connection was undeniable, and she longed to tell Carmen, to make sense of it. Emma had told her to do so, after all, but hesitation stirred deep inside. She couldn't tell Johnna. It felt like a violation, and while the thought felt irrational, Jamis didn't want to push her away.

She dressed, gathered the files, pictures, notes, and Maggie's report, tucking them in her bag. Emma had been in her dreams for months, and the realization left her jittery and tired. She drove in a daze, stopping at Starbucks, drinking two venti quad shot lattes, one after another. The caffeine stirred her body to life, and her heart pounded with the rush. It was only a little after eight, though it felt like she'd been up for days.

She queried the police station address. The station was a dark brick building, nondescript, just a few miles away. It didn't take long to get there. Inside, there was a desk in the middle of the foyer, behind a counter with glass that closed off the police station from the outside world.

Jamis pressed the bell. A few moments later, the door behind the desk opened. "Yes?" A cop in uniform stared at her.

"I need to talk to a detective. I have evidence in a cold case."

"You look familiar."

"I'm Jamis Bachman."

"I should know that name, but I don't?"

"I used to have a television show," Jamis said, shifting the bag on her shoulder.

"Ah, okay. What was it?"

"*Ghastly Incidents*," Jamis said.

"Oh hell. No way," she exclaimed. "My mom loves that show. She watches the reruns." Another mother. Check. "You have evidence for a cold case?"

"I do, yeah."

"Okay. Wait here. Let me get someone."

Jamis watched the street through the lobby windows. Perhaps Stephanie would rest after today. Jamis knew pain and trauma were not human defaults. It's not where anyone was meant to begin or end. And what moved people beyond it varied. For Stephanie, it was anger, which was always a mighty catalyst. Anger moved enough objects to get Jamis to Utah, but it wasn't enough to free Stephanie. For that, she needed truth, justice, and love.

To the right, a door opened. It was a middle-aged man in a blue suit. "Detective Daniels."

Jamis followed him through the door. The room was large and open. The detective led them into a small conference room. There was a Keurig on a table. He pointed to it, a question for her. "I've had enough," Jamis said. He turned to fill his cup as the Keurig whirred to life and spit coffee. She unpacked her bag and formed piles with the papers.

He turned to her. She looked at him. In this light, she saw the gray at the edges of his hairline. He pushed his glasses up his nose. She handed him a photo of Stephanie on the autopsy table. He took it from her hand. "That's Stephanie Gardner. Murdered in March, 1992." He sipped his coffee. She handed him Maggie's report. "That's a report from Mayday Forensics in Phoenix that asks that Stephanie's body be exhumed. Dr. Maggie Kirkpatrick, well known forensic scientist, took a look at all of this evidence and concluded Stephanie was not killed by Richard Crespin."

He read the report.

"I've documented a series of conversations I've had over the past week, since arriving here. I've also documented evidence I found and sent to Maggie," Jamis said.

"You sent evidence somewhere other than here?"

"In retrospect, it probably wasn't the best choice. I'll concede that. But I'm new to this murder solving stuff." Jamis paused, waiting for him. He said nothing else. "Anyway, I have reason to believe that Mitch Reynolds Jr. killed Stephanie because she was pregnant with his child and threatened to blackmail him. I'm told she wanted to leave town, start over. His father was the police chief, and I believe he covered up her murder."

"I know who he is," Detective Daniels said, motioning to the papers in front of Jamis. He opened the folder and scanned the paperwork in silence. Finally, he took off his glasses. "Do you realize what you're suggesting here?"

"I do."

"If this isn't real, the chief will have my ass. Chief Reynolds is a legend. An old west type, well liked and respected." He stared intently at Jamis.

"You're either going to be brave enough to ask questions for Stephanie, or I'll talk to someone else here. If no one is brave enough, I'll take it to social media, the local paper, and national news." He put his arms on the table. "I assume you know who I am."

"I know who you are," he said. "Does it occur to you that you shouldn't threaten the person you're asking to help you?"

"I'm not asking you to help me. I need you to help Stephanie." And also Emma, she thought, but she wasn't sure how. "It's the right thing to do. There is enough there to open the case. Look at it for yourself. Maybe I'm wrong and I missed something. But at least look."

"I plan to. Regardless of the consequences." He looked at Jamis. "Just so you know, with or without your threats, it's my responsibility to look into this."

"Okay. Don't jerk me around, then. Just listen to me and I won't threaten you," she said.

He sighed and put his hands up in defeat. "Why are you here? Why does this matter?"

"It's long and complicated and not so complicated at all. And I'm pretty sure you won't believe me." He shrugged as if to offer no certainty about his reaction. "I received an email from a couple renting her house." She motioned to the pictures. "They said it was haunted. Asked me to come. I did, and found all of that."

"An email got you to this?" His eyes narrowed behind the lenses of his glasses.

"And Stephanie's poltergeist." He laughed incredulously, and she zipped up her bag. "It doesn't matter if you believe me or not. What matters is that you help her rest."

He watched her for a few moments. "Don't go anywhere. Let's go through all of this in detail. Let me get my laptop." He left and she relaxed into her chair. She closed her eyes for a moment, looked for Emma in the field. She didn't find her.

Detective Daniels was back. "Okay. Start at the beginning. When did you get the email that brought you here?"

Jamis began talking.

Jamis had paused to use the restroom and respond to a handful of text messages, but other than that, she relayed, in exacting detail, everything she'd done and learned since arriving a week before. She omitted the dimensional hopping episodes and dreams, and completely avoided talking about Emma. Her focus was Stephanie, and it was her who Detective Daniels could help. Midway through the interview, he stopped and asked Jamis to call him John. He ordered in Chinese food, and Jamis ate fried rice while she talked about the tree falling in the house.

Once done, he shook her hand and assured her that he'd keep in touch as he was able and that he would officially reopen her murder case. Jamis left, exhausted and surprised she wasn't happier. She felt aimless. The sun fell eerily into the back of the sky and the falling dusk unsettled her. Shadows of tree branches danced faintly on the asphalt. She drove slowly to her hotel room.

She'd expected to feel better after sharing information with the police. But instead, she felt heavy and burdened. Her hotel room felt hollow and empty. She texted Johnna, Sapphire, Sam, and Carmen, wanting anyone to respond to her. She texted her friend Rachel in Phoenix. She responded first but told her she was on surgical rotation at the hospital. Jamis wanted to go home and also never wanted to leave Sage Creek.

She turned on the television to a local channel and tried to watch the news. Johnna texted her back and told her that Sam and Sapphire were at dinner, and she was still at the clinic. She looked at the text, happy and uncertain what to say next when Johnna sent her a shorter reply, inviting her to stop by.

Jamis splashed cold water on her face before she left, focused on the sensations in her body, the overwhelming despondency still present. She hoped they'd dissipate some as she drove to Johnna's clinic, but instead, anxiety joined them, and Jamis almost turned around to go back to the hotel room.

At the clinic, she stepped tentatively into the waiting room, hoping to avoid a run-in with Gloria, but found it empty.

"I'll be right out," Johnna said, calling from the back of the office.

Jamis crept to the swinging door and peeked in. Johnna was washing her hands at a large steel sink, in blue scrubs, her hair tied back under a cap.

"Can I come in?"

"Of course," Johnna said, seeing her. Her eyes were bright and smile big. "If you don't mind the smell. It's been a bad day here."

"What happened?" Jamis moved to stand by the end of the metal table, just on the other side of Johnna.

"Someone found a box of puppies with parvo today. Three died. I have two in doggy ICU. Someone else brought me seven kittens. Thrown out with trash and found at the dump. Another client's dog got out and was hit by a car. I had to amputate his leg. And that smell, well, my overnight guest there," Johnna pointed at a kennel, "couldn't hold it. We just got it cleaned up."

"Oh my God," Jamis said. "Are you okay?"

"Tired," Johnna said, laughing. "How was your day?"

"I went to the police. They're going to open Stephanie's case," Jamis said.

"I bet you're relieved," Johnna said, drying off her hands. She waved for Jamis to follow her. They sat down in a small office. Johnna poured coffee for them both.

"I don't know. I just feel like it's not done somehow," Jamis said.

"Has this happened before?" Johnna set the coffee down and opened the fridge. "I'm going to snack. Do you want something?"

"No, I'm fine," Jamis said. "And no, not like this." Johnna ate a protein bar, sipped her coffee. "I'm not keeping you am I?"

"No," Johnna said, reassuring her. "I need to wait for a couple of hours before I head out."

"Is Virginia here?"

"Sam took her home," Johnna said. She took another sip of her coffee.

"Can I ask you a question?"

"Of course," Johnna said.

"Tell me about your mom. About Emma. I'd like to know more about her." Johnna looked thoughtful, pensive. "Who was she?"

"Why do you want to know about my mom?"

"I'd just like to know." She worried her thumb ring back and forth, then took her glasses off. She folded them and hung them on her shirt. "How did she come out?"

"With fireworks. She came out with fireworks." Johnna smiled, her eyes shining. "Sometimes I think I'm so quiet about it because my mom did all the work for me." She stared forward, lost in memory. "It was like she lit a bonfire, put illegal Fourth of July fireworks in it, and then dared anyone to say anything as they exploded. She set the town on fire. Scandalized my grandma and grandpa. They all pretend it didn't happen, now, since she died. They've revised history." She said this with distaste. "I think she lived for so long, so repressed, that when she finally found her voice, there was no slowing her down."

Jamis listened as Johnna continued to talk, enjoying her voice as much as anything else. Jamis longed for the kinds of connections that powered these stories. People she loved so much their stories were as close as her own. When Johnna stopped talking, Jamis waited quietly, to be certain she was finished.

"Thank you," she said, truly grateful. Johnna was across from her, not more than twenty inches, the table small. Johnna felt like home. Her energy beckoned her, called to her, and it was unlike anything she'd ever felt before.

"Johnna," Jamis said, "I love the way you walk, talk, and hold your fork to eat. I even love the way you hold your coffee cup." Johnna froze, unmoving, across the table. "When I see you again, after I've not seen you for an hour or a day, my heart pulls me forward and I'm flooded with emotion. Since I've met you, every day, I think, how can I see Johnna?"

"Jamis," Johnna said, standing up, "I thought we talked about getting to know one another."

"We did," Jamis said, standing too. "Does my telling you this change that? I'm not trying to. I just want you to know."

Johnna nodded, wiped her hands on her scrubs, and turned to leave the room. Jamis reached out, hand on her forearm, and Johnna paused, held still. Jamis stepped tentatively toward her, moving her hand to her back. Jamis turned her to face her, and Johnna put her hands on Jamis's neck, pressed her forehead down, against her own. Jamis felt the warmth of her skin for the first time and responded by holding her wrists. It wasn't simply desire she felt. She wanted to love her. Take walks in the evening. Adopt three more dogs. Bring her coffee every day. Wake every morning next to her. The impulse was absurd. She'd just met her, but she felt what she felt.

"Jamis," Johnna said, pulling away. "You're going to leave."

"Who says?" Jamis dipped her head down, pressed her lips against Johnna's, gentle, soft, and pulled back and away. Johnna pulled her back, arms around her neck, and kissed her, firmly, hands on her face now.

"We'll see," Johnna said, letting go. Jamis embraced her, arms around her waist.

"Yeah, we will," Jamis said, another soft kiss on Johnna's nose, chin, and cheek, before she said good-bye with a kiss on her lips. "I'll let you get back to work. I'll see you later."

Chapter Nineteen

Saturday, August 24, 1991

Emma ran a brush through her hair. It fell in long strands around her face and touched her shoulders. She didn't typically look at herself in the mirror so long but could not look away. She applied lipstick with a shaking hand and grimaced as it slid across her cheek. She dropped the tube and scrubbed at her face with a washcloth. She breathed deep, steadied herself, and tried again. She set down the tube and picked up her mascara. She moved closer to the mirror, applied it gently, finished, and set the tube down. She ran her left index finger over the lines framing her eyes and fought back tears. With desperate want, she patted her face with powder to cover up the signs of her age. Hopelessness surged with her obsessive fixation on appearance, and she stopped and put the makeup away. She wanted to be who she was and not cover it up.

Travertine tiles lined the shower and the floor. Emma wiped down the new powder white cabinets with a washcloth. Stephen's promotion the year before allowed them to upgrade aspects of the house they had neglected for years. Disgust rose in her at the thought of him. She pushed it down. He worked in Logan, and rather than commute, he rented a small apartment. He was only home every other weekend, and she was sure he was as relieved as she was. When he was home, she slept on the couch. Anger rose unbidden in her chest, and she clenched her jaw, furious.

Once again, Emma looked closely at herself. There were lines around her mouth that were not there the last time she saw herself so clearly, and the skin on her neck was weathered, but her hair was still reddish blond. She looked at her hands. They looked like her mother's hands when she was young.

She pulled back from the mirror, picked up her makeup, and placed it heavily in the bag. She tossed it in the drawer and closed it with some force. She wanted to tear the bathroom apart with her bare hands, down to the studs, yank up the tile, take a crowbar to the cabinets. She walked into the bedroom. Johnna sat in the middle of the bed, a book in her lap. Her hair spilled out of her ponytail, and she looked up with simple regard and a smile. Emma smiled back involuntarily, so complete was her affection. The anger dispelled, swallowed by love, and she sighed as her chest relaxed. She wrapped Johnna in her arms. She kissed her head, smelled her freshly washed hair. "I love you to the moon and back."

Johnna rested in her arms. "I love you to the far side of the moon and back." Emma kissed her head again and squished her tighter with both arms. Johnna giggled but didn't pull away.

"I love you to Pluto and back." Emma held her and then let go. She tipped Johnna's face to her with a finger on her chin. "To the far end of the universe and back. Through time and space, heaven and earth. From this life to the next and every life after. You're stuck with me. That's how much I love you." Johnna rested her head on Emma's shoulder. She'd told Johnna this every day since she opened her eyes on planet Earth. Johnna never tired of hearing it. Sam and Jacob flailed and pulled out of her arms, but Johnna always stayed, even if she knew it by heart.

"I have to go to Mrs. Ojeda's funeral today, and I feel very anxious about it," Emma told her quietly.

"Want me to go?" Emma shook her head and kissed Johnna's forehead. She didn't know how her children got to be who they were, but she was grateful something in the long arc of her unhappiness manifested in love.

"No, you don't need to." She studied Johnna and hugged her again, not able to stop herself. She closed her eyes and hoped to any being who might hear her prayers that Johnna's path would unfurl with more gentleness and ease than her own. When Johnna came home to tell her she was gay, she would celebrate with her, and weather every unkind reaction for her. Then she'd pack her up and move her far away, so she could live the life she wanted.

"What?"

Emma smiled. Johnna was intuitive and sensitive, even if she tucked it away. "Afterward, do you want to go get dinner and see a movie? We won't let Sam or Jacob pick." Johnna's head moved only a little in agreement, but Emma felt it. Emma squeezed her tight again. "I don't know what to wear." Johnna tilted her head. "Any ideas?"

"Not the black flowery dress. I hate that."

Emma laughed. Flower barged into the room, looking for Johnna, and with a leap, jumped into the middle of the bed. Emma ignored the fact that a ninety-pound dog, of undetermined mixed breed, was in the middle of her bed. Stephen didn't like that Flower was allowed in the house, but Johnna loved her. Emma fought and won that battle with him, and silently she was proud of it.

"What's so funny?" She turned at the sound of Johnna's giggles.

Johnna pointed at Flower's feet, covered in mud. "Dad would have a cow." Emma sighed at the paw prints on the bed and the bedspread. "Don't worry. I'll clean it up before you get back."

Emma stood forlorn in front of the closet. Nothing in her life felt like it fit, including her skin.

"Wear the yellow dress," Johnna said. "I love that color. It's my favorite."

"You don't think it would be rude to wear a yellow dress to a funeral?"

"I think everyone at the funeral will be sad and seeing you in it will make them feel better. Because you're so beautiful," Johnna said. Emma turned to look at her, met her eyes, and smiled.

"So are you," Emma said. Johnna grinned and shrugged. "Yellow it is. For my baby girl."

Emma slipped the simple yellow dress over her shoulders. It flowed to her ankles. It was still warm outside, so she decided against nylons and slipped on sandals. She held up her arms and turned, eyebrows raised at Johnna. Johnna held up a thumb. Emma touched Johnna's shoulder as she bent to adjust her sandal. "I'll be back in a few hours. Make sure your brothers don't burn down the house." Johnna and Flower followed her from the room.

They stopped together in the kitchen. The counters were covered with white powder. "Sam, Jacob. Get in here." Sam and Jacob raced down the steps, their footfalls heavy and loud. Johnna perched on a barstool to watch. "What is this?"

"What?" Sam answered nonchalantly, arrogantly, his hand on his hips. Jacob hid behind him and looked at her from behind Sam's arm.

"What?" Emma said, pointing to the white substance all over the counter and floor in the kitchen. "What is this?"

"Cocaine," Sam said. Johnna laughed and punched his arm.

Emma smiled at him, though she tried to remain stern. "Both of you need to clean this up. What were you doing?"

"I was helping Jacob with a science project. We mixed vinegar and baking soda together. Boom." He smiled, eyes gleaming.

"Well, that's fine, but clean it up now." Sam started to speak, and Emma raised her finger. "No argument, no nothing. Now." Sam turned to open the closet to get the broom. Jacob wiped the counter. "I'll be gone a few hours. Don't go anywhere. We're going to go eat tonight and see a movie."

In the car, Emma turned off the radio and drove in silence to the Catholic church. She had known Mrs. Ojeda her entire life. Her time there with Carmen was the best in her childhood. Carmen's house was always busier than hers. Carmen's sisters and brothers, eight in total, were constantly moving in and out with their spouses and kids. The kitchen thrummed with activity, and the house always smelled of freshly cooked food. Emma remembered Mrs. Ojeda's home as one of emotional abundance and warmth and tried to re-create it for her own children.

Emma remembered this with the clarity reserved for memories of total presence and peace. The air in the car was hot, and she rolled down the window. The wind brushed against her face, and she tucked her hair behind her ear. Emma pulled into a parking space. She looked in the mirror, blotted her lipstick, and then rested her head on the steering wheel. Anxiety crept through every limb. Her hands tingled, and she moved her legs to be certain she wasn't paralyzed. Her stomach knotted.

Her episodes had begun years before, a year or two after Jacob's birth. She'd lost track of time. The first one came while she was in the kitchen, putting a plate in the cupboard. Suddenly, the ground beneath her feet gave out and the atoms in her body rearranged themselves, or so it felt to her, and she fell through the earth. Her thoughts had careened through the length of her body, and her identity had leaked out the soles of her feet. She came back to her body, pulled through the atoms she'd traveled, and found herself on her knees. They were bruised the next day. Jacob cried from his booster seat.

She felt this downward movement of her consciousness, as though she was dropping through her own body, and grasped the steering wheel. She closed her eyes and counted, only focusing on the numbers. In May that year, she'd gone to a healer in Salt Lake City whose advertisement she saw on the corkboard at the public library. It read "Mildred. Healer. Intuitive. Psychotherapist. Can I help you?" She pulled the number from the sheet and called. She planned a trip to the doctor on the same day as an excuse. A physical, she told everyone. She'd be gone until late afternoon.

She told Mildred about her episodes, in the dimly lit small room in the back of Caravan, Salt Lake City's only new age bookstore. Mildred held up her hands. "You pack so much psychic discord," she told her. "I can barely breathe near you. How do you breathe? You're living a life you were never meant to live. You sold your soul. For what? For nothing." Emma collapsed on the small couch and cried harder than she'd ever cried before. The words pierced her carefully manicured shields, and she felt hopeless, weakened, and empty.

Mildred held her hand. "This is why you're having attacks. When we are out of alignment, our body tells us. You're awake and aware, and you can only pretend to be asleep for so long before your body can't handle it anymore. You say you feel like your atoms are rearranging themselves. That is what they are doing. They're trying to make sense of this life you are living. Are you ready to be brave, Emma?"

Carmen. Twenty years ago, she'd begged Emma to leave Sage Creek. It was a different time, and it was not easy. She last saw Carmen the night she returned home from the hospital where her parents sent her when they discovered her secret. Carmen called from below her window, and she climbed out, as she had done so many times before. They stole quietly down the street to the park, on a bench far away from the overhead lights. Carmen held her hand, but Emma couldn't look at her. She was ashamed, scared, confused. Sitting in her car that day, she couldn't remember if this version was justification or the truth. "Go away, Carmen," she said. "Just leave town. Go somewhere else. Live your life." Then she left, but Carmen wouldn't let her go alone. Emma sobbed remembering how Carmen escorted her home.

At her window, Carmen said, "Please, Emma. We can do it together. You and me." Emma climbed into her window and closed it behind her. She'd not seen Carmen since.

After she left Mildred, she wondered about this moment. Why hadn't she gone with Carmen? It felt so far away. Where once the certainty resided, she now felt the awful weight of realization. Her awakening punctuated itself through her being. She was afraid to leave her mom and dad. She was all they had. She couldn't leave the town. It was all she knew. She couldn't reconcile who she was, a pervert, with what she had been taught. She had images of outer darkness awaiting her with death, of her family basking in the eternal light of Heavenly Father, in the celestial kingdom with God while she was condemned for unnatural desires, in hell.

The doctors at the hospital told her that her desire for other women was unnatural and she needed to be saved. They forced horrible medicine into her mouth. The pills at night put her to sleep. As she drifted to sleep, her chest tightened, and her breathing slowed so much she prayed and hoped she'd not wake up. She held her breath and imagined her lungs empty of air, shriveling and dying. But morning came, and the pills upset her stomach, and she threw up each day after breakfast. The afternoon medicine gave her hives, and she picked at her arms until sores opened on her skin. The doctors and staff forced her to repent and share her secrets with the others there. They excommunicated her, and then baptized her again, and for three awful months, she suffered, and finally believed them when they told her she could not be that person.

The burden of her culture's fears wrapped around her legs, like the chains of the condemned, and she carried them with her for twenty years. She saw them dragging behind her, and as they did, they pulled parts of her soul to them. The best parts of her dragged behind, wrapped in the weight of the iron. The episodes began when too much of her soul had leaked into those chains and she could no longer function. Her transgression was not loving Carmen. It was believing it was more vital to her salvation to be Mormon than gay. She lifted her head and looked through the windshield.

How could a whole group of functioning, somewhat rational human beings, get it so wrong?

Her wounds called out for healing. Was it time? How could she have known? How could she begin? She wiped the mascara from her cheeks. She had a funeral to attend. Emma climbed from the car, pushed down the awful weight of her wasted life, took a deep breath, and put on a perfect smile.

She walked into the church with confidence and purpose and wondered if the chains bound to her legs were silenced by the force of her smile. She smiled at people she had known all her life, and greeted them all by name. Emma Addens Yager, the beautiful only child of Rose and William Addens, homecoming queen, valedictorian, wife of Stephen Yager, and mother to Sara, Johnna, Sam, and Jacob, always greeted everyone by name. The perfectly molded, sculpted, untouchable Emma Addens Yager remembered everyone's birthdays and children's names, and could talk to anyone about anything. She grimaced inwardly, thinking she'd just written her own obituary.

She settled into an aisle seat in the back row of the church and crossed her legs. Her mother was six rows ahead and waved at her to sit with her. Emma ignored her. She scanned the crowd and found Carmen on the end of the first row. She stood, bending toward her sister, unrepentantly wearing black pants and a gray shirt. Her hair was short. Emma's heart lurched and face flushed. She ducked her head, not ready for Carmen to see her.

The hymnal began, the procession music played as the casket moved up the aisle. Emma settled back into her seat. She remembered lying in Carmen's arms, snuggled into a sleeping bag on the eve of her seventeenth birthday. There was Carmen's mouth on her neck, her hands as they roamed over her body, unlocking her. She remembered the utter pleasure of the moment, the feeling of wholeness. She took a deep breath and remembered the warmth and softness of Carmen's skin pressed against her. She wiped tears from her cheeks, surprised by them.

The tent was where her mother would find them a few months later. She pulled Emma by her hair while she screamed and threatened to kill Carmen. Carmen left to run home to her mother, who came to the house to try to talk to her mom. Her mom screamed at Mrs. Ojeda to leave them alone. Emma clenched her hands in her lap and struggled to leave the memory.

Emma looked up, finding Carmen again. She had long hair when she saw her last, always pulled up and away from her face.

She liked it better short. She wondered if it still felt the same way, or if like hers, was coarse with time. Emma crossed her fingers in her lap, looked at her wedding band. Ashamed again, she slipped it from her finger and slid it into her purse. She rubbed where her skin was whitened by time and clenched her hands tighter.

She slipped from the church unseen as the funeral ended. The procession to the cemetery would take time, and she didn't want to go. Instead, she drove across town to the park and bench where she rejected Carmen all those years ago. She waited in silence, enveloped by the weight of her grief.

Chapter Twenty

Saturday, August 24, 1991

When she arrived at the town recreation center, the room was loud with voices and music. Emma slipped into the side door. Her mother was with her friends, whispering. Emma approached them. Her mother touched her shoulder. "You look so nice. I wish you'd do this more often." She waved her hands in front of Emma's face. Emma smiled, perfectly obliging to her mother.

She looked again for Carmen and wanted nothing more than to talk to her, to whisk back in time with her and say, "Yes. I'll go with you." She clasped her hands neatly in her lap and resented her mother, even as she fought to keep the emotion from her face. She listened to the women half-heartedly and excused herself after fifteen minutes to talk with Maria, who cried by herself in the front of the room. Just three years younger than Carmen, Maria had occupied a prominent place in Emma's young life.

"Maria?" Emma spoke quietly, waiting for her to respond.

Maria turned to look at her. "Emma." She hugged her tight. Emma returned the embrace, and then pulled back. "You are as beautiful as ever."

Emma ignored the compliment. "I'm so sorry about your mom, Maria. She was a remarkable woman." Maria looked sad again. "How are you? Where are you living now?"

"Colorado. My husband and I moved there years ago." She smiled, touching Emma's cheek. "And you?"

"Here. I'm still just here." They chatted until someone else recognized Maria. Emma waved at her to attend to the interruption and then was alone. Her thoughts pulled her inward, but she felt a presence call to her and looked up to see Carmen standing in front of her, staring. She took a deep breath and rose to walk toward her. Carmen's color faded.

"Emma," Carmen said. Emma looked in her eyes, still so brown they were almost black, and still gentle. She smiled at Carmen, barely, and wanted to touch her. "How are you?" Carmen struggled to recover.

Emma didn't know what to say, and so said, "Okay. I'm sorry about your mom, Carmen."

Emma looked down at her sandals, studied the knots in the wood on the basketball court floor, and tried to look up again. She couldn't. Tears threatened her. "Thanks for coming," Carmen finally said.

"How long are you staying?" It felt like the most important question Emma had ever asked.

"Forever. I'm moving into Mom's house and taking over the store. She asked me to." Emma's heart raced. She continued to stare at her feet.

Mustering courage, Emma looked up again. She couldn't talk or respond.

"Carmen." They both looked to Maria, who was waving to Carmen. "Come here." Carmen held up her finger. Emma retreated and stepped back.

"I won't keep you. Take care, Carmen." She turned to leave, and Carmen grabbed her arm, gently. Emma felt the contact to the center of her soul. She hadn't realized that nothing had touched her since Carmen left. She also realized Carmen was always asking her to stay.

"Don't go. I'll be right back," she pleaded, her eyes warm, questioning.

"I shouldn't. I should go." Emma turned, panicked, fled from the recreation center, and rushed to her car.

❖

At dinner, Sam and Johnna huddled over the same menu, their shoulders touching. Jacob was next to Emma, bored and restless. Emma put her arm around him and squeezed his shoulders. He pulled away and she kissed his cheek and ruffled his hair. He shook his head, disgusted. Emma laughed, and Sam pulled a pouty face at him.

"Mom, how was the funeral? Were there a lot of people?" Sam looked over the top of the menu.

"Yes. She was loved." Johnna twirled a straw wrapper in her fingers. Sam was so confident, such a juxtaposition to Johnna. As extroverted as she was introverted, as jovial as she was serious. And as short as she was tall. Their hair and eyes were the same color, mannerisms were the same, but they were so fundamentally different in every other way. Twins who were mirror images of each other. Jacob's dark hair spilled over his ears. He needed a haircut. She felt a rush of affection for them and then fear. Had she condemned them to the same sort of life she lived, one rife with fear and ritual? Of Sunday morning church services and Wednesday night church activities. A life where they must heed the words of a madman named Joseph Smith or fear they would be condemned to hell. She teared up, looking down at the menu.

"Are you going crazy, Mom?" Sam put his elbows on the table, trying to get closer to her.

Johnna hit him. "You're such a jerk. Leave her alone. Someone died." Emma laughed despite her grief and tears, nearing hysteria. Jacob and Sam giggled, but Johnna didn't.

"Doesn't my gorgeous face make you smile?" Emma touched Sam's hair and smiled. She took a deep breath and wiped her tears as their waitress approached the table.

"Hi, Tina," Emma said.

"You okay, Emma? You look like you've been crying."

"She went to Mrs. Ojeda's funeral today," Johnna explained, so Emma didn't need to answer. Emma dabbed her eyes with a napkin.

"I understand. She was a wonderful woman, wasn't she?" Emma fought tears again. "Well, what can I get for you?"

❖

Emma sat on the couch with a glass of water. She talked with Stephen. It was a cordial but cold conversation. He was as much aware of their problems as she was, so they talked only about the bills and the kids. She sighed, running her hand through her hair. Johnna was on the other end of the couch, twirling her toes in Flower's fur, reading a book. They decided not to go to a movie but stopped at Blockbuster to rent one. Sam picked *Defending Your Life,* just out on VHS. Sam and Jacob lay on the floor. Emma missed Sara and rose to call her from the kitchen phone. "Mom, you're going to miss the movie."

"Let me call Sara real quick. I'll be right back. Hit pause." Sam obliged and poked Jacob in the side. They began to wrestle.

Emma dialed Sara's dorm room at Brigham Young University, longed to hear her voice. The phone rang only once, and Sara answered. "Hello, sweetie. It's Mom."

"Hi, Mom. How are you? What are you guys doing tonight? Dad came and took me to lunch today and then a movie. I just got home."

"That's what he said. Are you studying?"

"No, I should be, but I'm just lying here, looking at the wall. My roommate is on a date, so I'm alone. I have a hard time concentrating when I'm alone." Emma worried about that and started to ask about Sara's emotions, but didn't get a chance. "How is everyone?"

"Fine. Sitting right here. We're watching a movie. Do you want to talk to them?"

"No, that's okay. I was just wondering. I'm going to run. I need to study since I shouldn't tomorrow. I love you, Mom."

"I love you too, Sara. I'll talk to you soon." Emma returned to the front room.

Sam looked at Emma with his eyes crossed. "Can I hit play and watch the movie now?" Emma tossed a pillow at him from the couch and he swatted it away, giggling.

They watched the movie in silence. At some point, Johnna put her book on the table next to the couch to participate. Emma wiped her eyes as the story of a life review played before her with serendipitous and painful synchronicity. Johnna scooted down the couch and curled up against Emma's side, head on her shoulder.

"I'm going to bed," Johnna said, as the movie credits ran. Flower followed her down the hall and into the bathroom where the shower ran.

Emma rested her head on the back of the couch, listened to the quiet sounds of the house, and felt anxious. She rose. "Boys, don't stay up too late. Soon, you'll have to get back to your school schedules." They grimaced, even as Sam connected the Nintendo. In the bedroom, Emma slipped off her pants and shirt and looked at the white garments covering her body.

She'd worn them since she married Stephen in the temple. They represented the vows she took when they married and the covenants she made with God. She tried to find solace in those vows, tried to believe that her sacrifice—her marriage—fulfilled a higher purpose. She tried to believe that through her commitment, belief and faith in the restored Church of Jesus Christ of Latter Day Saints, she could be whole, saved, and happy. It was insane. She was insane. She wrapped her arms around her waist and held tight. It was a self-soothing gesture she'd done her whole life, when unable to do anything else.

The truth weighed heavily on her heart and pressed into her stomach. It was part of the burden that pushed her atoms down through her feet, into the earth. She wondered if she could really just let go of it. She turned on the tub faucet, and slid out of her garments, the white nylon falling to the tile in a heap. She poured bubbles into the bath and remembered she neglected to shut the door. She did this and watched the tub fill. She ran her hands across her stomach and traced a finger down her stretch marks.

She should have never married Stephen, but she did, and now she had four children and they all left a mark behind. She knew which mark came from each one, and traced her finger across them, remembering. She studied the veins on the insides of her thighs and down her legs. She slipped into the hot water, sank in deep, and rested her head against the edge.

She closed her eyes, wondering. What would her life have been if she'd left with Carmen? Who might she have become? Maybe they would have had kids together. She opened her eyes and stared at the condensation on the shower tiles. Before, she was able to justify her angst with faith in her sacrifice, but that changed. God, who would equate a marriage with sacrifice? Who would make your core, fundamental self a burden to be carried? It was so wrong she couldn't grasp it. Yet, she lived with it for twenty years.

Since Stephen started working away, Emma had space, and in that space something in her changed. Something stirred deep inside her as it stirred the world. The Soviet Union was collapsing. On Headline News in June, she saw gays marching in parades all over the country. That day, she'd shifted uncomfortably on the couch and thought, silently and powerfully, "Maybe that could be me." She'd not spoken it aloud, but it teetered around inside her, asking to be expressed, in all its terrifying glory.

Tears spilled down her cheeks, and she began to sink through her body again as her atoms reorganized themselves. It was late, and she worried about getting the kids up early for church, but then paused. Why should she go to church? She didn't want to go. She could choose to no longer have her reality defined by Biblical passages and the Book of Mormon. She was awake and uncertain how it happened. She remembered her bishop's face as he told her on the day of her marriage, "Heavenly Father gives us all challenges. Heavenly Father has a greater plan for us all." She felt the urge to claw his eyes out with her fingernails. He smiled at her with paternal pandering. He and Stephen talked in the fluorescent hallway, using the hushed voices male Mormons used when talking about things of the priesthood they believed women could not fully understand.

Almost an hour later, she rose from the bath and lifted a towel from the cupboard to dry. She wrapped herself up and went into the bedroom. She picked garments from the dresser and felt furious, threw them on the ground and kicked at them. She opened the door into the backyard, grabbed her robe, and wrapped it around her, striding into the middle of the yard.

Emma stared up at the night sky.

She was humbled by the size and scope of the sky and the gleam of the moon, and the five billion other people who existed with her on the planet. Humbled knowing billions existed before and billions would exist after. She knew nothing of what really was and had lived her entire life not daring to do what she really wanted to do, because of what she was told to do. Why had she done that?

There was a time when life was bright, when she wanted to be alive and live in the world. Once, life was not a burden, but a gift. When she was young, the beating of her heart powered her movements through the world. Now, she listened to it with panic. Life was burden, pain, sacrifice, and resignation. Emma didn't want that any longer. Air filled her lungs, and her skin tingled.

She walked into the house, pulled off her robe, dressed in jeans and a T-shirt, no garments, no bra, and slipped on sandals. She looked in on the kids. They all slept soundly. She quietly lifted her keys from the holder, stepped into the driveway, and locked the door behind her. She started the car and backed out of the driveway, following a familiar route.

She parked in the Ojedas' driveway. She panicked for a moment, realizing her mom would see her car. Then she dismissed the idea. It no longer mattered. At the door, Emma rang the bell.

A few agonizing moments passed, then the light flickered on the porch.

The inside wooden door opened, and there was Carmen. Emma said, "Hello." Carmen watched her, unmoving, and then came back to herself and pushed open the screen door. Emma stepped inside, not sure what to say. Carmen's arms hung at her sides, unmoving.

Emma raised her hands and dropped them again. Carmen stepped forward, grabbed her, and Emma knotted her fingers in Carmen's hair as she held her tight. "Please forgive me. I'm so sorry I didn't go with you. I'm so sorry I ruined it for us. Please forgive me." Carmen's arms around her were desperate, trying to pull her tighter.

"I should have fought harder for you. I should not have left until you went with me," Carmen said.

Emma sobbed in her arms and pulled back, placed both hands on her face. "I love you. I've never stopped." Carmen kissed her, silenced her, and they pulled at each other. Emma reveled in the feeling of being who she was and no one else, of being only Emma, with Carmen again. She reveled in the freedom, of losing herself, of groaning and moaning and finding release, again and again. She reveled in the feeling of Carmen's skin against hers, and with her head thrown back and her body arching, she looked out the open window, into the night sky, and was humbled by how little she understood about being alive, and for these few moments, was in awe of the wonder of it.

CHAPTER TWENTY-ONE

Sunday, August 25, 1991

Emma closed her eyes as Carmen traced a finger down her face, around her jaw, to her chin. Emma scooted closer, arm around her waist, and placed a kiss on her nose. Carmen said, "I hate to ask, but what comes next? Is it just this, Emma?"

"I'm done. If you ask me to go with you this time, I will. If you still want me. If you can forgive me." She couldn't get close enough and so pulled Carmen on top of her, wrapped her arms and legs around her. "I have additional baggage this time around. Three of four still live at home with me."

Carmen buried her face in her neck. "Tell me about them."

Emma smiled and moved her hand to Carmen's face. "Sara is the oldest. She's at Brigham Young, in school. She wants everything to be perfect all the time but spends all of her time worrying about everyone and everything because deep down she knows it isn't perfect and so she's secretly miserable. But she can't admit it." Emma kissed Carmen on the cheek, nose, forehead. "She's going to age prematurely, I think." She kissed Carmen's lips, lingering.

"It's going to take you a long time if you keep pausing to kiss me," Carmen said. "But I don't mind."

"Well, that's good. Better get used to it." Emma kissed all over her face in a flurry of movement. Carmen laughed, returning the kisses, nuzzling her neck until Emma moaned.

"Then there's Sam and Johnna. Twins. Sam is flamboyant and funny. He's so funny. Johnna is serious, studied, concerned. I expect Johnna to come home one day to tell me she's gay. I think Sam will figure it out before Johnna and tell her she is. She's incredibly smart, but is so self-contained, she misses the world around her."

"Really?"

"Yes." She trailed off. "Then there's Jacob. He's quiet, like Johnna. But he loves sports and is really gifted. The only athlete. I need to spend more time with him."

"Stephen?" Emma grabbed her face when she saw the flash of pain in her eyes.

"Thankfully, far away. God, he's such a son of a bitch," Emma said. "I'm sorry. Excuse me. I'm filing for divorce. It's done. I'm sorry."

"Do you really think you need to say that to me? To apologize for calling him names?"

"Habit." Emma smiled through tears. How could Carmen forgive her? Be interested in her children? This was what love looked and felt like. How could she have ever believed anything else?

"Who do the kids look like? You?"

"Sara and Jacob look like Stephen's side, with dark hair. But Sara has my color eyes. Jacob has brown eyes. Sam and Johnna look like me." Emma pulled Carmen closer.

Emma willed herself to stop thinking, to concentrate only on Carmen, on the moment. She pressed into her. "Come meet them later today. We'll go on a picnic or something, enjoy the last remaining days of summer."

Carmen responded to her pressure. "Do you need to get home?" Emma looked at the clock. Five forty-five a.m. She had time before they woke up.

"I have some more time," she said, running her hands down Carmen's back. Carmen mumbled something into her neck, and Emma laughed. "What?"

"I said that's good because I'm not finished yet." Emma shuddered at her breath on her neck and her intention and relaxed, submitting.

"Do whatever you want. You have an hour."

❖

Emma drove home with the windows down. The air was crisp, but she liked how it felt moving over her skin. Every nerve in her body was alive. She ran her hands through her hair. The gravel of the driveway crunched under the tires. She paused for a moment to revel in the morning. Everything would be different now. She opened the back door to the house.

Johnna was watching television, with Flower curled up next to her. "Grandma called. She wanted to talk to you. She sounded really wound up."

"When?"

"About an hour ago. I told her you were still sleeping." Johnna looked at her from the corner of her eyes.

"You didn't need to lie."

"I didn't know what was going on." She paused and turned to face her. "What is going on?"

"Nothing. I just needed to get out, take care of some things." Emma knew she didn't accept it. "Johnna, I'm sorry."

"Don't apologize," Johnna said.

"Later, let's go on a picnic. I'd like you all to meet an old friend of mine." Johnna stretched.

"I'm going back to bed." Emma watched her and Flower walk away.

Emma picked up the phone and dialed her mother. After a single ring, she answered. "Emma?"

"Johnna told me you called."

"I thought I saw your car at the Ojedas' this morning when I got the paper. Johnna said you were still sleeping."

"You did."

"What?"

"You did see my car. I was there," Emma said.

"What were you doing there?"

"You know, I've given birth to four children. I've managed to take care of myself for quite some time now. Understand when I tell you to mind your own business. I mean it." Emma twirled the phone cord in her fingers and smiled. The tightness around her chest lessened, and the air she breathed felt new.

"Emma, I think you need to call Stephen. He needs to not travel so much, come home."

"I'm going to call Stephen. To tell him I want a divorce. I'll let you know how it goes." Emma smiled, proud of herself, and felt a bit reckless.

"Emma, you're not thinking straight. You've had a stressful year, with Sara leaving for college, Stephen gone."

"Mom, I love you. But buckle down, you're about to have one hell of a year." Emma hung up the phone and climbed into bed. She figured she had about thirty minutes to sleep before her mom showed up, and so nestled down under the covers, strangely at peace.

❖

Emma felt her mother's presence before she said anything. She opened her eyes "Hi, Mom."

Her mother was on the foot of the bed. "What are you doing?"

"Sleeping?"

"Don't be cute. You know what I mean."

"No, Mom, I don't." Emma swung her legs over the side of the bed.

"Emma, you are not thinking clearly. Get up, get dressed, and let's go to church. You can talk to the bishop."

Emma laughed, bending forward. "You're kidding me." Her mother stared at her. "You think that will fix it?" She went into the bathroom. "I need to shower, get dressed." She stripped off her clothes, started the water, pulled back the shower curtain, and climbed inside.

Her mother followed her into the bathroom. "You're being ridiculous. What are you going to do? Move in with her?" She spat this out. "The minute I heard she was coming back here, I knew there would be trouble. She's no good. She's always made you do things." Emma laughed. "What is so funny?"

"You make me do things. Dad makes me do things. Stephen makes me do things. It's ironic that the only person who has never made me do anything I didn't want to do is the one person you can't stand." Emma finished rinsing off. "Hand me a towel." Her mother handed it over the shower curtain. Emma dried off.

"Mom, stay out of it. It can be nice and easy, or it can be rough. It's really your choice. This is sort of like a hostage situation. I can make it an international incident, or I can handle it quietly, making sure no cameras are rolling. But if you get in my way, everyone in this town will know by nightfall that your beautiful only child is leaving her husband for a woman."

She pulled back the shower curtain and stepped out. She stood in front of her mother naked. "I'm tired of it, Mom. You ruined me. You ruined my life, but I know I was a willing accomplice. Now I'm done being a willing accomplice. So, with whatever time I have left, I'm going to do what I want." She moved closer to her mom. "I suppose the reconditioning you sent me for so many years ago kind of wore off, huh?" She hissed this at her mother and turned away. Emma hadn't realized she was this angry. Her heart pounded in her chest.

"I don't know why you'd do this to me and your father, and your kids. Poor Stephen." Her mother began to cry.

"The kids will be fine because I love them. And as far as Stephen goes, well, he's fucked me for the last time."

"Emma. Your language," her mother said, crying. "Why are you doing this to me?"

"This has nothing to do with you or Dad. Stay out of it."

Her mother tried to steady herself against the doorframe. "Emma, I can't believe you'd do this to your family."

"What? Make myself happy? I'm the picture of selfishness, aren't I, Mom?"

"I don't even know you anymore," her mother said, crying.

"You've never known me. Go on now, get out. Come back when you're ready to start getting to know me." Emma put on jeans and a blouse. She took the blouse off with fluster and grabbed a bra from the dresser. She turned away from her mom to put it on and then put the blouse back on.

"You're kicking me out?"

Emma paused and tipped her head. "I guess I am. I've said everything I wanted to say. For now, at least." She held perfectly still, holding her mother's gaze.

"You'll regret this, Emma."

"I regret plenty, Mom, but this won't be one of those things." She heard her mom leave, the door to the outside echoing behind her, and wondered if she shouldn't be more upset. She searched her emotions, wondering if concern for her mother was hidden somewhere, but found nothing. She dressed quickly and went to check on the kids.

Sam and Johnna were together and she smiled at them. "Grandma seems a bit mad," Sam said.

"So it goes," Emma said.

"You and Dad getting a divorce?"

"I think so," Emma said. "We'll be okay. I love you. You know that, right?"

"Yeah," Sam said. "Does he know yet?" Emma shook her head. "When are you going to tell him?"

"Soon." Emma left, leaving Johnna and Sam in silence.

Sam leaped off the bed and ran into the hallway. "Hey, Mom."

Emma turned. "Yes?"

"Good for you," Sam said

"Thank you, Sam." Emma came back and hugged him, kissed his forehead, and turned away again.

"Go, Mom. Really, she's cracking up. But it's cool." Johnna looked at him, her expression serious. "This is going to get interesting." He paused a moment. "We're staying with her, right?" Johnna's look was incredulous. "I just wanted to check. You're the boss."

Emma moved into the kitchen, pulling pots and pans out for breakfast. She busied her hands, whipping eggs, buttering toast, and called for her kids. Johnna and Sam looked at each other, but not at her. Jacob still slept, and she let him. At the table, she took a bite of food, starving. "I don't want this to be hard on you kids, but your dad will try to take you."

"We won't go," Sam said.

"You may not have a choice."

"He can take me, but I won't stay," Johnna said.

"I go where she goes," Sam said.

"I'm sorry you overheard that conversation with your grandma. She and I will make up and be fine. Eventually. It's not how I would have planned to tell you." Emma took a bite.

"I don't really like Dad." Sam lifted more pancakes to his plate.

"Sam," Emma said.

"What? I don't. He thinks I'm too tiny."

"I don't know why all of this is happening now, but it is. I promise to keep us together, okay?" Sam and Johnna nodded earnestly. "Always. You're stuck with me. I'm never going to let you go." She smiled and felt the burden of love roll from her stomach to her chest. Once again, she was struck with urgency. There was so much to do, and she was running out of time. She willed her inner emotions to slow. She would call Carmen after she cleaned up breakfast to tell her she planned to see her every day, from that moment forward.

Then she would call Stephen and tell him she was filing for divorce. She would stay with Carmen, if necessary, assuming she'd want her to, because Stephen would race home as soon as she called. She mapped the timeline silently in her head as she watched her twins eat and wiped a tear from her eye.

Life was meant for the present, not the unknown space after death assigned as heaven or hell. It was just this, and she felt the weight of it on her shoulders. If she created this, she could create something else.

So she did.

CHAPTER TWENTY-TWO

Jamis stopped in the office to pay for the week. Jamis waited while Tess rang up another customer and then slowly moved to the counter. "You look like one of my dogs after they pee on a toy."

"Don't yell at me anymore," Jamis said.

"I'm not mad. You're just nuts."

"I don't disagree. I came to pay my bill and see if I can book another week. I'm heading up to Salt Lake, but I'm not ready to leave yet."

"If you promise not to flail around like an idiot on my sidewalk."

Jamis really hoped she wouldn't. Tess handed her the credit card receipt. "I'll see you later tonight or tomorrow."

Her phone chirped. It was Sapphire. She texted back that she'd stop on her way out of town. After leaving Johnna the night before, Jamis decided to visit Mildred in Salt Lake. Johnna said her mom's visit to the store gave her the strength she needed to change. Johnna admitted she'd never visited. She only knew about it because Carmen told her the story. Jamis understood. It made sense to want to hold it in sacred space, not soil it with reality. She didn't tell Johnna her plans to visit. Maybe later, if she found resolution.

Sapphire waited outside the municipal building, wearing a light sweater. The weather had warmed to forty degrees, and people acted like it was summer. Jamis pulled into a parking spot. Sapphire jogged to the passenger door and climbed in.

"Did you have a good time at dinner?"

"Um, yes." Sapphire looked at her clasped hands. "You said something, didn't you?"

"I just pointed out the obvious."

"What's that?" Sapphire looked at her from the corners of her eyes.

"That you're brilliant, amazing, beautiful, and he's a fool. Because you've waited." Sapphire lunged across the seat and hugged Jamis's neck.

"You act distant and cool, but you're so soft and kind. Decent," Sapphire said.

"No, I'm not. But I'm trying to be better," Jamis said.

"What are you doing? Are you okay?"

"I'm fine. Going to Salt Lake. I've got some stuff to do. But I'm coming back. I want to see Stephanie exhumed. Maggie will come up," Jamis said.

"Okay. Well, text me when you're there and safe. I'm going to work on the video feed some today, see if can enhance the resolution and such of those images."

Sapphire waved at Jamis as she drove away. She wound her way back to Salt Lake. The path was less menacing this time, because her expectations were set. Everything was less scary the second time around. The only stuff she had to do in Salt Lake was see Mildred at Caravan.

Jamis parked in front of the store. The parking lot was empty but for a scooter chained to a hose pipe by the front door. Caravan was a small, wooden framed building, standing alone in a half-acre lot, circled by a cement sidewalk. Jamis turned in a full circle to look at the Wasatch Mountains, which gave way to the valley, reaching to the Great Salt Lake, and then to the Salt Flats beyond. It was breathtaking, and she imagined Emma standing there in 1991.

Warm air soaked with incense greeted her when she stepped inside. There were shelves of crystals, books, rings, necklaces, and earrings. It was a lot to take in, so she focused on the woman behind the counter.

"Hi," Jamis said. The woman looked at her. Her hair was gray, long, and pulled into a loose ponytail. She wore a purple crystal around her neck and a small silver ring on her thumb. Her linen dress hung loosely on her shoulders.

"Can I help you?"

"I'm looking for Mildred," Jamis said. The woman's eyes were piercing blue and Jamis felt unsettled by her stare.

"I'm she." She tipped her head, watching Jamis. "You've come a long way to see me."

"I was in Sage Creek." Mildred was silent. "I came to Utah looking for a ghost. A poltergeist." Jamis stumbled over her words.

"That's not why you came."

"No, it is. I got a video."

Mildred laughed and set down her magazine. "Well, that is the external causation for your arrival. But you've always come here. There is never a time you don't come here." She tipped her head. "You've got stuff to work out. This is where it happens. Time and time again."

"I actually came to talk to you about someone else. Not me," Jamis said, stepping back.

"Someone else is you. Others are mirrors of ourselves. We only see them when we're ready to see ourselves."

"Okay. Yeah. Well, I won't keep you." Jamis wanted to flee. Despite everything she'd seen, from alien epitaphs to moaning specters, Mildred's new age thought meets Freud, triggered the landmines in her. So many things came to mind to say. "What the fuck, Mildred?" was on top of her mind, but she didn't say it.

Instead, Jamis waited for more, expecting some long-winded spiel about how her negative energy created everything bad in her life. "Emma. I just want to talk about Emma Yager."

Mildred pushed the stool against the counter, turned off the radio playing nature music, walked past Jamis, and locked the door. She flipped off the open light and pointed to beads hanging in a doorway. "I need a snack and some tea. Join me?"

Jamis's desire to talk about Emma outweighed her cynicism. The beads swooshed. Mildred turned on a small electric kettle. "Go ahead and sit," Mildred said, pointing to a small couch. "What kind of tea would you like?"

"I'll have whatever you're having." Mildred busied herself with the tea. Tapestries of brilliant red, blue, purple, and yellow hung on the walls. There were deep purple rugs on the floor. Mildred poured the hot water into a glass, settled a tea bag in it, and brought two cups to the couch. She handed one to Jamis. "Are you a gypsy?"

"Oh, probably in one life or another." Mildred joined her on the couch. "So, Emma."

"Do you remember her?"

"I see a lot of people," she said, blowing on her tea.

"That's not really an answer," Jamis said. She set the tea on her knee and stared straight ahead.

"I know it isn't. I'm trying to decide what to tell you."

"You do remember," Jamis said.

"Of course. But I don't think this is about Emma." Her eyes at once softened with compassion and indomitable strength. There was no pushing this conversation. "This is about you." Jamis shook her head. "If you think you know so much, why did you come to me?"

Jamis was pissed and felt it from her abdomen to her face. "Look, if you want to help me, fine, but don't give me tea and do some Dumbledore shit with me. Either answer the question or don't. If not, I'll leave."

"Stop it," Mildred ordered. "You're angry, but it's not at me. Who are you so pissed at? Your mom? Life? Yourself? Who?"

Sadness welled up behind Jamis's rage, and she fought back a sob. She put the tea on the table next to the couch. Mildred didn't move. "Just tell me about Emma." Why was she so emotional?

"You already know everything you need to know about Emma. You're connected, that's how you communicate. I don't know anything more than that. You came here today, just as she came here, all those years ago, to find answers from me you already have inside yourself." She sipped her tea.

"You love her daughter. You always have. You're just seeing it now. She's your path, by the way. Look no further. It's the only way you'll evolve past the self-obsessed boob you are now." Jamis was shocked and insulted, but paused before she said anything. Mildred was right, and how did she know about Johnna? "The other spirit. The angry spirit and Emma. Somehow, they're connected. I don't know how, but you'll find out soon."

Jamis listened quietly, less agitated. Mildred wasn't a new age hack who fed on people's guilt and fears. Maybe she was legit. "It's all really happening now, you know. Nothing happens that doesn't happen in the now."

"I have no idea what you're talking about," Jamis said, hands up.

"You will." Mildred turned to face her. "I need to go back to work."

"I don't even know what to say," Jamis said.

"That's good, actually, because you talk too much."

"I make a living talking," Jamis said, defensive.

Then Mildred hugged her, quickly but tightly. "Now go on. Be a hero. Love. Live your life. It'll all come together in the next few days." Jamis's agitation returned. Mildred controlled their entire exchange. She felt like a puppet, strings yanked. "You need to be careful, though. It's a passage between light and dark, and a lot is being transmuted. Share the burden. Tell someone else."

"That's what she said. Emma. Told me to tell Carmen." Jamis paused, the door opened wide.

"Then do it," Mildred said.

"What if she gets angry and doesn't believe me?"

"The spirit of a dead woman told you to do something." Jamis waited for something else, but nothing came. Mildred held up her hands in front of her, palms up.

"Right," Jamis said. "It's crazy to not just listen."

"Now you're getting it." Jamis turned and left, pausing to look at the view one more time. The sun had passed the midpoint of the sky. She wouldn't return to Sage Creek for the night. She'd find a hotel, head back in the morning. She needed a break from whatever was happening to her there, and needed to muster the courage to share everything with Carmen.

CHAPTER TWENTY-THREE

Jamis tossed and turned in the hotel bed all night, dreaming of her mom. Sleep came in spurts, finally taking her deep around three a.m., where she remained until noon. She rushed to leave, anxious and frantic, feeling in a hurry though there was nowhere to be. The conversation with Mildred triggered a lot of emotion buried under layers of practiced detachment.

Jamis was consumed by death. Death was her life. It's why she chased ghosts. Dr. Frank was right. She was bound by her mother's death, trapped in a cycle of repetition, where in large and small ways, the trauma replayed. Never finding proof meant never achieving closure. It meant Jamis was a walking, breathing, hungry ghost.

She drove hectically, only half-conscious of the GPS directions. She knew that when people died, there was an authentic, chemical reaction to the loss of their presence. The pathways in our brains which form our experience of reality had to be rewritten. She was rewritten by grief, all those years ago, and because it happened at such a formative age, she never stopped living out the same story.

It was all madness. She was absurd.

Her head swam with darkness. She liked it there a little too much and always had. She just needed to get clear of what was happening in Sage Creek, back to the sunlight in Los Angeles, and figure out what came next. She'd reform. Get a real job. Maybe go back to school, be a real archaeologist. If any decent academic program would have her. She'd stop visiting women like Mildred, entertaining these fanciful ideas that did nothing but reinforce her delusions that her mom remained after she died. That's what the counselors in the group homes called it. Delusions.

It was all too much, so Jamis did what she always did. She struggled to detach as the skyline of Sage Creek came into view. Once there, she stopped at the police station, sought out Detective Daniels, and pressed to find the status of Stephanie's case. He assured her the case was re-opened and that he contacted Maggie. He needed to wait until Monday to get an order to exhume the body. She accepted his responses and talked with him about the process for some time and left satisfied but not satiated. She liked him and trusted he'd do the right thing.

Which is why her increasing alarm worried her. She'd woken unhinged, ruminating on grief and death, when her mood should have been settling. Stephanie's death would be investigated. Mildred told her she'd figure out what she needed to learn from Emma. But the knots in her stomach called for her attention. She texted Johnna again. She'd kept her up to date and wanted to see her but knew there was no avoiding Carmen any longer. She told Johnna she was going to stop by Carmen's and would reach out later.

She dialed Carmen and waited for her to answer. Her call rolled to voice mail, and she hung up and tucked the phone in the center console.

Her phone rang, and she jumped. "Carmen?"

"Yeah. Did you call?"

"I was wondering if you could talk. I mean, I need to talk. Are you free?"

"Sure. Just come by. I'll text you my address."

"Okay," Jamis said.

"You okay?" Carmen asked, concern in her voice.

"I'm just leaving the police station. I think I'm just unsettled by it all."

"Well, come over. I was just watching TV." Carmen covered the phone and she heard her talking.

"If someone is there, I don't need to come over," Jamis said.

"No one is here. I was talking to the dog Johnna stuck me with me. He's some sort of mutt, maybe shepherd and poodle? He's deaf and confused all the time. Someone brought him into the clinic six months ago for her to put down." Jamis heard the affection in her voice and it warmed her and slowed her nerves. "Obviously, she couldn't."

"His name?"

"T-Rex. But I just call him Rex." Jamis grinned despite the weight of her limbs.

"I'm on my way." Jamis hung up, querying the address Carmen texted. Saturday night was slow in Sage Creek. There was a time in life when Saturday night meant chaos, mayhem, and partying all night. Now, she was more likely to be home with Netflix. She'd somehow managed to evolve with time, not just grow old with it. Maybe she was healthier than she thought.

At Carmen's house, she raised her hand to knock on the door. Carmen opened it proactively and smiled. She wore a simple gray T-shirt and dark blue jeans. She'd gotten a haircut since she'd seen her last and it was buzzed against her head. Tears spilled onto Jamis's cheeks.

"Kid, what is wrong?" Carmen hugged her, pulling her into the house. Jamis stiffened and then relaxed. It was comforting, and she wasn't used to such feelings. Carmen patted her back and pulled away, hands on her shoulders, dark eyes soft. "What's wrong?"

Her concern was wrapped in authentic kindness, which caused Jamis to cry more. Carmen put her arm around her shoulders and pulled her toward the couch. Jamis followed wordlessly. Carmen settled her on the couch and turned away. She left the room and returned a few minutes later with a box of tissues and T-Rex, who followed behind her and erupted with joy when he saw Jamis. He rushed to her and planted his front feet in her lap, licking her face as he wagged his tail. He climbed to the side of her on the couch. Jamis laughed through her tears and rubbed his chest. Carmen handed her the tissues.

"What's going on?" Jamis looked at her, saw time on her face and hands. She saw her loss in her warmth and patience. Carmen's house was sparsely decorated and immaculately clean. There was just a couch and a television, mounted on the wall. She looked up to the built-in bookshelves and saw Emma's photo in the middle of the center shelf. There was nothing else on them. On the shelf to the right of the door, a picture of Johnna and Sam faced the couch. Jamis cried harder.

"I don't know what's wrong. But I have to tell you something." Carmen waited. Jamis looked down at her hands and put her right one on T-Rex's chest. He wagged his tail. She said, before she lost her courage, "Emma."

Carmen's posture changed. Her back grew rigid. She scooted back and away from Jamis. Jamis grasped her forearm. "Wait. Please. Just listen," Jamis said.

Carmen was alarmed, jaw clenched, but she didn't move so Jamis continued. "For months before I came here, I started having these dreams of a field. It was so beautiful. The sun was always just right. I was always alarmed to be there, but once I learned to just let myself be, I felt better there than I ever have in my life." She wiped tears from her cheeks.

"Then I saw this woman. In a yellow dress. She was far away, and I couldn't see her. I so wanted to talk to her, and I tried all the time, but the closer I got, the farther away she got. I couldn't reach her." She let go of Carmen's forearm and wiped her nose in a tissue. "I couldn't reach her." She put her hands on her thighs. "I didn't think much of it. Just thought it was some trauma or something working itself out. I had a lot of those growing up."

She crumpled up the tissues and put them on her leg. "Then Vince and Darcy sent me that video. All this started. It's only been a week, but it feels like my entire life has been rewritten. Everything is different. Nothing will be the same now." She looked up at Carmen, pleading. “Friday night I talked to the woman in my dream. She told me she knew I’d be coming here. She told me to be careful, that someone was coming, to tell you. I didn’t know who she was until Wednesday night. At Paul and Sara’s house. I saw Emma’s picture.”

Carmen jerked up and off the couch, stumbled backward, and caught herself on the doorframe leading down the hallway. Jamis sensed her rage and tried to move toward her.

“What the fuck is wrong with you? What are you playing at?” Carmen stepped back as though Jamis was diseased.

“I swear to God I’m not. I know how this looks, Carmen. How crazy it sounds. She asked me to tell you.”

“It doesn’t work that way. You are fucking crazy,” she yelled at her, taking huge strides to the door, yanking it open. “Get the fuck out of my house and don’t ever contact me again.”

Jamis didn’t move. “Please don’t do this. I’m telling you the truth. I know how much this must hurt. I know how much you loved her.”

Carmen strode toward Jamis, and for a moment, Jamis was afraid. Carmen backed her to the door. “You have no idea of anything. I spent my whole life loving her, wanting her, and when I finally got her back, she died. She left me. She always left me.” Now there were tears in Carmen’s eyes, under the anger. “No one grieved with me, Jamis. No one asked me if I was okay. Her ex-husband got all that sympathy. Not me. I was here in my house and thought about all the ways I could die. How I could cut my veins and just bleed out. How I could put a gun in my mouth and pull the trigger. How I could swallow pills and never wake up.” The veins in her neck bulged. “One day, I was ready to do it. Probably three weeks after she left me again. I heard a knock on the door, just moments before I was ready to pull the trigger. I got up and looked. I don’t know why. It could have been a Jehovah’s Witness, for all I know. A fucking Mormon.”

Jamis held on to the door to withstand Carmen’s onslaught. “It was little Johnna. Just thirteen years old. She still had a cast on her arm. She had a tin of cookies and she held them out to me and asked if she could come in." Carmen took another step toward Jamis, inches from her face. "You stay away from her. Don't you dare tell her any of this. I'm only even alive because she showed up with cookies and kept coming back. You stay away from me. You have no idea what you're talking about. I would give anything to have her back. To talk to her one more time. To see her and feel her close. Anything. For you to stand here and tell me you did and lie to me about something this important and this real? You can fuck off and die. Get the hell out of my house." She pushed Jamis from the doorway with a single, forceful shove.

Jamis stumbled backward, caught herself on the railing, as the door slammed. "Well, hell," she said, and gulped back tears. Carmen's reaction was surprising and terrifying. She anticipated disbelief, but she'd not expected that level of anger. It was violent in its force and it filled the room with its potency. Jamis felt nauseous from it.

She started the car and left. She imagined that Carmen would call Johnna, so she picked up her phone and turned off the sound. She tossed it in the front seat and hit her fists against the steering wheel, driving aimlessly. She stopped at a small sushi house with an open sign in the window, choosing a seat at the long counter. She ordered four rolls, starving. Her body shook from the encounter with Carmen. She tucked her legs around the long legs of the stool and ducked her head. Her thoughts returned to her own mother.

On a Saturday morning not long before her death, she'd awakened Jamis early. They went for a long walk and stopped in for breakfast at a storefront cafe in downtown La Jolla. The sea breeze blew softly against them. Her mother laughed when Jamis bit into her croissant and the crumbs covered her chest and arms. Her eyes gleamed and her smile was wide, and she hugged Jamis to her while she brushed the crumbs from her shirt. They spent the day on the couch, watching movies together.

Jamis sobbed at this memory, of her mother's face vivid in her mind, and then fought to gain control. What was wrong with her? She made her way to the bathroom as the world spun. She splashed cold water in her face, saw her own eyes in the mirror, bloodshot from tears. Her nose was red, skin looked clammy and pale. She wiped her face with a cold paper towel. Mildred and Carmen shook her up, but she needed to pull it together.

She was learning to surrender to discomfort, embrace it, allow it to unfold. She didn't need to react and try to fix it with something or chase it away. Jamis was going to sit at the counter, eat her sushi rolls, drink a Diet Coke, stop by Stephanie's house for the cameras, and then go to the hotel, get some sleep, wake, pack her bags, and leave town. Just as Carmen asked her to do. She'd respect that.

She'd send Johnna a letter, tell her everything, let her decide if they had a path forward. She couldn't imagine telling her in person and getting a negative reaction. She'd not done anything wrong. If anything, she was the victim in this whole affair, swept this way and that by forces she couldn't possibly understand. A puppet! Mildred upset her so because she made her aware of it.

For the moment, her self-talk helped and Jamis felt moderately reassured, though still terrified of not seeing Johnna again. But she had to do what was necessary. This was done. Her last chase complete. She was going home. Dr. Frank would be pleased.

Her food waited for her at the counter. She ate greedily, left cash, and hustled to the house. Night had fallen, and with it, the air chilled to below freezing. The house was cold when she arrived, probably from the gaping hole in the hallway. She turned on the light in the front room and peeked upstairs. She'd called the property management company to let them know about the accident, and they said they'd send a contractor to begin repairs. The wall was patched with a piece of plywood and sealed with plastic.

Just as Jamis touched the camera to dismantle it, something clanged in the kitchen and then dropped. A muffled voice told Jamis she wasn't alone. She took the stairs three at a time, grabbed the front door handle, and then something struck her head. She felt a sharp stab of pain and her vision tightened into a single point of light. Someone hit her, but even as she wrestled with this knowledge and tried to consider her next steps, an arm, holding a lamp, came down at her again. Instinctively, she put up her hands to try to stop it but couldn't counter the force. The lamp hit above her right eyebrow.

She fell back against the front door, sliding down it. The pain of the blow ricocheted through her skull and the wood scraped her back where her shirt pulled up. She sensed everything around her—the breathing of the man who hit her, the hum of the central air, the red blinking eye of the camera at the top of the stairs.

She tried to speak, but nothing would come out of her mouth. She couldn't move her legs and arms. The pain behind her eyes was unbearable and her back was bleeding. Then someone bent down to look at her and the world went dark.

Jamis floated above the field in her dream. The sky was brilliant blue. A soft breeze blew. She smelled gardenia and soared toward the sun, then dipped back down and landed softly on her feet in the field. "Emma?" she called, but no one came. Strong hands grasped her shoulders and pulled her backward. The field faded and she was sucked into a long tunnel of darkness. The hands on her shoulders locked around her chest and pulled her. She pulled at the arms, gray and clammy around her, and struggled, but couldn't free herself. She landed with a strong thud on a carpeted floor. She was in Stephanie's house, but it looked older and dirtier. She touched the carpet, brown and white, faded and worn. There was a black couch with colored flowers. There was wood paneling on the walls. Jamis rolled to her side and screamed.

A man held Stephanie by her throat with both hands. Stephanie fought him, scratching his arms. He let go of her throat and punched her in the face. She screamed and kicked at him. He pulled back from her and punched her in the stomach. Jamis screamed and rushed at him but fell through him. She stumbled and came at him again, but couldn't grab hold. He yanked Stephanie's pants down. Jamis screamed and ran to him again, flailing her arms back and forth, praying she could somehow make contact with him. It was over as quickly as it began. He zipped his pants and kicked Stephanie in the head. She lay stunned on the ground. Jamis turned with him to see his face.

It was Bobby Reynolds. "You son of a bitch." She swung wildly at him, once again passing through him. She turned to Stephanie and fell to the ground next to her. Her hands passed through her. "Stephanie? Stephanie, oh my God." She felt helpless, kneeling by Stephanie's head. Bobby Reynolds paced through the house. Stephanie lay with her eyes half open, fading in and out of consciousness. Stephanie's head faced toward the corner of the room. It was the spot she stared at while Bobby Reynolds raped her. Jamis tasted acid in her throat. "I'm so sorry. You didn't deserve anything that's happened in this life."

Stephanie's gaze abruptly fixed on Jamis. Jamis jumped back startled, but Stephanie grabbed her arms and screamed. The sound shook the windows and rattled the cupboard doors in the kitchen. Jamis jerked, fell backward, and closed her eyes. When she opened them, Stephanie was gone, and something was stuck in her mouth. She tried to move her arms, but they were bound behind her back. Her legs were also tied. She flailed back and forth on the floor, struggling to sit up. She managed to roll to her side. Her eyes adjusted to the dark. There were voices in the kitchen. Jamis was in Stephanie's corner of the room. Her body began to shake.

She closed her eyes and focused on the voices. Did Bobby Reynolds kill Stephanie? Or did he just help his brother do it? Jamis wiggled again and knocked into the coffee table. A silhouette emerged from the kitchen. She fought frantically against her bindings. It was Bobby. She kicked out with her bound legs, trying to connect with him. He dropped to his knees and grabbed her by the front of her shirt, and slammed her against the ground with so much force the air left her lungs. The gag caught her breath.

"That's better, fuckin' dyke." He spit the words at her, his eyes hard and dark. Jamis looked over his shoulder. There was another man behind him by the stairs. "I should have some fun with you before I cut your throat."

"No," the man said. "You're lucky you didn't get caught last time." There was a long pause. Jamis recognized the voice but couldn't place it. "We need to figure out how to get rid of her quickly. We need to know what evidence she's found and deal with that. The last thing I need is you leaving DNA in her. Find someone else for that. We need to cut our losses here."

Bobby looked over his shoulder and back at Jamis. "You don't tell me what to do here. You never did."

"That's enough," the other man said, voice firm.

"I saved your ass all those years ago. She was going to tell your wife how much you liked fucking her while she was pregnant with my brother's baby. You'd have been ruined if it weren't for me. I'll do whatever I want with my dyke ghost hunter." The man behind him stepped forward. Bobby turned to face him. "You're going to listen to me this time. None of this would matter if you hadn't packed all her shit up and put it in the attic."

"I cleaned up. How was I to know this would happen?"

"I told you to get rid of all of her stuff. Take it to the fucking landfill. Instead, you pack it all up and put it upstairs? Did you want someone to find it?" Bobby yelled at him. "What the fuck were you thinking?"

"I wasn't thinking. Not only did you kill Stephanie that day, you also killed Emma, her son, and that truck driver, you stupid, reckless son of a bitch." The man swung his fist at Bobby and connected with his jaw. Bobby recovered and hit back. They both stumbled in place, bent over, hands on their jaws.

"You told me to get out of town. You told me to hurry. How was it my fault that fucking trucker jackknifed? He hit black ice. It might not have been because of me," Bobby shouted, one hand on his knee, one on his chin.

"It was you. Admit it." The other man rushed him, and they fell into a standing wrestle, fighting for control. "Admit it."

"Fine. I watched them all die in my rearview mirror. But I left, did my part. You packed up Stephanie's stuff and sealed it in an attic." Bobby threw another punch, connecting with the man's stomach.

Jamis squirreled farther into the corner. She bit at the rag in her mouth, pulled with her teeth, back and forth, until it loosened and fell free. She took a deep breath. The moonlight fell through the cracks in the drapes on the front window. It met the light from the streetlights and fell on the second stranger. "Dan Abbey? Oh my God, Dan Abbey? You killed her?" Bobby turned quickly. Dan lurched forward and pushed him out of the way.

His eyes were clouded and unreadable. "I'm so sorry," he said, and hit her with a stun gun.

Chapter Twenty-four

Friday, March 13, 1992

Emma stretched, opened her eyes to the sun slipping through the cracks of the blinds, and arched her back. She slipped from bed to the bathroom and stole back under the covers when she was done. While spring began to hint at its return, the night still belonged to winter. Frost settled on the window where icicles dripped water during the day. She scooted over and put an arm around Carmen's middle and shook her lightly. "You awake?"

"Since someone shook me, yes," she said and turned on her side away from Emma.

"Hey," Emma said, scooting closer. "Turn around. I brushed my teeth."

"That's good because your morning breath is atrocious." Emma grabbed her side and pulled her back. Carmen laughed, turned, and pulled her close. "I love you unconditionally, but I can't lie." Emma stretched out on the length of her. "I'll be right back, okay?"

Emma reluctantly let her go, rolling back into the middle of the bed. "What are you doing today? Do you have to go into the store?"

Carmen came back in the bedroom, toothpaste in her mouth, foam building in the corners. "I should," she mumbled with the toothbrush between her teeth.

"You're cute," Emma said. Carmen smiled. "Let's play hooky today. I don't work."

"You're a bad influence," Carmen said, disappearing around the corner.

Emma looked at the ceiling. A long crack spread from the right corner to the middle. The house needed a lot of work, but they'd get to it, room by room. She'd taken a job as an assistant at the library in early September, and while it wasn't much, it gave her enough for her independence and insurance benefits. Shortly after she told Stephen she wanted a divorce, he threatened to take the house, assets, and kids. She willingly let go of the house and assets, but she planned to fight him until the end of time for the kids. She might lose, but she would go down swinging. She wanted nothing but her children.

Carmen reappeared and scooted back into bed next to her. "Hand me the phone," Emma said. Carmen lifted the large cordless phone from the base on the end table and put it in her outstretched hand. "This thing weighs ten pounds."

"It does not," Carmen said.

"Can't we just have an old-fashioned rotary phone? With a big dial?" Emma asked as she punched in her home number.

"It's the dawn of a new millennium. Embrace change." Emma made a puffing noise with her lips and hit dial.

The speaker of the cordless phone broadcast the sound. "It's so loud too," she said. Johnna's voice was audible. "Hi, baby," Emma said. "You up for school?"

"Yeah," Johnna said.

"How are you doing? Are you okay? What about Sam and Jacob?"

"We're okay, but I miss you so much. I want to be where you are. Why won't dad just let us come with you?"

"Honey, I know. I want to be where you are too. I'm picking you up from school tonight and we'll have the weekend, okay? We can do whatever you want. Jacob has his scouting thing, and Sam is staying over at a friend's house, so I am all yours. Sound good?"

"Yeah," Johnna said. "I just don't feel good when I don't get to see you."

"I know baby," Emma said, her voice soft. "We'll get through this, okay? I promise. We will. I love you to the far end of the universe and back. Through time and space, heaven and earth. From this life to the next, and every life after. You're stuck with me. That's how much I love you. That's right. I'll see you in about seven hours, okay? You got it. Be strong."

"Okay. Seven hours. I love you, Mom," Johnna said. Emma punched the end button and handed Carmen the phone.

She turned on her side, propped her head on her hand, elbow on the bed. "She's having the worst time."

"We can do something else. Whatever we need to do for them. I want you, but I don't want your kids not to have you."

"We've talked about this. I want to live my life. Some people might think it's the ultimate act of selfishness. But I can't live any other way. I think sometimes we mistakenly think we can protect children from all and any disruption, but we can't. Life on Earth is messy business. I feel at peace. I'm not to blame. My mother might be to blame, but I'm not." She smiled, and Carmen matched it. "I'll work with Johnna through this. All of them. We'll find our peace. It might not be tomorrow or next month, or next year, but somewhere, we'll transcend all of this. We'll punch through it, let it go, and move forward." She smiled at Carmen. "I'll put that out there to the universe."

"Am I playing hooky today with you?" Emma grinned, nodding. "Any reason why?"

"Does there need to be?" She touched the end of Carmen's nose with her finger. "If this were your last day alive, what would you want to do?"

"Is this the twenty question game?"

"Yes," Emma said.

"What question is this?"

"Eighteen," Emma said. They'd played the twenty questions game since they were children. They resumed it with some rules the fall before. Each question had to be meaningful, and they had to respond with the next question in the designated time frame. If they forgot or defaulted, the penalties ranged from dishes to late night romantic activities. Very little had changed from when they were ten years old, but for their bodies and the lines around their eyes. The game solidified that and Emma loved it. She never let Carmen forget.

"Really? We're at eighteen?"

"Yup," Emma said.

"Okay, well, if this were my last day alive, I'd just want to spend it with you. Cuddling in bed, making love, eating grilled cheese." Emma grinned, encouraging her. "Maybe crawl out to the couch, watch a movie, naked, wrapped in a quilt with you."

"I like the way you think."

Carmen rested her head in her hand. "Are we going to act out number eighteen today?"

"Please?"

"Twist my arm," Carmen said.

"You have to think of number nineteen by nine p.m. or you lose the game."

Carmen pressed her back, lips on her neck. "I'll see what I can do."

Emma was wrapped in a quilt, waiting for Carmen to return with their grilled cheese sandwiches. She'd flipped off the movie they'd barely watched and stared blankly at Headline News. She felt deep sadness in her chest. It came upon her quickly and she wanted to tuck it way before Carmen felt it or saw it, but her eyes stung with it. She'd been clingy with Carmen today. She couldn't get her close enough, wouldn't let her from her sight for long. It was worse today than it had been for a while, though it was an ongoing issue. A month or so earlier, over dinner, before Carmen needed to broach the topic, she blurted, "I know I'm needy." She said it with so much honesty and innocence Carmen choked on her soda, and it came out of her nose. Since then, they'd been able to talk about how, from time to time, it was a good idea for Carmen to have some space. She knew it, and constantly monitored herself for signs of being a crazy girlfriend who wouldn't let her partner breathe.

She'd teased it apart in her mind, first tracing it back to the night she told Carmen no, closing the window. Then she teased it back further, to the hospital where the pills made her throw up, and she cried at night for her. She unwound the sensation, from front to end, the way only a person who experienced anxiety could; she analyzed it obsessively. Until one day, Carmen told her to stop worrying about it. That she didn't mind her need to be close. If she ever felt smothered, she'd tell her. "As long as you're not boiling a live rabbit on the stove because I talked to another woman, I think we're in the clear."

Emma tightened the blanket around her shoulders. At times, she knew she was mentally unstable. Anxiety and hysteria crept up on her like evil monsters in a horror movie. She'd read a number of books over the years about depression and anxiety. She worked hard to keep all the pieces together and not break apart, but she wasn't always successful. Admittedly, she'd found greater mental peace since September than the twenty years before.

She backslid, from time to time, swept away as her atoms rearranged themselves, but her ability to pull them back together, in her desired form, was so much easier with Carmen by her side. She believed her inner life was a direct reflection of her outer, and moving more into alignment with her truth meant the broken pieces inside her could fall back into place. Every day, she'd become a bit more whole.

One day she would feel entirely healed. Carmen returned with two grilled cheese sandwiches. Emma opened her quilt and shifted on the couch. Carmen climbed inside with her. Their legs tangled, and they struggled to wrap the other quilt around them. "You look awfully serious," Carmen said.

Emma bit into her grilled cheese. "I was just thinking I'm mentally ill and you're in love with a crazy woman."

"If you were mentally ill, I don't think you'd be that aware. Do you?" Emma shrugged. She wasn't sure. "Anyway, I'll love you even if you are nuts. It doesn't matter. Just don't go anywhere. If you're going to be crazy, be crazy here with me."

Emma dressed quietly, the same sadness deep in her chest. It welled up to her eyes and spilled over onto her cheeks. Carmen wrapped her arms around her from behind. "What's going on today?"

Emma turned to her, arms around her neck. "I'm emotional. I just feel sad, clingy, and needy." Carmen tightened her arms around her waist. "I woke up like this."

"I'm going to go into the store for a few hours, while you get the kids, get everyone settled, and then I'll be back early. By six or so. That work? We can spend the rest of the evening together. Do whatever Johnna wants to do?"

"That works. I'll be okay. It's just one of those days."

"Sure. It's fine. I love you." Carmen cupped her face in her hands and kissed her gently. Emma held her hands and pressed her forehead against Carmen's. "Should we go?"

They walked out of the house together, fingers intertwined. Emma tossed her purse in the front seat of the Pontiac she'd bought used a few months before. Carmen opened her door for her. "You're so gallant."

"Don't you know it." Emma climbed behind the wheel of the car and looked up at Carmen, who kissed her lightly on the lips. "See you later." As she went to pull away, Emma grabbed her T-shirt, and pulled her back for a longer, more intense kiss. She let her go reluctantly and pulled the door closed. Emma watched Carmen in the rearview mirror all the way to the grocery store. She honked as she passed Carmen, turning into the store parking lot.

She waited in line for Jacob first. He climbed into the seat behind the driver's seat, sullen and quiet. Her efforts to engage him in conversation failed, and she stopped trying when Sam and Johnna opened the doors and climbed in. Sam kissed her cheek and fastened his seat belt. She made eye contact with Johnna and pulled slowly from the school parking lot. "How are you both?"

"Good. I canceled my plans so I can stay with you, if that's all right," Sam said.

"Of course, it's all right," she said. "It's always all right. Jacob? Are you still going with the Scouts this weekend?" He shrugged, noncommittal in the back seat.

"Dude. Parents get divorced," Sam said. "You gotta get over it, man."

"Leave him alone," Johnna said.

Emma interrupted before it became an argument. "How about if all of us just take a deep breath for a minute, realize that a lot of stuff is going on, and be kind to each other, okay? If Jacob needs to be quiet, he can."

"Whatever." Sam stared straight ahead and crossed his arms.

"Let's just get home, take a break, and figure out what the weekend will look like, okay?" Emma said. "Let's do that." She turned to get on the interstate to bypass afternoon traffic backing up on the surface roads. It was just a mile or two, but she thought it prudent to get the kids out of the car as quickly as possible. She was not mother of the year, but she had enough experience to know the best way to avoid escalation and dramatic upheaval was to let them all decompress in separate corners. She pulled onto the interstate, found it largely empty, and drifted to the left lane to pass a slow moving car on the right.

Chapter Twenty-five

Jamis opened her eyes to the front room. Dan Abbey was by the front door, hands in his pockets. "I should have destroyed everything. I know. I think I felt guilty. And I was worried about getting it out of the house. I was worried if I threw out the carousel, someone would find it. Just like they found her body. I thought it would be safer here. I closed up the attic."

"You were always too soft, Danny," Bobby sneered. "I've spent my whole life being your muscle when you're too pussy to do it. Just like that little girl at camp that year."

"Don't put it on me. You loved every moment of everything you did to Stephanie and that girl."

"Yeah, well, I'm not the one that dipped my dick into her to waive her rent."

"We all make horrible mistakes," Dan said. He turned toward Jamis. She closed her eyes, feigned unconsciousness. "What are we going to do with her?"

"I'll take care of her," Bobby said. He went into the kitchen. "I need to find something to do it with." Dan followed him.

Jamis wiggled around so her back was against the wall. They'd replaced the gag in her mouth and it was tight. She fought against the bindings on her wrists but was unable to untie them. She fell slightly forward and struck her head on the corner of an end table. Dazed again, breathing through the discomfort, she felt fingers on her wrists, as the ropes fell away. She felt loved and warm and closed her eyes. She heard a whisper, "Don't close your eyes. You have to get up. Carmen is coming."

Jamis cried out from the painful contraction of her muscles. She fell forward and shook her arms awake. They tingled painfully. She fell still, blood rushing to her extremities, listening to Bobby and Dan in the kitchen.

"It's too late to do anything but kill her," she heard Dan say. "She's seen both of us. But we need to be better at getting rid of her. She's popular, but she's also not from here. We have to think this through."

"We can think it through after she's dead," Bobby said. Jamis untied the rope around her feet. She felt nauseous and woozy from the blows to her head, and the stun gun made her innards feel microwaved. The world moved up and down in waves. She climbed to her feet, rushing to the front door. She yanked it open. Dan and Bobby yelled. She was unsteady from her injuries and fell from the house, landing on her hands and knees.

Dan seized her by her hair and yanked her back into the house. She kicked and waged war against him, connecting multiple blows to his face with her elbows and fists once he let go. Bobby joined the struggle and put his hand over her mouth. She bit down on his fingers and tasted blood. He yanked his hand back and grabbed her shoulders, throwing her into the middle of the room. He ran at her and hit her in the face with his fist once, twice, and pulled back for a third time. But before he was able to connect, the room erupted.

Curtains billowed, chairs tipped over, and the cry Jamis first heard filled the house and smothered all other sound. A dark, angry figure with a swelling stomach lurched up in the corner of the room, climbing up the wall and into the ceiling. Dan screamed and tried to run for the front door, but a force struck him at the threshold and sent him flying backward. Bobby was thrown back by the same force, hitting the banister so hard it cracked. He tried to come at Jamis but was hit again.

Jamis held her jaw, wondering if it was broken, and used the wall as leverage to stand. It was fight or die, so she grabbed a lamp from the table and rushed at Dan. She hit him on the back of the neck, and he dropped to his knees, stunned. She kicked out and connected with his face. He fell to his side. He struggled to stand back up, and while poised halfway up from the ground, feet unsteady, Jamis shoved him forward through the window. The glass shattered as he fell through, into the front yard, grabbing at shards of glass embedded in his flesh.

Blood spilled down Jamis's forehead, into her eyes, and she wiped at it, making it worse. Bobby Reynolds would kill her unless she got to him first. Once again, Jamis was surrounded by warmth, and though her head pounded, she was suffused with clarity.

He lurched toward her, with a maniacal look in his eyes. His grin was menacing and pure evil, his eyes empty orbs. "I am going to kill you if it's the last thing I do. You should have let this be." They clashed in the middle of the room. He grabbed her hair and pulled. Jamis kicked and connected with his groin.

"You're a sissy hair puller," Jamis yelled, wrenching away from him. He swung his arms wildly at her. She grabbed his wrist and twisted like she'd learned in self-defense class. She pulled his arm down and back and shoved him forward. He stumbled but came back at her, head down, shoulder in the front, and he connected with her stomach. It knocked the wind out of her, and she stumbled.

"You dyke bitch." He kicked her knees from behind and she dropped to them on the ground.

"Oh, get original, you fucktard." He lunged for her throat, but she pushed up with surreal strength, her limbs flooded with adrenaline. She connected with him, her full body against his and they both stumbled toward the kitchen. "I'm not a delicate flower, Bobby. How does it feel to fight someone you can't overpower so easily?" She grabbed his ears as they stumbled, yanking them, and then let go of one to stick her thumb in his right eye. It popped and she flipped what felt like jelly off her thumb. He screamed and shoved her back. She hit the doorframe leading into the kitchen with the space between her shoulder blades and cried out in pain.

Somehow, he seized the moment to grab her shirt from behind, pulling it tight against her neck, wrapping his arm around her throat. "Can't talk now can you?" Jamis dug at his arm but couldn't budge it. He'd restricted her oxygen supply. The cupboard doors began to open and close on their own. From the corner of her eye, Jamis saw Stephanie standing in the middle of the kitchen, mouth opened in a scream. The fridge door opened and slammed into Bobby. He stumbled forward with Jamis in his grasp.

She resolved not to die this way, and thrashed wildly, from right to left, yanking forward and backward. She connected her foot to his instep, and then his shin. His arm loosened some and then reasserted itself. The pressure on her neck hurt, and she had to get free of it. She continued to thrash when suddenly, he let go. She fell to her knees. Her throat and lungs burned and throbbed.

Bobby lay in front of her, blood pooling from his head. Through the blood in her eyes, Jamis saw Carmen, bat raised above her head, ready to strike again. Stephanie was beside her, quiet. When he didn't move, Carmen dropped the bat and knelt to touch Jamis.

"Don't fuck with a dyke holding a softball bat," Jamis said.

"Do you ever stop?" Carmen's hands were on Jamis's face, shoulder, and arms, checking for breaks.

"Lesbians should not be fucked with. Fuck you," Jamis screamed at Bobby. Lying prone on the floor, she kicked him in the back of the head. "Lesbians should band together and take over the fucking world." She kicked him again. "I'm pretty sure he's dead, Carmen." She kicked one more time. "She told me you were coming. Untied me. It was your Emma. Said you were on your way." She rolled onto her back and looked at the ceiling. "I don't feel very good. I can't see good. My head feels real woozy."

"We need to get out of here. The upstairs is on fire." Carmen pulled her up, hands under her armpits. Jamis stumbled forward, toward the front door, all her weight against Carmen.

"Dan Abbey. He's in the front yard," Jamis said, slurring. "Watch for him. He stun gunned me, the son of a bitch." She was pissed. "Take me to him. Fuck you, Dan Abbey. You stun gunned me?"

"He's unconscious. Come on, you gotta help a little," Carmen said, and Jamis tried to focus, as Carmen pulled her from the house. On the porch, Carmen stepped below her, and hoisted Jamis over her shoulder like a sack of potatoes. She carried her through the front yard, and leaned her against the truck's wheel. She'd stopped right in the middle of the street. Carmen dialed 911 as a car sped around the corner, up the road toward them, and came to rest behind her truck.

Sapphire jumped from the car and ran to Jamis and Carmen. "Oh my God. Are you okay?" Sapphire cupped Jamis's face in her hands. "Are you there?"

"Maybe," Jamis mumbled. "I got hit in the head a lot."

Carmen spoke on her phone. "I need an ambulance. Maybe more than one. Fire trucks. There's fire and injuries. Third Street. In front of the campus." Her voice wavered. She set her cell phone on the truck, even though the call was still there.

"Should we get the guy in the house?" Sapphire spoke to Carmen, over the top of Jamis's head.

"No, just wait for the cops," Carmen said.

The flames on the second floor leaped and grew, running down the front of the house, as if they were tasked with what they were about to do. The whole house erupted in fire.

Sapphire rushed to her car and came back to Jamis with a towel.

"I called the cops, too," Sapphire said, wiping Jamis's face, trying to clean the blood from her eyes. Carmen slid down the side of the truck to sit next to Jamis. Jamis dozed in and out of consciousness, aware of the heat from the house.

"Dan Abbey," Jamis mumbled, pointing at the front yard. Sapphire moved forward, but Carmen grabbed her arm.

"Let the cops get him," Carmen said.

Jamis fell forward, unable to sit up. Carmen held Jamis against her, sitting side by side.

"It's okay, kid. Just hang in there," Carmen said. Sapphire pressed the towel against the open wound on Jamis's forehead. "You need to stay awake. You probably have a severe concussion. Paramedics will be here any moment." Jamis tried to nod, but her vision blurred.

"How did you know?" Sapphire asked Carmen, pointing at the chaos around them. "How could you know? Did she call you?"

"She came by earlier. We had a fight. I tried to go to sleep, but I couldn't. I just had this overwhelming sense that she was in danger. I just felt like I had to find her."

"Thank you," Jamis said, but it came out garbled.

"I found her like this. Bobby Reynolds was about to kill her. I think they killed Stephanie and they tried to kill her for figuring it out."

Sirens filled the air. An ambulance skidded to a stop in front of Carmen's truck. Paramedics rushed to them. Carmen let go of Jamis. Sapphire pointed to Dan Abbey and told them another man was in the house. They rushed in through the kitchen and came out less than a minute later with Bobby Reynolds on a stretcher. Another set of paramedics rushed to Dan. Jamis looked up into the night sky at the full moon as they lifted her into the ambulance. It was so bright she could see as if it were dusk. The night was beautiful and would have been perfect to spend with Johnna, in front of the fire.

In the ambulance, Carmen held Jamis's hand. The paramedic hooked up an IV and attached monitors to Jamis. "It'll be okay," Carmen said. "I'm sorry. It's going to be okay now."

Jamis heard her voice even as she drifted away. As she faded from consciousness, she tried to tell Carmen to call Johnna, but words would not come out.

❖

Bright light stretched endlessly in all directions. Jamis lifted her hand to her head, touched above her eyebrow, expecting to see blood. There was nothing. She studied her exterior for sensations of pain and found none. Either she was dead, or she had slipped into another dimensional loop, but she couldn't be sure. "You're not dead." She turned and saw Emma about twenty feet from her.

"You're Emma," Jamis said.

"I am," she said.

"I'm not dead?"

"No, but you got close. Really close." She walked toward her. "I think you're in the hospital right now. Probably unconscious."

"I wouldn't have let him kill me," Jamis insisted.

Emma smiled and stopped just a few feet from her. She took Jamis's hand. "You almost did, though. I'm glad he didn't."

"Where am I? Is this like the field?"

"Honestly, I'm not sure. This is a new place for me. I didn't do it. Didn't bring you or myself here."

"It's so bright," Jamis said with some derision.

"Let's break a few light bulbs, see if the light comes down." Emma laughed and smiled at Jamis, eyes bright.

"You really are beautiful," Jamis said.

"I've heard. It's just a projection, you know. It all is. I wonder why I chose it," Emma said.

"Maybe it's just the most authentic representation of your soul," Jamis said.

"Well, that's what we do, isn't it? We fixate on these ideas of ourselves, and then we insist upon them in the world, again and again. We try to create permanence where there is none, including in ourselves," Emma said. "I'd like to sit down." Two high-backed chairs appeared to the right of them. "Will you look at that."

"Did you know that would happen?"

"Oh my God, no. But such power could be dangerous." Emma crossed her legs and patted the seat beside her. "Come sit."

Jamis did and sighed. "God, I'm tired."

"Yeah, well, you've been busy."

"I really have. It's been a weird week."

"I think it's been going on longer than that, though. I can't quite grasp it all, but this is the crescendo and final arc of one long chapter in your journey. You had a lot of shit to work through. Now, you're into new beginnings. The next chapter." Jamis laughed at her language. It felt out of place in the bright light. "No one tells you while you're alive what's going to happen, how long it will take to work through it, and how painful the process will be. Our inclination is usually to hang on when we should just let go."

"Unless you're hanging on a ledge," Jamis said.

"I suppose it depends on the ledge and the timing of your descent," Emma said. She uncrossed her legs and turned to face Jamis. "You helped me, my kids, and Carmen work through it. Somehow." She waved her hand in the air. "I'm not quite sure how, but it feels better now. Like I can move on."

"I don't want you to go. Will I see you again?"

"Yeah. But you already are. It's already happening." Emma stared at a spot over her shoulder, a small smile on her lips. "Everything is happening from this point in the eternal now. Does that make sense?" Jamis indicated it did not. "It will. I think it does for me because I'm really dead to this life." She closed her eyes and took a deep breath, though Jamis wasn't sure they were breathing. "I do. I have to let this life go. I didn't think it was my time, all those years ago, but that doesn't matter. Suffering is between what we think we should have and what actually is."

"That's very Buddhist."

"They got a lot right." Emma grinned. "We're connected. Me and you. Somehow. Maybe we ran into each other during the Dark Ages, thought it might be fun to stay in touch. Really, though, I think you needed a mom. Of all the things I did wrong, the thing I did best was be a mom. It's so weird, isn't it? I was only a mom because I turned my back on who I was. It goes to show you that love is always possible, no matter what."

Jamis sobbed, put her hand over her mouth. A dark well of hurt moved out of her then, and Emma held her. "Thank you," Jamis said. "I think you're right."

"I think so too," Emma said. "But, all things as they are, I think my time here is up. Got to move on. The other Emmas need this part of me with them." Jamis held up her hands, not understanding. "I didn't understand either. I think it's because when you're in there," she tapped Jamis's head, "behind these eyes, your vision is fixed to what they can see, for the most part." She touched Jamis's cheek, then dropped her hand. "Unless some crazy woman breaks into your dreams."

"Where's Stephanie? I thought she'd be here."

"She's already back, I think. She has a lot to work out. But you helped her. I felt her with me, but I don't anymore." They shared silence. "Do me a favor?"

"Anything," Jamis said.

"Tell Carmen she lost the game. She never asked me question nineteen."

"What does that mean?"

Emma stood and held out her hand to Jamis. "She'll know." Then she pulled Jamis close and kissed her cheek. "Now, love my daughter and wake up. You have to wake up now."

CHAPTER TWENTY-SIX

Jamis woke to sunlight through a small window in the wall above her bed. The ceiling was white, industrial foam-like material with metal strips holding it all together. The walls were beige and the metal trim around the door was blue. Johnna was next to her and Carmen was at the foot of her bed. Sapphire and Sara were on a small light blue couch near Sam.

"You're awake," Johnna said, taking her hand in hers. Jamis tried to smile, but it hurt too much.

"Don't try to smile yet. We thought your jaw was broken," Johnna said. "But it's not. I looked at your X-ray. You're just really bruised and swollen. It might be hard to talk."

"That's going to be hard for her," Carmen said. Jamis wanted to laugh, but could only hold up the middle finger on her left hand.

"You have four broken ribs," Johnna said. "There was concern you might have a skull fracture or brain swelling from all the blows, but the CAT scan came back clear. You're just really beaten up, Jamis." Johnna's eyes were soft with concern.

"Carmen told us what happened," Sam said, moving toward the bed.

"Or at least as much as I understand," Carmen said. "The paramedics picked up Dan Abbey. They removed about thirty pieces of glass from his body. One nicked an artery and he almost bled out when they removed it, but they saved him. He's in ICU down the hall. Bobby is dead."

Jamis tried to wet her lips with her tongue, but her mouth was dry. Johnna saw it. "Do you want some water?"

"Yeah," Jamis said.

Johnna poured water over ice, handing it to her. Jamis struggled to drink it.

"Here," Johnna said, "Let me lift the bed for you." Jamis's head pounded as she struggled upward. Jamis took the water from Johnna's hands and sipped. She swished it around her mouth. She set the water on her thigh. "How long have I been unconscious?"

"They kept you under, medically induced, for hours. It's Monday morning," Johnna said, twisting her arm to look at her watch. "About ten a.m. We were getting worried you weren't going to wake up."

"I don't think I wanted to." Jamis sipped the water again. "Carmen, the cops. Bobby. It was self-defense."

"You mean because I clocked him with a bat?"

"Yes," Jamis said. "He was going to kill me. You saved me."

"The official cause of death was suffocation." Jamis was confused. "I don't know. I clocked him good. He looked dead. But when they got him here, they found he'd inhaled smoke. Had scars in his throat and esophagus from smoke inhalation. Pronounced him dead about six hours after they got him back here."

"I pulled the video feed for them, Jamis," Sapphire said. "They didn't see the camera you had at the top of the stairs. It got everything. It recorded their conversation. They got there about three minutes before you. They broke in through the back door and took down the cameras on the first floor. But they missed the one at the top of the stairs. They were looking to go into the attic like we did, but you interrupted them. We have a video of them assaulting you. From that angle, you could see the whole front room. All of it was recorded up until the point they yanked you back into the house. Right when I logged in and saw it live. I think I accidentally stopped the recording. I was so frantic. I'm sorry."

"So, we didn't get the poltergeist throwing shit around the room?" Jamis should just be happy to be alive.

"I'm so sorry. I was so scared," Sapphire said. "I just had to get to you."

"It's okay. You two saved me," Jamis said.

"The cops will still want to talk to you, but I think it will be fine," Sapphire said.

Jamis closed her eyes. Stephanie had raged downstairs and she'd seen her, materialized. Once again, proof was missing. She didn't want to be upset about that.

Johnna tugged at her fingers. Jamis turned to her, seeing only her as the room faded away. "Sapphire told us. About my mom and Jacob. Sam. Bobby making that driver jackknife." Her eyes filled with tears.

Sapphire spoke again. "Jamis, the thing I don't get though…" Jamis turned her eyes back to her. "They tied you up. We watched it on the video. How did you get free?"

Jamis drank the rest of the water, and Johnna took the cup. "I don't expect any of you to believe me, but someone untied the ropes on my hands." She looked at Carmen. "She told me I had to get up because Carmen was coming."

"What?" Sapphire came to her.

"Carmen," Jamis continued. Carmen had deep circles under her eyes and looked so stressed and tired. "She told me to tell you that you lost the game. You didn't give her question nineteen." Carmen's shoulders dropped, and she cried. Sapphire put her arm around her shoulders.

"My mom," Johnna said.

"I have no idea what's going on here," Sara said, speaking for the first time.

"I'm pretty sure I do," Sapphire said, "but I think we can wait for Carmen to tell us." Sam took Sapphire's hand. She looked at him with tenderness and love. He held her hand delicately on his shoulder, not making eye contact. Jamis saw it and smiled.

A knock on the door interrupted them. It was Detective Daniels, who also had dark circles under his eyes. Jamis kept everyone awake. "If I may, I need to talk to Jamis." Everyone but Johnna readied to leave. "Alone," he added, looking at Johnna.

She sighed and turned to look at Jamis, squeezing her hand, leaving the room reluctantly.

"I saw the video," Detective Daniels said as he sat in the chair.

"So they said," Jamis answered.

"You were right and wrong, all at once."

"It often goes that way with me," Jamis answered, closing her eyes again. "My brain feels like jelly."

"Dan Abbey is awake. He lawyered up. Claims that Bobby Reynolds had him under duress, had nothing to do with any of it. That he just found the body after Bobby killed her."

"He's a liar."

"Well, we'll build a case. Our district attorney recused himself. Conflict of interest. Since it's his uncle," he said.

"I didn't even think of that. What will you do?"

"We're talking to the attorney general. Getting guidance. Charges are being filed. Second degree murder. Accessory to murder. Interference with justice. Kidnapping. That's you. Attempted murder. That's also you. I'm digging up as many charges as I can find." He tapped his knees with his fingers. "Shame I didn't get to try Bobby."

"He was a monster. The world is better without him," Jamis said with venom.

"They think he came to in the house as the smoke descended from upstairs. Took in too much, too fast. Had burns inside his throat. Third degree burns on forty-five percent of his body. Can you imagine?"

"I hope he suffered," Jamis said, happy he was dead.

"He did. For about six hours," he said. The door opened. A nurse came in.

"Wait. I had all of Stephanie's stuff moved into a shed. Tess's nephew can tell you where. It didn't burn in the house," Jamis said.

"I don't know if I'm angry or grateful."

"I need to look at Jamis now," the nurse said. "You can talk to her later." She checked the IV bag.

"Yeah, that's fine. I'm sure she'll see a lot of me. One more thing though. We got the order to exhume Stephanie. But we're waiting to do it until we figure out jurisdiction. We'll do it as part of the charges."

"Thank you," Jamis said, managing a weak smile.

He held up his hand. "Not me. You almost got killed. Just stay in touch. I will need official statements when you're well enough, and you'll likely need to testify at trial." He left, and as the door opened, Johnna came back in.

The nurse had put something in her IV. The pain dissipated and time stilled. Johnna's breath was on her neck, and her lips, and barely a whisper in her ear. "Don't go. Stay here. With me. I love the way my house feels when you're in it." Jamis closed her eyes and lifted both hands to Johnna's face.

"Yes. We'll figure it out," Jamis said. "We're each other's karmic reward."

About the Author

Jen Jensen lives in Phoenix, Arizona, with a pack of rescued senior dogs, lovely family and friends, and spends too much time reading books.

Books Available from Bold Strokes Books

Flight to the Horizon by Julie Tizard. Airline captain Kerri Sullivan and flight attendant Janine Case struggle to survive an emergency water landing and overcome dark secrets to give love a chance to fly. (978-1-63555-331-4)

In Helen's Hands by Nanisi Barrett D'Arnuk. As her mistress, Helen pushes Mickey to her sensual limits, delivering the pleasure only a BDSM lifestyle can provide her. (978-1-63555-639-1)

Jamis Bachman, Ghost Hunter by Jen Jensen. In Sage Creek, Utah, a poltergeist stirs to life and past secrets emerge. (978-1-63555-605-6)

Moon Shadow by Suzie Clarke. Add betrayal, season with survival, then serve revenge smokin' hot with a sharp knife. (978-1-63555-584-4)

Spellbound by Jean Copeland and Jackie D. When the supernatural worlds of good and evil face off, love might be what saves them all. (978-1-63555-564-6)

Temptation by Kris Bryant. Can experienced nanny Cassie Miller deny her growing attraction and keep her relationship with her boss professional? Or will they sidestep propriety and give in to temptation? (978-1-63555-508-0)

The Inheritance by Ali Vali. Family ties bring Tucker Delacroix and Willow Vernon together, but they could also tear them, and any chance they have at love, apart. (978-1-63555-303-1)

Thief of the Heart by MJ Williamz. Kit Hanson makes a living seducing rich women in casinos and relieving them of the expensive jewelry most won't even miss. But her streak ends when she meets beautiful FBI agent Savannah Brown. (978-1-63555-572-1)

Date Night by Raven Sky. Quinn and Riley are celebrating their one-year anniversary. Such an important milestone is bound to result in some extraordinary sexual adventures, but precisely how extraordinary is up to you, dear reader. (978-1-63555-655-1)

Face Off by PJ Trebelhorn. Hockey player Savannah Wells rarely spends more than a night with any one woman, but when photographer Madison Scott buys the house next door, she's forced to rethink what she expects out of life. (978-1-63555-480-9)

Hot Ice by Aurora Rey, Elle Spencer, Erin Zak. Can falling in love melt the hearts of the iciest ice queens? Join Aurora Rey, Elle Spencer, and Erin Zak to find out! (978-1-63555-513-4)

Line of Duty by VK Powell. Dr. Dylan Carlyle's professional and personal life is turned upside down when a tragic event at Fairview Station pits her against ambitious, handsome police officer Finley Masters. (978-1-63555-486-1)

London Undone by Nan Higgins. London Craft reinvents her life after reading a childhood letter to her future self and in doing so finds the love she truly wants. (978-1-63555-562-2)

Lunar Eclipse by Gun Brooke. Moon De Cruz lives alone on an uninhabited planet after being shipwrecked in space. Her life changes forever when Captain Beaux Lestarion's arrival threatens the planet and Moon's freedom. (978-1-63555-460-1)

One Small Step by Michelle Binfield. Iris and Cam discover the meaning of taking chances and following your heart, even if it means getting hurt. (978-1-63555-596-7)

Shadows of a Dream by Nicole Disney. Rainn has the talent to take her rock band all the way, but falling in love is a powerful distraction, and her new girlfriend's meth addiction might just take them both down. (978-1-63555-598-1)

Someone to Love by Jenny Frame. When Davina Trent is given an unexpected family, can she let nanny Wendy Darling teach her to open her heart to the children and to Wendy? (978-1-63555-468-7)

Tinsel by Kris Bryant. Did a sweet kitten show up to help Jessica Raymond and Taylor Mitchell find each other? Or is the holiday spirit to blame for their special connection? (978-1-63555-641-4)

Uncharted by Robyn Nyx. As Rayne Marcellus and Chase Stinsen track the legendary Golden Trinity, they must learn to put their differences aside and depend on one another to survive. (978-1-63555-325-3)

Where We Are by Annie McDonald. Can two women discover a way to walk on the same path together and discover the gift of staying in one spot, in time, in space, and in love? (978-1-63555-581-3)

A Moment in Time by Lisa Moreau. A longstanding family feud separates two women who unexpectedly fall in love at an antique clock shop in a small Louisiana town. (978-1-63555-419-9)

Aspen in Moonlight by Kelly Wacker. When art historian Melissa Warren meets Sula Johansen, director of a local bear conservancy, she discovers that love can come in unexpected and unusual forms. (978-1-63555-470-0)

Back to September by Melissa Brayden. Small bookshop owner Hannah Shepard and famous romance novelist Parker Bristow maneuver the landscape of their two very different worlds to find out if love can win out in the end. (978-1-63555-576-9)

Changing Course by Brey Willows. When the woman of your dreams falls from the sky, you'd better be ready to catch her. (978-1-63555-335-2)

Cost of Honor by Radclyffe. First Daughter Blair Powell and Homeland Security Director Cameron Roberts face adversity when their enemies stop at nothing to prevent President Andrew Powell's reelection. (978-1-63555-582-0)

Fearless by Tina Michele. Determined to overcome her debilitating fear through exposure therapy, Laura Carter all but fails before she's even begun until dolphin trainer Jillian Marshall dedicates herself to helping Laura defeat the nightmares of her past. (978-1-63555-495-3)

Not Dead Enough by J.M. Redmann. A woman who may or may not be dead drags Micky Knight into a messy con game. (978-1-63555-543-1)

Not Since You by Fiona Riley. When Charlotte boards her honeymoon cruise single and comes face-to-face with Lexi, the high school love she left behind, she questions every decision she has ever made. (978-1-63555-474-8)

Not Your Average Love Spell by Barbara Ann Wright. Four women struggle with who to love and who to hate while fighting to rid a kingdom of an evil invading force. (978-1-63555-327-7)

Tennessee Whiskey by Donna K. Ford. Dane Foster wants to put her life on pause and ask for a redo, a chance for something that matters. Emma Reynolds is that chance. (978-1-63555-556-1)

30 Dates in 30 Days by Elle Spencer. A busy lawyer tries to find love the fast way—thirty dates in thirty days. (978-1-63555-498-4)

Finding Sky by Cass Sellars. Skylar Addison's search for a career intersects with her new boss's search for butterflies, but Skylar can't forgive Jess's intrusion into her life. (978-1-63555-521-9)

Hammers, Strings, and Beautiful Things by Morgan Lee Miller. While on tour with the biggest pop star in the world, rising musician Blair Bennett falls in love for the first time while coping with loss and depression. (978-1-63555-538-7)

Heart of a Killer by Yolanda Wallace. Contract killer Santana Masters's only interest is her next assignment—until a chance meeting with a beautiful stranger tempts her to change her ways. (978-1-63555-547-9)

Leading the Witness by Carsen Taite. When defense attorney Catherine Landauer reluctantly becomes the key witness in prosecutor Starr Rio's latest criminal trial, their hearts, careers, and lives may be at risk. (978-1-63555-512-7)

No Experience Required by Kimberly Cooper Griffin. Izzy Treadway has resigned herself to a life without romance because of her bipolar illness but wonders what she's gotten herself into when she agrees to write a book about love. (978-1-63555-561-5)

One Walk in Winter by Georgia Beers. Olivia Santini and Hayley Boyd Markham might be rivals at work, but they discover that lonely hearts often find company in the most unexpected of places. (978-1-63555-541-7)

The Inn at Netherfield Green by Aurora Rey. Advertising executive Lauren Montgomery and gin distiller Camden Crawley don't agree on anything except saving the Rose & Crown, the old English pub that's brought them together. (978-1-63555-445-8)

Top of Her Game by M. Ullrich. When it comes to life on the field and matters of the heart, losing isn't an option for pro athletes Kenzie Shaw and Sutton Flores. (978-1-63555-500-4)

Vanished by Eden Darry. A storm is coming, and Ellery and Loveday must find the chosen one or humanity won't survive it. (978-1-63555-437-3)

All She Wants by Larkin Rose. Marci Jones and Tessa Dalton get more than they bargained for when their plans for a one-night stand turn into an opportunity for love. (978-1-63555-476-2)

Beautiful Accidents by Erin Zak. Stevie Adams and Bernadette Thompson discover that sometimes the best things in life happen purely by accident. (978-1-63555-497-7)

Before Now by Joy Argento. Can Delany and Jade overcome the betrayal that spans the centuries to reignite a love that can't be broken? (978-1-63555-525-7)

Breathe by Cari Hunter. Paramedic Jemima Pardon's chronic bad luck seems to be improving when she meets police officer Rosie Jones. But they face a battle to survive before they can find love. (978-1-63555-523-3)

Double-Crossed by Ali Vali. Hired thief and killer Reed Gable finds something in her scope that will change her life forever when she gets a contract to end casino accountant Brinley Myers's life. (978-1-63555-302-4)

False Horizons by CJ Birch. Jordan and Ash struggle with different views on the alien agenda and must find their way back to each other before they're swallowed up by a centuries-old war. (978-1-63555-519-6)

Legacy by Charlotte Greene. When five women hike to a remote cabin deep inside a national park, unsettling events suggest that they should have stayed home. (978-1-63555-490-8)

Royal Street Reveillon by Greg Herren. Someone is killing the stars of a reality show, and it's up to Scotty Bradley and the boys to find out who. (978-1-63555-545-5)

Somewhere Along the Way by Kathleen Knowles. When Maxine Cooper moves to San Francisco during the summer of 1981, she learns that wherever you run, you cannot escape yourself. (978-1-63555-383-3)

Bold Strokes Books
Quality and Diversity in LGBTQ Literature